Promised Land

by
Bob Adamov

Packard Island Publishing

Other *Emerson Moore* Adventures by Bob Adamov
Rainbow's End   Released October 2002
Pierce the Veil   Released May 2004
When Rainbows Walk   Released June 2005

Next *Emerson Moore* Adventure
The Other Side of Hell To be released Summer 2007

The following publications provided reference material:

MORE SWAMP COOKING by Dana Holyfield, Copyright 2001
Ten Speed Press

LOST STORIES: YESTERDAY AND TODAY AT PUT-IN-BAY by
Ronald L. Stuckey, Copyright 2002 RLS Creations

ISBN: 0-9786184-0-8
978-0-9786184-0-7

Library of Congress Control Number: 2006904091

Cover art by John Joyce, Red, Incorporated

Submit all requests for reprinting to:
BookMasters, Inc.
2541 Ashland Road
P.O. Box 2139
Mansfield, OH 44905
Published in the United States by:

Packard Island Publishing, Cuyahoga Falls, Ohio

www.bookmasters.com
www.packardislandpublishing.com
www.BobAdamov.com

First Edition—July 2006

Printed in the United States of America

Acknowledgments

I'd like to acknowledge the support and wealth of guidance that I received from the following: Judy and Bob Bransome, the Cohen Family at James H. Cohen & Sons—Rare Coins, Captain Doc Holly of the *Natchez* steamboat, Luka Cutura, Jimmy Van Hoose, at Jimmy's Café for the introductions in New Orleans, Rafael Goyeneche and Anthony "Tony" Radosti, at the Metropolitan Crime Commission, Ralph Schillaci, Detective Dan Lance, Dr. Bob Dull, Dr. Mike Rollins, Dr. Joe Jasser, Wayne Williamson, and my friends at the New Orleans Steamboat Company. I'd also like to thank two special French Quarter friends, Chellie and Tricia Smith.

A special thank you to my team of advisors and editors for their invaluable support: Joe Weinstein, Hank Inman with Goldfinch Communications, Sam Adamov, Bob Adamov Jr., and Rhonda Sharp of BookMasters.

As they say in New Orleans: *Laissez les bon temps rouler* or "Let the good times roll!"

The National Multiple Sclerosis Society will receive a portion of the proceeds from the sale of this book.

They that wait upon the Lord shall renew their strength; they shall mount up with wings as eagles; they shall run, and not be weary; and they shall walk, and not faint.
—Isaiah 40:31

Page Dedicated to the *Excellence in Law Enforcement Award* Recipients Awarded by the Metropolitan Crime Commission in New Orleans

On March 22, 2006, the Metropolitan Crime Commission's President, Rafael Goyeneche, and Vice President, Anthony "Tony" Radosti, recognized three law enforcement officers for their heroic efforts during the aftermath of Hurricane Katrina. The national criticism on the shortcomings of a few bad officers cannot cast a shadow on the Herculean efforts and unswerving dedication of the New Orleans Police Department's (NOPD) officers, who served with honor and distinction during the darkest hours in New Orleans' history. During this unprecedented disaster, officers inspired each other to overcome fatigue and despair to accomplish the impossible by rescuing fellow citizens and restoring order.

NOPD CAPTAIN TIMOTHY P. BAYARD
Captain Bayard led boat rescue operations from the foot of Canal Street, deployed personnel in search and rescue operations, assisted the Tactical Unit in clearing buildings, and took the lead in secondary sweeps by wading through chest-deep water, in the sweltering heat, and going door to door through neighborhoods looking for survivors, saving stranded pets, and recovering Katrina's casualties.

NOPD CAPTAIN JEFFREY J. "JEFF" WINN
Captain Winn led his Tactical Unit in deploying boats, in the swiftly moving water, and saved hundreds of lives. Often, they abandoned the relative safety of their boats and swam into homes to rescue homeowners, stranded by the rapidly rising water. His team also participated in numerous SWAT and building clearing situations.

HARBOR POLICE DEPARTMENT
CHIEF ROBERT HECKER

Despite orders to the contrary, Chief Hecker and two of his officers remained on duty while Hurricane Katrina ravaged the city. Chief Hecker led rooftop rescue efforts through flooded neighborhoods, in the sweltering heat. He and his team patrolled the Port of New Orleans properties and the city, as well as rescuing hundreds from the Lower Ninth Ward, including the legendary musician, Fats Domino.

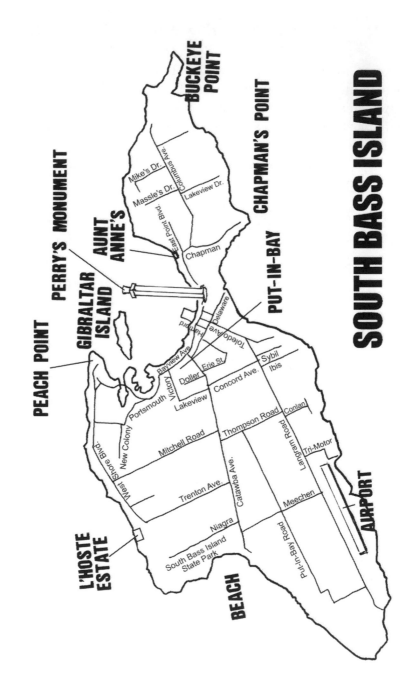

SOUTH BASS ISLAND

BUCKEYE POINT

CHAPMAN'S POINT

PERRY'S MONUMENT

AUNT ANNE'S

PUT-IN-BAY

GIBRALTAR ISLAND

PEACH POINT

L'HOSTE ESTATE

BEACH

AIRPORT

Mike's Dr.

Massle's Dr.

Columbus Ave.

Lakeview Dr.

East Point Blvd.

Chapman

Delaware

Hartford

Toledo Ave.

Bayview Ave.

Victory

Doller

Erie St.

Sybil

Ibis

Concord Ave.

Lakeview

Portsmouth

Thompson Road

Conlan

Langram Road

Tri-Motor

New Colony

Mitchell Road

West Shore Blvd.

Catawba Ave.

Trenton Ave.

Meechen

Niagra

Put-In-Bay Road

South Bass Island
State Park

New Orleans' French Quarter

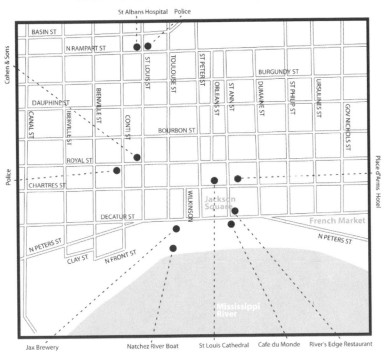

St Albans Hospital   Police

Cohen & Sons

BASIN ST

N RAMPART ST

ST LOUIS ST

TOULOUSE ST

ST PETER ST

BURGUNDY ST

BIENVILLE ST

DAUPHINE ST

CONTI ST

ST ANN ST

DUMAINE ST

ST PHILIP ST

URSULINES ST

GOV NICHOLS ST

ORLEANS ST

CANAL ST

IBERVILLE ST

BOURBON ST

ROYAL ST

Police

CHARTRES ST

Place d'Arms Hotel

WILKINSON

Jackson Square

DECATUR ST

French Market

N PETERS ST

N PETERS ST

CLAY ST   N FRONT ST

Mississippi River

Jax Brewery   Natchez River Boat   St Louis Cathedral   Cafe du Monde   River's Edge Restaurant

Prologue

A Note to Readers

For years, New Orleans has been one of my favorite cities to visit. In May 2005, I finished preliminary site research and interviews for this book. I was looking forward to working out the plot details, and was writing in late August, with one eye on the news reports about the approaching Hurricane Katrina. Like many other Americans, I watched in horror at the devastation caused by the hurricane, and subsequent destruction caused by the flooding. As September turned into October, I saw the progress being made in the city and decided that Katrina was too big for me not to include. I didn't want to write a story about the hurricane; instead, I wanted to allow it to interrupt the plot and throw some twists in the way. I hope the story captures the sense of the disaster, while at the same time heightening the tension at the end of the book.

From my post-Katrina follow-up visit to New Orleans, it appeared that the national media struggled in ascertaining and reporting the truth about Katrina's aftermath. Conjecture and whispered rumors served as the basis for many of the reports, as the networks worked furiously to keep abreast of breaking developments.

As citizens fled New Orleans and resettled throughout the United States, they took with them a bit of the multicultural ethnic stew, that had been simmering over the last two centuries in New Orleans. And now, many parts of the United States are being enhanced by the flavor of New Orleans gumbo and the city's celebratory spirit as the evacuees resettle into new homes in new locations.

To date, the number of confirmed fatalities in Louisiana is more than 1,100 people. They are still discovering people's remains. This book, in part, is dedicated to those hardy New Orleanians, who have lost so much, but are working so hard to rebuild their beautiful city.

Pulitzer Prize Winner

On April 17, 2006, it was announced that *The Times-Picayune* of New Orleans won the Pulitzer Prize for Public Service for their dauntless coverage of Hurricane Katrina and its aftermath. They also won the Pulitzer in breaking news reporting for their Katrina coverage. Working from a bunker within their building and making dangerous newsgathering forays into the storm and its aftermath, these committed reporters and employees epitomized self-sacrifice and dedication. This book is dedicated, in part, to them for their unequalled devotion—and congratulations on the Pulitzer recognition!

Book One

Off the Coast of Spain
October 21, 1805
Late Morning

～

Cannon fire, explosions, and the din of the battling ships filled the warm morning air. One of the *Redoubtable*'s lethal cannon balls honed in on a figure standing on the *Victory*'s quarterdeck, cutting the man in half and killing him instantly. He was Lord Horatio Nelson's personal secretary.

Nelson momentarily diverted his attention from directing the battle to glance at John Scott's scattered remains. Crimson-red blood flooded the deck where Scott had been standing just moments ago. *The horrors of war,* Nelson thought, as his face filled with remorse at the loss of his loyal secretary, who had chosen to forgo the safety below deck to station himself near his commander.

Scott wasn't the first good man that Nelson had lost from his crew. He turned his attention back to the battle and the living as two crewmembers approached to haul the body parts away.

Off the Coast of Spain
Earlier That Morning

～

On the horizon the slightest hint of morning light began to show, announcing the arrival of a new day. *It would be a day filled with death and the screams of the wounded,* Admiral Lord

Horatio Nelson thought as he cast his eyes astern, piercing the diminishing darkness to see the shadowy outline of his squadron strung out behind his flagship, *HMS Victory.*

A wave lifted the *Victory* and Nelson looked upward at the topsail as the wind freshened and filled it. *Today's the day,* he thought. They would catch Napoleon's fleet today, he was sure.

Nelson was resplendent in his bright blue jacket with nine gold buttons and their gold loops. The three gold stars on his epaulets and the three gold braids on his cuffs clearly signified his rank as admiral.

"Good morning, Sir."

Nelson turned upon hearing the familiar voice. "Ah, Hardy," Nelson began, "it will be a better morning once we catch the coalition's ships."

Hardy smiled. "That it will, Sir. That it will."

Hardy returned to his morning rounds as Nelson watched him. Thomas Hardy was his flag captain and had been with him during their victories at the Nile and Copenhagen. He counted on Hardy for his disciplined approach and attention to details, character traits that freed Nelson to focus on his strategic tasks.

Nelson had his own reputation—one of a brilliant strategist, with a sometime disregard for orders. It had been at the Battle of Copenhagen, in 1801, when Nelson had ignored orders to cease action by putting his telescope to his blind eye, claiming he couldn't see the signal. His defiance enabled him to win the battle. He had lost the sight of his right eye during the Battle at Calvi in 1793 and lost his right arm at the Battle of Santa Cruz de Tenerife in 1797. The amputation of his right arm was due to multiple fractures caused by an enemy musket ball.

As the wind snapped the sails, Nelson's eyes scanned the deck of *the Victory,* a 100-gun ship of the line. *The watch would be ending soon and the ship's crew would be awakening to a day of victory,* Nelson thought.

Three decks below on the lower gun deck, Bernard Thompson awoke as six bells tolled 7:00 a.m. To the shouted orders of "Up all! Hammocks away!" Thompson rolled his five-foot frame out of his hammock with the rest of the crew in the sweat-filled close quarters. The entire ship's crew set to rolling up and stowing the 460 hammocks, which had been hung from the deckhead.

As he rolled up his hammock the ruddy-complexioned Thompson thought how he had adjusted quickly, but reluctantly—to daily life on board a ship of the line. He would make the best of his circumstances until an opportunity to jump ship presented itself. This wasn't his war. He was British on his father's side and French on his mother's side. He hadn't chosen a side during this war. The war chose for him.

Months ago, Thompson had been in Portsmouth, the British naval port on the country's southern shore. He had been trying to find passage back to France and his mother's farm after visiting his father's family in Brighton.

One night he had had too many tankards at the Red Stallion pub and, when he left—stumbling down the street—he had been picked up by one of the press gangs. When he awoke in the morning he was at sea. They may have impressed him, but he was looking for the first opportunity to jump ship.

As they were piped to breakfast at 8:00 a.m., Thompson moved to join his messmates, who were seated on benches around a small table hung from the deckhead and between two 32-pounder cannons. His mates were relatively quiet that morning in anticipation of the action that was rumored to take place later that day. His crew cook returned with their meal of porridge sweetened with molasses and ship's biscuits. It was a high carbohydrate meal.

Thompson ate his meal from the wooden square dish that was served to him. One thing about the British Navy, they made sure that you got your three square meals a day. He drank his Scottish coffee, which was made of charred ship's biscuit and sweetened with sugar. He then downed the two servings of grog that had been distributed to each man. *Two servings of grog is surely a sign that we will see action later this day,* Thompson thought.

Eight bells signaled the start of the morning watch and Thompson found himself in a party of men who were practicing swordplay with their cutlasses. It seemed like each day had been filled with drills as the men were pushed to sharpen their skills. If it wasn't practicing with the cutlasses, it was small arms or gunnery training plus the daily chores required to keep the Admiral's ship in good repair. But today's morning cutlass drill seemed more intense as rumors spread around the ship about the upcoming battle.

Killing people wasn't something new to Thompson. He committed petty thievery and had killed a couple of the people during a robbery when they had foolishly resisted surrendering their purses to him.

The cutlass drill was interrupted when a lookout spotted the 33-ship French and Spanish fleet which outnumbered Nelson's 29-ship fleet. Immediately, Nelson ordered on more sail. They began to gain on the enemy fleet as the decks cleared for action.

In Nelson's quarters at the stern, the movable wooden bulkheads—the cabin walls—which separated his dining cabin from his bedplace, were removed and stored, along with the wooden veneers lining his quarters. His captain's cot, which consisted of canvas stretched over a wooden sleeping box and hung from the deckhead between two 12-pounder stern chasers, was removed and stowed. His leather armchair, his sidebar, and other furniture were carried to the hold and stored so the crew would have unencumbered access to all fighting areas of the ship. The stern windows were covered with wood to protect the stern chaser gunners from flying glass.

The crew worked efficiently as they stowed the officers' furniture in the hold and the bulkheads. They laid out the fire hoses on each on the decks. After wetting the decks, they sprinkled the decks with sand to prevent them from slipping during the upcoming battle. The sand also acted to deactivate any loose powder that might spill on the decks during the gun-loading process.

As the crew stood down to await the call to battle, Nelson took a walk through each of his gun decks to encourage them. On the upper gun deck, armed with its long 12-pounders, Nelson bent to inspect the tackle that was attached to the closed end of one of the 12-pounders and through its breech ring. He stood up after his inspection and placed one foot on its elm-constructed gun carriage. "Make sure she's secure," he said to the gun crew. "Don't need her breaking loose and a loose cannon running around the deck."

"Aye, Sir," the gun captain agreed as he quickly ordered two of the gun crewman to tighten the tackle.

Nelson continued his inspection walk through the middle deck with 28 24-pounders and the lower gun deck, which contained the 32-pounders. At times, he paused to give inspiring words to his men as he allowed his eye to inspect their areas. They were well prepared due to the relentless training they had been given. The training provided the British with an advantage over Villeneuve's fleet, which had been blockaded in a harbor while the English fleet stood off and was able to practiced gunnery fire. The British crews had advanced to the point where they could reload and fire within 90 seconds, far faster than the French.

Nelson's eyes swept the various types of shot that would be used during the battle. The round-shot, solid cast-iron balls, would splinter hulls. Chain-shot, the double-headed shot, would spin when fired, breaking spars and rigging upon impact. Bar-shot, two round cast-iron balls connected by a metal bar; and grape-shot, the small metal balls and pieces of metal, would be used against people and small boats with devastating effect.

Before the battle started, Nelson took a few moments to make a change to his Will and to write a prayer. He had a premonition about dying during this battle. The prayer he wrote was: *"May the great God, whom I worship, grant to my Country and for the benefit of Europe, a Great and Glorious Victory; and may no misconduct, in any one, tarnish it; and may humanity after battle be the predominant feature of the British Fleet. For myself individually, I commit my life to Him who made me and may His blessing light upon my endeavors for serving my country faithfully. To Him, I resign myself and the just cause which is entrusted to me to defend. Amen. Amen. Amen."*

Nelson stowed his writing material and his notes and returned to the quarterdeck.

Seeing Villeneuve's fleet sailing northward in a single irregular line, Nelson split his fleet into two squadrons. One squadron would attack the rear of the French line and the other squadron, led by Nelson, would disrupt the French line by cutting through its middle. This was contrary to typical naval battle strategy that called for ships to sail parallel to each other with blazing guns. By the time the leading ships of the French line turned to attack, the two British forces would have reunited presenting a superior force to the remaining coalition ships.

At 11:40 a.m., Nelson ordered Hardy to alter course to starboard and break the French line behind the *Bucentaure*. As they sailed into battle, Nelson signaled his fleet at 11:50 a.m. with the message: "England expects that every man will do his duty." He then ordered his ship to commence firing on Villeneuve's ship, the *Bucentaure*.

Within minutes, the *Victory* began to receive fire from the enemy ships. It was during this initial fire that Nelson's servant, who had been conversing with Captain Hardy, was cut in half by a round shot. Moments later, eight Royal Marines, on the quarterdeck, were killed by a second round. Seeing this, Nelson ordered the remaining Marines to other areas of the ship, leaving the quarterdeck unprotected from enemy snipers.

As the *Victory* closed on the French fleet, grape shot was loaded into the 12-pounders on the quarterdeck. The two 68-pound carronades on the forecastle that were nicknamed the "smashers" for their ability to deliver devastating damage to enemy ships, were loaded with round shot and a keg of 500 musket balls. The heavy shot was fired at a low velocity so that when it struck, it would cause massive splinters to shoot throughout a ship, killing and maiming the gun crews.

The larboard "smasher" fired first and at the weakest part of the enemy ship, its stern. Its shot struck the stern of the *Bucentaure* with fatal effect as splinters streaked like deadly missiles the length of its gun deck. The *Victory* continued past the stern of the *Bucentaure* with each gun on the larboard side firing as it came to bear. This methodical firing caused 360 casualties and dismounted 20 of the *Bucentaure* guns.

After crippling the *Bucentaure,* the *Victory* sailed into the open to identify a new target. It set its sights on the *Redoubtable.*

On the *Victory*'s gun decks, the gun crews reloaded and prepared for their next victim. While reloading, they rammed a damp sponge down each gun barrel to extinguish any burning debris. Next, they rammed a cartridge, which was gunpowder in a flannel bag, down the barrel. The cartridge was quickly followed by the iron shot and a section of junk rope, which prevented the shot from rolling out of the gun barrel. After ramming this deep into the gun's deadly bowels, the gun was run out for firing. Through the vent on top of the gun, the cartridge bag was pricked and the gun captain inserted the fuse and primed the gun with gunpowder from his powder horn.

Using handspikes, two gun mates maneuvered the gun to the left or right, up or down, as directed by the gun captain who sighted on his target. Ordering the crew to stand clear, the gun captain pulled the lanyard and stepped back. The hammer with its flint struck the primer pan, creating a spark, which ignited the primer in the pan. The flash flew through the flash hole and ignited the fuse, which, in turn, caused the cartridge's gunpowder to explode and send the shot hurtling on its deadly mission.

On the quarterdeck, a flaming piece of rigging plummeted to the *Victory*'s quarterdeck. It narrowly missed the one-eyed, one-armed, five-foot-four admiral, who was pacing as he directed the battle. His 100-gun, man-of-war moved in as the French warship's main sail was ripped to pieces by the *Victory*'s grapeshot. As the ships fired at point blank range and closed, they became entangled in each other.

Well-trained French snipers, in the tops, poured down fire on the decks of the *Victory*.

Stationed high in the *Redoubtable*'s mizzen top, one French sharpshooter had been carefully targeting and shooting at the *Victory*'s officers. At 1:15 p.m., he found the most important target of the battle. On the *Victory*'s quarterdeck, he spied an officer, who had refused to discard his cloak with its ribbons, clearly signaling that he was a senior British officer to anyone on the French ship. The officer in his sights was Admiral Horatio Nelson.

The French sniper aimed and squeezed the trigger. The musket ball whistled through the air, quickly crossing the narrow space between the two fighting ships. Despite the typical inaccuracy of a musket, the ships' movements on the swells, and the dense, hanging smoke from the cannons, the musket ball found its target. It passed through Nelson's shoulder, pierced his lung and came to a final stop near the spine. Nelson collapsed to the deck that was still bloody from the death of his personal secretary.

Nearby crewmembers rushed to transport Nelson to sick bay four decks below on the orlop deck. As he was carried below, Nelson covered his face with his only arm. It was a feeble attempt to hide who he was from his crew so as not to demoralize them.

Below deck, the order was given to prepare for boarding. One man from each gun crew had been detailed as part of the boarding party. They moved quickly from their stations to prepare for boarding the *Redoubtable*. Thompson, who had been chosen from his gun crew, made his way to the carnage on the *Victory*'s main deck. He grasped his cutlass tightly as he emerged and saw the bodies scattered on the main deck. He looked upward and saw that the *Victory* had lost her fore topmast and her entire mizzenmast. Her bowsprit, except for the piece nearest the ship's bow, had been entirely shot away. He couldn't see them, but both anchors on the starboard side of the forecastle had also been shot away.

As the grappling hooks were thrown at the *Redoubtable*, the men prepared for boarding. The Royal Marines' muskets filled the air with explosions and more smoke, as they helped clear the French deck. From the forecastle, the 68-pounders were loaded with grapeshot and the barrels depressed to fire onto the *Redoubtable*'s decks. From the *Victory*'s stern, the 12-pounders also were filled with grapeshot and their barrels depressed to fire upon the *Redoubtable*'s decks.

Shot, smoke, and screams from the wounded filled the air as the boarders began to charge onto the *Redoubtable*. Thompson leapt aboard the enemy ship, swinging his cutlass and screaming his loudest as he surged with adrenaline. He had two goals in mind. First, he was going to do his best to avoid being killed, by working his way below deck to a safer sanctuary. Second, he was looking for valuables to steal.

Dropping below deck, Thompson fought to the *Redoubtable*'s middle gun deck, which was littered with bodies from the carnage wrought by the *Victory*'s fire. He stepped over bodies, looking for dead officers who might have valuables on their person. In a few cases, he heard moans from wounded seaman and thrust his cutlass into them to silence them permanently. On the far side of an overturned 24-pounder, he spotted a portly priest lying on the wooden deck. Dead bodies were scattered around the cannon and the priest, who had a two-foot wooden splinter protruding into his abdomen and two smaller splinters stuck in his skull, just above his eyes.

An hour earlier, the priest had been comforting the wounded when a British round exploded through the gun deck and sent the splinters flying. It was only a matter of time until he would enter the world of the dead.

As he lay there praying, he thought back to the secret mission that had been entrusted to him by Pope Pius VII. Of all the missions he had been assigned by the Pope, this one was the most important. The others had been to gather information, to address disciplinary issues with other priests, to assist in negotiating treaties, and to meet with leaders of nations in order to influence their policies. This mission would challenge the legitimacy of one of the world's newest nations, the United States.

Time passed and the din of the battle began to subside, but he had no idea who was winning. When he heard the approaching footsteps, he hoped it was one of the Frenchmen. Then, he could have the person arrange to return his parcel to the Pope, and let the Pope know that he wouldn't be able to complete this mission.

He raised his head to look at the approaching man. "Who is it?" the richly-robed priest inquired in French as he looked through his bloodied eyes. The red haze prevented him from distinguishing that his visitor was in a, now-tattered, British seaman's uniform.

"Who is it?" the priest asked again as pain went through his body in waves.

"It's not important who I am," Thompson replied in his native French.

"Are you a Catholic?"

"Of course," Thompson lied. "What are you doing here?" Thompson asked again.

The priest sighed with painful relief at his good fortune at being found by a Catholic Frenchman, someone he could trust.

"Tell me. Who has won the battle?"

"The British, mon pere," Thompson said.

The priest frowned with disappointment. "I have something that I need you to give to your captain," he pleaded as he reached back into the inner folds of his garment. "The British must not get their hands on this."

Thompson's eyes widened at the thought of stealing something valuable, if that was what the priest was reaching for.

"You will have to explain this to the captain. He doesn't know anything about this," the priest groaned as he produced an eight-inch-long gold cross. It was adorned with one green emerald.

Thompson's eyes widened as he looked at the cross. It was worth a small fortune. His hands reached eagerly for it, but the priest gripped it tightly, and wouldn't release it.

"Not yet. You must promise to give this and a message to your captain."

"Of course, I promise," Thompson lied eagerly.

"Tell him that Pope Pius sent me on a secret mission to the United States and that the French saved me when the ship I was traveling on sank. I had no intention of getting mixed up in a naval battle." The priest paused to take a deep breath. "This must be delivered to the United States' President, Thomas Jefferson."

"And why is it so important that this be delivered to him?" Thompson asked as he raised his head to see if anyone was nearby.

"It's about the promised land."

"The promised land?" Thompson asked, not understanding.

"Yes, this is very important. Will you help me?"

Thompson's attention was focused on the cross. He didn't hear the question.

The priest asked him again. "Will you help me?"

Pulling his eyes away from the prize, he raised his cutlass. "I will help you." Thompson's mouth broke into an evil smile. "I'll help you get to the promised land!" Thompson said slyly as he leaned closer to the dying priest, and drew his cutlass blade across the priest's throat.

"No no! You don't understand!" the priest gurgled as the blood streamed from the opening in his throat. "There's more to my story!" His life bled red onto the deck.

"I understand much more than you think," replied Thompson as he pulled the cross from the priest's weakening grip. He cut a length of rope and tied it under his shirt and around his waist. He then tied the longer end to the cross and dropped the cross inside his wide pant leg to conceal it.

Thompson hurriedly returned to the main deck and blended in with the victorious British sailors celebrating their capture of the *Redoubtable.*

The Orlop Deck
HMS Victory

∼

Below decks, the mood was much more somber. Nelson was propped against the hull and surrounded by a number of his men. He could be heard calling out for Captain Hardy who finally made a visit to his dying commander. Three hours had elapsed since the start of the battle.

"How goes the battle?" Nelson questioned weakly.

"The day is yours, Sir!" Hardy replied.

Nelson smiled.

"Not over the side, Hardy. Not over the side," Nelson requested.

"Yes, Sir. I understand," Hardy responded.

"I have done my duty. I praise God for it," Nelson said weakly as his body began to relax. A few moments later, he died.

Normally, officers killed in battle were placed in their wooden sleeping beds that resembled caskets hanging from the ceiling, and buried at sea. This contrasted with the burial of seamen, who were sewn up in their canvas sleeping hammocks by the ship's sailmaker, before being buried at sea.

Hardy turned to the surgeon who was standing next to him. "We'll honor his request for burial, but we'll have to put into Gibraltar for repairs before we can return his body to England. How can we preserve him?"

"Brandy, Captain!" the surgeon answered. "We'll put his body in one of the large, empty water casks and fill it with brandy."

"And what's to prevent the crew from tapping the cask to drink the brandy?"

"I'll add a touch of camphor oil to ruin the taste," the surgeon said, innovatively.

"Have at it. I'm returning to the quarterdeck to see how it goes with our French prize ship."

The battle was over at 5:00 p.m. with the sinking of 13 of the 33 French ships and 7,000 Franco-Spanish taken prisoner, including Villeneuve. The British had 1,500 men either killed or wounded, but didn't lose any ships.

Besides damages throughout the ship, the *Victory* incurred damages to the bow figurehead. The figurehead on the bow consisted of two cupids supporting the royal coat of arms, topped by a gold crown. Each cupid wore a colored sash. The red sash indicated a seraphim, the highest order of angels and represented the love of God. The blue sash represented a cherubim, the second order of angels, and indicated wisdom. During the battle, the starboard cherubim's leg was shot away and the larboard seraphim had its arm shot away.

The *Victory* arrived in Gibraltar on October 28th. During the time that she was being repaired, Thompson was able to slip over the side and swim ashore where he made arrangements for passage home to France, with money that he had stolen from his sleeping shipmates and the dead French sailors.

A few weeks later, he arrived at his mother's small farm in southern France. Before entering the farmhouse, he snuck into the barn and hid the cross in a corner after wrapping it in a sack.

Thompson would never have the opportunity to sell the cross and enjoy the proceeds. Two days later, he visited a nearby village. As he rounded a corner, he was killed when he stepped in front of a runaway carriage and its two horses. A few years later, the cross was found and sold. It has now been sold several times, throughout the years, without anyone finding its hidden secret. Ironically, it was purchased by a antiquities dealer and transported to the United States in the late 1800s.

The *Victory* returned to Portsmouth in December and Nelson's body, which had been remarkably well preserved by the brandy, was transported to London where it lay in state and was buried at St. Paul's Cathedral. His deathbed request was fulfilled. His body had not been put over the side and buried at sea.

Book Two

The scream broke the early morning tranquility of the French Quarter. Gasping for breath as he looked at the dead body, the city sanitation worker lurched back. The body was partially covered by trash bags, waiting for the morning's pickup. Its lifeless eyes stared pleadingly at the worker as if begging for help.

"What is it?" the driver called as he jumped from the cab and walked to the truck's rear.

"It's another one."

The rotund driver bent over the body and peered closely at the victim. Squinting his eyes, he saw the red cross drawn in blood on the dead man's forehead. "It sure is. I thought we were done with these."

It had been three weeks since the last serial murder had taken place in the Quarter. This one would bring the count to 13 in the last five months. Each of the corpses had a red cross, drawn in the victim's blood, on the forehead. The police had determined that the murdered males, who were mostly tourists, had been killed elsewhere, and their bodies dumped in the Quarter's streets. *The Times-Picayune*'s crime reporter reported as much about the grisly murders as he could, including scathing stories about the lack of progress by the New Orleans Police Department toward solving the mysterious deaths.

Retrieving his cell phone from the cab, the driver called the police and was connected with the crime unit. After identifying himself, he explained, "We're over here on St. Philip Street, just off Decatur. We just found another body in the curbside trash. He's got a red cross on his forehead." He paused for a second, then continued, "Looks like your serial killer is back."

Catawba Island Club
Western Lake Erie
Early Thursday Evening

~

Ignoring the posted speed limit, the green rental car careened through a left turn from Sand Road and flew up the private road leading to the Catawba Island Club. Past the golf course and the tennis courts, the car sped. It turned right onto the road, which led to the clubhouse, and came to a screeching halt as an entranceway guard blocked the car's path.

Shaking his head, the guard approached the car as the driver's window lowered. "I just bet you didn't see the speed limit sign back there," he said tongue-in-cheek as he pointed toward Sand Road.

The driver stuck his head out the window. He appeared stressed. "Listen, boy, I'm late and it won't happen again," the dark-haired driver groused with a deep, southern accent.

"That would be a good thing. We've got children here and you need to be careful."

The driver heard the screams of a group of children playing at the nearby bathhouse's playground.

"Okay, I'll be careful," he said, anxious to move on.

Looking at the car's windshield and not seeing the membership decal, the guard asked, "You're not a member here, are you?"

"No, I'm meeting one of your members, Dr. Rick Schenk. He invited me to go boating."

"Sure. I know Dr. Schenk. He's a surgeon and a real nice fellow from Detroit. His boat is at 'A' dock. It's the . . ."

"Cutting Edge," the driver finished for the guard and smiled. It had been the first time that he had smiled in 24 hours.

"Right. It used to be called Hatteras row," the guard grinned. He then directed the driver to a parking spot. "Have fun boating. Weather should hold for the weekend."

The driver slowly drove forward to the designated parking spot. As he drove, he took in the ambiance of the club grounds and the 330-slip marina, which was filled with a variety of boats. There was a peacefulness about the area that he found restful. It was a 180-degree difference from the previous day's stressful call and subsequent crisis.

His bags were packed, and he was ready to leave his antebellum home in the New Orleans Garden District for the airport, to catch his early morning flight to Detroit, where he was going to meet his old college roommate, Rick Schenk. With a couple of Schenk's fellow surgeons, they were going to take Schenk's 40-foot Hatteras, from its berth on Lake St. Clair, down the Detroit River, and to the Catawba Island Club, northeast of Port Clinton on Lake Erie.

A phone call interrupted his weekend boating getaway plans. When he answered it, it was a call from St. Alban's Hospital.

"Dr. Thibadaux," the caller had begun.

"Yes," Thibadaux had replied irritably as he glanced at his watch.

The caller explained to the hospital's chief of cardiology that one of his patients had just been admitted with a blocked carotid artery. The patient was being stabilized and given blood thinners, but would require immediate surgery to open the artery.

"I'll be right there," Thibadaux said as he swore under his breath. If it had been any other patient, he might have let someone else handle the operation. This one, though, was a big financial supporter to the hospital. Thibadaux knew that he'd better be the one doing the procedure.

Dr. Truman Thibadaux left his bags in his home's vestibule and raced to his Cadillac. Pulling out of the driveway, he dialed his cell phone and called Schenk. He let him know that he would be delayed and made alternative plans for catching up with him. They had agreed that he would fly to Cleveland that afternoon and drive to Catawba Island Club to meet them for the balance of the weekend.

Upon reaching St. Alban's Hospital, Thibadaux successfully conducted the surgery and began searching for a flight to Cleveland, while he rested in the doctor's lounge. He had located a nonstop Continental flight from New Orleans to Cleveland, which would arrive late that afternoon. There, he'd pick up a rental car for the hour or so drive west to the Catawba Peninsula.

Thibadaux eased his five-foot-seven, muscular body out of the rental car and stretched. He took a deep breath of the fresh lake air as his eyes swept over the boat-filled harbor. He was still tense from the pressure caused by missing the start of the boating excursion from Lake St. Clair. He spotted "A" dock and started to walk toward it.

"Tru!" a voice yelled from "A" dock. "It's about time you got here. Any later and we'd have you walking the plank!"

A smile crossed Thibadaux's ruddy face and the 46-year-old called back, "Yeah—and then I'd show you how I walk on water!" He grabbed his duffel bag and quickly strode to the dock, and on board the *Cutting Edge*. "Nice dinghy you've got here," he teased.

"My practice has been lucrative," Schenk replied as he looked at his old friend, whose dark hair was beginning to show streaks of gray. "Let me introduce you to the rest of our crew for the weekend. Meet Len Wildman. He's in cardiology, also."

"Welcome aboard," the large-framed Wildman said as he and Thibadaux shook hands.

"And this is Henry Inman, a neurologist. He's our resident quiet guy," Schenk offered as he introduced the gray-haired doctor with a slight build.

"I'm anything but quiet," Inman said with a mischievous look.

Thibadaux shook hands as he looked over the group. They all appeared to be in their mid-forties and successful practitioners. "I'm looking forward to a fun-filled weekend, and maybe breaking a few hearts," he said arrogantly.

"Heartbreaking has to wait until tomorrow!" Schenk said. "We'll have dinner tonight at the clubhouse and have drinks up there." He pointed to an open-air bar on the second story of a building, which offered views of the lake and harbor as well as boats entering and leaving the channel to the harbor.

The three guests nodded their heads in agreement.

"Tomorrow, we're heading to Put-in-Bay," he grinned.

"Put-in-where?" Thibadaux asked.

"Put-in-Bay. It's a little resort town a short cruise from here. It's on the north side of South Bass Island and a lot of fun. We're having dinner tomorrow night at the Crew's Nest and taking a short walk through town, and then it's back to the *Cutting Edge* for poker! I'll take all of your money! Just like in med school. Right, Tru?" Schenk teased.

Thibadaux groaned aloud as he recalled how much he had lost to Schenk during those all-night marathon poker games. Wildman and Inman laughed.

"But before we go, I've got these for everyone to wear." Schenk pulled out and held up a white T-shirt for everyone to see. Lettered across the front were the words, *"Cutting Edge."* "Now you know why I wanted your shirt sizes. If you're going to be a part of the crew on the *Cutting Edge,* you have to dress the part," the affable Schenk teased as he tossed a shirt to Thibadaux. "This one's yours." He then tossed the remaining shirts to the other two doctors. "You can wear these tomorrow."

They stowed Thibadaux's bags on board and then walked to the clubhouse of Catawba Island Club, which was also known as "the finest country club on the Great Lakes." Walking down the hallway, they turned right into the cozy Cove Bar with its wood plank floors, walls, and ceilings. To the right of the entrance was an L-shaped bar with bar stools. Dark pine tables and chairs were positioned throughout the bar and nautical-type decorations abounded. From the exposed timber beams hung old lanterns that cast a warm yellow light throughout the premises, adding to its mystique.

After having drinks and a light dinner, the group left the bar and walked along the lakefront and past the tented pavilion where a band was playing and club members were dancing.

"We're going up to the Burgee Bar," Schenk explained as they approached the stairs to the second-floor, open-air bar. When they emerged onto the second floor, they saw the well-known CIC yellow burgee, edged in navy, hanging from the bar. Also hanging from the bar were other burgees.

Schenk produced cigars, and the group sat back with their drinks, smoked, and watched the sun set in Lake Erie's western basin. They caught up on past events in their lives and talked about their plans for the next day.

The Boardwalk
Put-in-Bay

◆

The twenty-pound sack of potatoes sailed through the air, narrowly missing Eric Booker before it thudded heavily on the floor. Booker jumped and turned as a deep, guttural laugh filled the air. Seeing the source of the laughter, the Boardwalk restaurant and bar owner smiled.

"Lanny, you trying to kill me?" Booker joked. How could anyone get mad at the likable Lanny Kualii? The rotund Hawaiian cook had signed on to work the summer season at the Boardwalk. Booker had met him while deep-sea fishing in the Hawaiian Islands and lured him to his restaurant.

"Sorry, Boss! I almost broke yo' head with da bag," the 57-year-old said, in a heavily accented mix of Hawaiian pidgin English. He laughed again at the thought of hitting his boss.

"Lanny, you need to be more careful when you're storing these. We don't want the potatoes bruised for our customers," Booker cautioned.

"Da no problem, Boss! I jus' going make mashed potatoes outta dem potatoes," he said, with a huge smile filling his fat face.

"Lanny, Lanny, Lanny. What are we going to do with you?"

"Eat ma food," the good-natured Hawaiian retorted as he bent to pick up the next bag of potatoes that he would carry carefully to the food storage area. "Lika I bean telling you, you needa put poi on da menu!"

Recalling the bland, pasty, sample batch that Lanny had made for him when he first arrived, Booker replied, "That won't sell well here."

"You needa listen to me, Boss. I helpa you make planny good money." Lanny paused for a moment, and then added, "Upstair on da deck. You needa have hula girls. They planny good for business."

Booker didn't respond. Lanny had pushed for hula dancers all season long.

"Yeah, with da little coconut tops and da grass skirts." Lanny began to sway his hips and move his hands and arms to some imaginary Hawaiian tune. "My seesstah, she gonna go make da grass skirts fo' da wahines. I gonna play ukulele and sing like Bruddah Iz or maybe you gonna lika Don Ho mo' bettah!" Lanny began singing *Tiny Bubbles*.

"The only bubbles you need to worry about are the ones you're going to see when you're washing these potatoes." Booker shook his head and walked to his office at the edge of the Boardwalk.

Nonplussed, Lanny continued singing as he walked into the kitchen to entertain the waiting potatoes.

Northeast of Port Clinton
In Lake Erie
Early Friday Afternoon

~

Floating, he closed his eyes and relished the warm weightless feeling surrounding him. He allowed himself to become lost in its comfortable womb.

Something hard bumped into his right shoulder. The diver was awakened from his brief and tranquil respite. Reality was calling. He opened his eyes and saw that the current had carried him in to the side of the shipwrecked dredge and he had bumped against its bow.

The tall, athletic, deeply-tanned man with dark hair quickly looked around for his diving buddy and gave him the thumbs-up signal. They were about thirty feet below the blue-green surface. Emerson Moore grinned as he looked through his mask and wished he had taken up scuba diving much earlier in his life. It had been two months since he had completed his certification at Port Clinton's New Wave Dive Center. Rob and Scuba Kat had been fun to learn from and had talked him into joining *BAD* and *LEWD*, Bay Area Divers and Lake Erie Wreck Divers. He was looking forward to taking dive trips with the two groups.

Today, he was diving with Tom Duke, one of the island's ice fishing guides. Duke and his thirty-foot-long *Tiara* had been hired to take a vacationing couple diving to one of the many shipwrecks, which dotted the western Lake Erie. They were one mile west of Rattlesnake Island, where a dredge from Toledo had sunk years ago.

He adjusted his regulator and looked at his pressure gauge to see how much air he had left. He had plenty. They had only been in the water for ten minutes.

The couple was giving Duke a difficult time as they continued to swim out of range in the murky water. When they disappeared again, Duke turned to Emerson and signaled for him to stay put while he went after them. Emerson acknowledged him with the okay signal using his right hand and waited.

Sinking lower, he soon found himself descending through a thermocline, where the water temperature changes drastically by four to six degrees. Since he hadn't donned a hood, gloves, or wetsuit for the dive, the intensely cold water caused a painful, intense headache, like one would get by eating ice cream too quickly.

With his head throbbing, Emerson quickly became disoriented and lost his awareness. He looked around with sense of panic and relaxed momentarily when he saw the approaching lake bottom. He lowered his hand to push off from the bottom but found his arm sinking into silt up to his armpit. Panicking again, the new diver added air to his buoyancy compensation device and began slowly rising out of the silt toward the surface.

Without realizing it, he had drifted closer to the dredge. As he was ascending, his mask struck a section of the dredge's rusty crane arm. The impact caused Emerson's mask to become dislodged, and water flooded into it. As he was taught, he calmly held the top of his mask to his forehead and exhaled into the mask so the air would displace the water that had accumulated in the mask, so that he could see again.

Emerson continued his ascent to the surface where he saw the two vacationing divers bobbing in the water and being lectured by Duke.

Approaching South Bass Island
Early Friday Afternoon

∽

"Looks like someone got lost in the fog," Thibadaux mused as he saw the ship's bow perched on a cliff on the island's southwest side. Looming majestically over the Lake Erie waters was the ominous, huge bow section of a Lake Erie freighter. Lettered on its bow was the name, *Sauvignon.* Below the ship's bow and running down along the cliff's face was an iron stairwell. At the bottom of the stairwell, the remains of a dock could be seen.

"Bet the captain had a good yarn to tell the ship's owner," Inman teased.

"Not really. The owner had it moved there. That's the *Sauvignon,* and that used to be the L'Hoste estate. L'Hoste ran the biggest fleet of freighters on the Great Lakes out of Cleveland. They cut off the bow of the *Sauvignon,* put it on a barge, and had it hauled to the island about 20 years ago. There used to be a stone French chateau behind it, but it caught on fire about a year ago. It was so badly damaged that they razed it and hauled away the stone. All that's left is the ship's bow. Car dealer in Sandusky bought it and uses it as a vacation home."

"Nice vacation home," Wildman commented appreciatively.

"Why'd the owner sell it?" Thibadaux asked.

"He got mixed up in something with nuclear waste. Heard he was killed. Reporter who lives in Put-in-Bay wrote it up and won a Pulitzer Prize."

"How do you know so much about this?" Thibadaux questioned.

"I don't really know that much. I try to boat down here at least twice a month in season. I usually spend most of my time at the Catawba Island Club, but get over to Put-in-Bay about four or five times. This is Peach Point," he said as they began to round a small peninsula on the northwest side of South Bass Island.

His three crewmembers turned their heads in unison as Put-in-Bay came into view. Rather than heading between Peach Point and Gibraltar Island, Schenk ran the *Hatteras* parallel to Gibraltar.

"Hey, I thought we were going to Put-in-Bay," Thibadaux said.

"We are. We're going around this small island and then into the harbor."

"Why not take that shortcut? It looked pretty direct to me," Thibadaux said with his deep, southern accent.

"Direct it is, but it doesn't go all the way through. Alligator Reef blocks the entrance to the harbor. Some boaters never read a chart and run through there, damaging their hull on the rocks."

Looking toward Gibraltar Island and seeing a number of cottages and a stone castle, Thibadaux asked, "And who owns that?"

"Ohio State University," Schenk replied. "Jay Fiske, the guy who helped finance the Civil War owned the island for a number of years. He was originally from Sandusky, but lived in Philadelphia. He built that castle as a summer retreat from the hot summers in Philly."

"What's it used for?" Inman asked.

"The Stone Lab runs studies on the water and water life. Ohio State students also attend summer classes there.

"Nice castle," Wildman murmured as they rounded the island.

The boat approached Lake Erie's crown jewel, Put-in-Bay. The picturesque resort town sees the island's population swell from 400 year-rounders to 20,000 on summer weekends, as tourists flock to enjoy its ambiance. Its natural harbor was the perfect haven for boaters and partying.

"That's Perry's Monument," Schenk said as he pointed to the tall, narrow limestone monument towering 350 feet above the ground. "They built it to honor Perry's victory over the British just northwest of here during the War of 1812."

"Impressive," Thibadaux said as Wildman and Inman nodded their heads. It wasn't the first time for either of them to gaze upon the monument as they had crewed with Schenk several times.

Schenk maneuvered the boat past the first set of docks and the Boardwalk to the docks owned by the Crew's Nest. "It's a little quieter down here. Not as rowdy," he explained.

"And what is wrong with a little rowdy now and then?" Thibadaux grinned.

"Depends on what you mean," Schenk responded before radioing in to the Crew's Nest dockmaster for his dock assignment.

In response to the call, Nancy radioed him docking instructions. "It's Doctor Schenk," she said to her coworker, Sue, "He's such a gentleman."

"Like my son, Robbie," Sue grinned.

Jet Express
Entering Put-in-Bay's Harbor
Early Friday Afternoon

～

As the *Jet Express* rounded Gibraltar Island, the fast, jet-powered catamaran slowed its engines. It had made the trip to South Bass Island from its Portage River dock in Port Clinton in 22 minutes. Its three levels were filled with a full load of weekend visitors looking forward to a fun-filled excursion to Put-in-Bay.

"Oh, I'm sorry, Sister," a 50-year-old man said as he lost his balance and bumped into a nun clothed head to toe in her black habit despite the building heat of the sunny afternoon.

"That's quite all right," she replied firmly. She had been studying an island map, which she had acquired at the ferry ticketing office.

The man wanted to ask her if she was carrying a concealed ruler as he thought back to his parochial school days and the many times his knuckles had been whacked by a ruler-wielding nun. He decided not to yield to his desire, which was probably a good thing for him. Sister Mary Margaret Mantel was a different breed of nun, a very serious and focused woman. She was on a singular mission to Put-in-Bay.

The *Jet Express* slowly nudged itself against its Put-in-Bay dock, and its passengers rushed to disembark. Seeing a waiting taxi, the nun flagged the driver and gave him the address to where she wanted to be driven.

It was a short ride past Perry's Monument to the green Victorian house at the curve. Paying the driver, the nun stepped out of the cab and opened the gate. She climbed the steps to the porch and knocked on the door.

"Coming," came the feminine reply from within.

While she waited, she looked around the screened-in porch, which was filled with comfortable wicker chairs. A good place for sitting and talking, she mused to herself. She turned to look toward the harbor and saw a dark-haired man at work on the motor of a small dinghy.

The white, gingerbread screen door swung open and an energetic 67-year-old woman with gray hair appeared. "Hello, Sister. May I help you?"

"You're Anne, right?"

"Yes."

The nun's face slowly broke into a smile. "Good. I was hoping to find you. I'm Sister Mary Margaret Mantel. I'm raising money for the Sisters of St. Mary Orphanage in Ethiopia, and wondered if I might be able to talk with you about it."

"Why sure. Come in. Come in," Anne said as she stepped back from the doorway to allow the nun to enter. Anne was always willing to help anyone in need. "Have a seat right here," she said as she pointed to one of the wicker chairs.

"Thank you," the nun said as she sat. She turned her head to look directly at Anne. "Usually, I like to talk to both the husband and wife when I'm fundraising. Is your husband around?"

"In spirit only," she said longingly. "Frank died a few years back."

"Oh, I am so sorry. I promise I will pray for his soul."

"Thank you," Anne replied appreciatively. "I can call in my nephew, Emerson. He's out on the dock fixing the dinghy's outboard."

The nun turned her face to look at the male figure working on the engine and smiled furtively. "No, that's quite all right. We girls will just chat." She smiled at Anne as she responded.

"Okay. Would you like some lemonade? It's a hot one today, and you must be warm," Anne said as she looked at the black habit.

"Yes. I'd like that."

"I'll just be a second." Anne turned and went into the house.

"I'll come with you and help," the nun offered as she quickly rose and followed Anne.

"No, I can manage. You just stay put. I'll be back in a second," Anne called as she entered the kitchen at the rear of the house. She walked directly to the back door and grasped the doorknob.

"I wouldn't do that!"

Anne turned and saw the nun with a sinister look striding rapidly towards her. The previously angelic face was filled with a devilish fury.

Aunt Anne's House
The Dock
∿

"What a beautiful view from here!"

Emerson looked up from his work on the engine to see a nun standing on the dock. She was looking around the busy harbor.

"Yes, it is," he replied as she turned her head and looked directly at him. Her pretty face struck him. Not what he would have expected from a nun. His eyes moved quickly from the top of her habit to the shiny glint of her shoes. "Can I help you?" he asked as he laid down a wrench and stood.

"I was just in the house talking with your aunt about funding an orphanage. She sent me out here to talk to you."

Strange, Emerson thought, *that my aunt didn't walk her out to meet me.* "Yes?" he asked as he tried to guess what this visit was really about. He was suspicious, but then again, he had a suspicious nature — as was common among good investigative reporters.

The nun taunted him, "You don't remember me. Do you?" She roughly pulled off her headdress. "Does this help?"

Emerson stared as she released the pin holding her long, blonde hair, and it fell over her shoulders.

"Now do you recognize me?" she asked.

"Yes, I do," Emerson said with immediate recognition. "You're Judith Beckwith. You worked for Max Ratek!" Emerson said as he recalled the Wall Street robber baron who had been involved in the takeover battle of Fallsview Tire. Ratek had died during a fight with Emerson. Beckwith had been one of Ratek's top assistants and had killed the slimeball, Grimes, with an ice pick during a drunken fight.

"You're responsible for the break-up of one of the most successful takeover firms in Wall Street history," she stormed.

"Now hold on a second," Emerson started. "Don't try to blame that on me! Ratek and the rest of you used coercion and murder to accomplish your little, dirty deeds so that you could take over companies. It wasn't anything that I did. Your evil just caught up to you."

"Only because you got involved with the whole business! You were responsible for Max's death and the demise of the company! I lost everything—my job and my boss and lover. Now, it's your turn to lose something," she said ominously. "Your life!"

Beckwith moved in closer to Emerson. She didn't like to waste time. From a pocket in her habit, she withdrew a knife and lunged at him.

Emerson dodged the lunge on the narrow dock.

"You better think about what you're doing here. It's not worth it. Besides, we're in plain sight of everyone in the harbor," Emerson said as he bought time and ran a number of scenarios through his mind for resolving the situation. He didn't get a chance to act on any of his ideas as she moved in close to him.

"I don't give a damn anymore," she said as her pretty face filled with rage, and she lunged at Emerson with the knife aimed at his lower abdomen.

Emerson grasped her knife hand and the two began to struggle. Their struggle carried them to the dock's edge where they lost their balance. They fell off the dock and into the water, which was eight feet deep. Sinking to the bottom, they continued to wrestle for control of the knife. Emerson began striking at Beckwith with his free fist.

Beckwith hadn't planned on being in the water and found her strength drained by the additional weight placed on her by her water-soaked habit. It was pulling her down. She and Emerson kicked up, and their heads broke the surface where they were able to gasp fresh air, before sinking below again. As they continued to fight, the knife slipped from Beckwith's hand and fell to the harbor floor. Emerson pulled his legs up to his chest between Beckwith and himself. He then power-fully extended them at her, thrusting her backwards and away from him. Unfortunately for her, his thrust carried her against one of the dock pilings, and she struck her head against it.

Emerson swam to the surface for another breath of air. When he broke the surface, he lingered to replenish his lungs and await Beckwith to surface for air. When she didn't, Emerson dove back underneath the water and began to search for Beckwith. He was careful when he dove down in the event that she had somehow recovered the knife.

Instead, he found her body under the dock. She had drowned while trying to free her habit, which had become snagged on several of the metal supports under the dock. When Emerson surfaced for air, he saw two Put-in-Bay police officers racing down the dock and a Coast Guard cutter, which patrols the harbor, bearing down on his aunt's dock.

"You okay?" one of the police officers asked Emerson as he bobbed on the water's surface. "We got a call from one of the waiters at Axel and Harry's about a fight here, something about two people going into the water." Axel and Harry's was the new restaurant at the east end of the harbor that was close to the dock where Emerson had been working.

"I'm fine, but the lady below the dock isn't doing so well."

One of the police officers ran to the dock's edge, discarded his shoes and appeared to be ready to dive into the water.

"No need to hurry. She drowned," he explained as he saw the cutter lower a dinghy containing two divers. "You'll find her under the dock here," he shouted to the divers as the police officers helped pull Emerson out of the water and onto the dock. He stood to his feet and ran his hand quickly through his wet hair. "We need to check on my aunt," he said as his eyes anxiously scanned the screened porch.

"Your aunt? What do you mean?" the police officer questioned as he followed Emerson who was walking rapidly toward the house.

"She met with my aunt before coming to talk to me."

As they walked, the officer probed as he tried to take notes. "What happened here? Was the nun someone you knew?"

"Yes, in a round-about way." Emerson quickly explained what had transpired on the dock, and his past run-in with Beckwith and her boss, Max Ratek.

"Oh, I recall hearing about that. Wasn't it connected to the explosion at the Monument, too?" the officer asked as they hurried to the house.

"Yep." Emerson related the incident with Grimes, another associate of Ratek's, and the attempt to murder Emerson at the Monument. He glanced at Perry's Monument as he remembered the fight on the observation deck, and how narrowly he had missed death. When they entered the house, Emerson kicked off his wet sandals and called out, "Aunt Anne? Where are you?"

They heard moaning from the kitchen and walked in to find his aunt tied to a chair with a gag in her mouth. Emerson quickly pulled the gag out of her mouth and knelt behind the chair to untie her.

"That woman was no nun. I was just sneaking out the back door to tell you that I needed you in the house. I think she was trying to scam me for money!" Aunt Anne said angrily. She was angry at allowing someone to take advantage of her.

"She was here to do more than scam for money," Emerson said as one of the police officers produced a pad and began to take notes. "How did you know she wasn't a nun?"

"Lipstick. In all my days, I never saw a nun wear lipstick!" Aunt Anne retorted.

"Good for you. It was the high-heeled shoes that gave her away to me. I saw them when I was kneeling on the dock, and she walked over. I didn't think that they were normal nun attire," Emerson observed. He quickly recounted to the Put-in-Bay police officer what had transpired, and Aunt Anne also recounted what had transpired between her and the nun.

"I'm just astonished that that woman would track you down to try to kill you," Aunt Anne said as they walked onto the front porch.

"You just never know," Emerson mused as they looked out the front porch where they had relocated and watched as Beckwith's body was pulled aboard the dinghy. "Some people have a hard time adjusting to losses."

They helped the officer complete his police report.

Tippers
Put-in-Bay
Friday Evening

~

Tippers was crowded with an older crowd, who had nicknamed the bar area the "Wrinkle Room." Most of the younger set were next door in the more raucous and cavernous Beer Barrel, which was known for having the world's longest bar.

Schenk, Thibadaux, and the rest of Schenk's guests were seated at the bar, enjoying post-dinner cocktails. Thibadaux was seated next to two empty stools. A couple of locals took the stools and placed their drink orders. Thibadaux noticed an attractive red-haired female with blue eyes, who sat down next to him. He decided to initiate a conversation when the barmaid returned with drinks for the ladies.

"Let me pay for that," he said. "It's not every day that I get to sit next to someone so pretty," he drawled.

The redhead turned to her friend and gave her a quick roll of her eyes. She knew that she was being hit on. While she was flattered, she was also very married. "Thank you," she said as she turned to the man and replied with a deep, southern accent. As soon as she did it, she realized that she made a mistake. It would only serve to open a conversation. She was right.

Thibadaux was taken aback. "You're from the south?" he asked.

"Used to be," she said as she dropped the accent. "I was raised in Georgia, and my accent was so thick you could have hung a hammock on it."

Thibadaux laughed at her joke. "Visiting here?"

"Here, yes," she said referring to Tippers. She then decided to go ahead and disarm the handsome stranger. "My husband and I own a bed and breakfast on the island," she smiled.

"Really! Which one?" Thibadaux questioned quickly as he try to hide his chagrin at hearing that she had a husband.

"Ashley's Island House. Just about two blocks from here."

"Owned it long?'

"My husband and I bought it about 10 years ago," she said, reinforcing that she was married.

"And where is your husband tonight? I'm not sure I'd want somebody as pretty as you out by herself," he leered.

She smiled briefly before replying. "He knows that he doesn't have anything to worry about. I'm a one-man woman. Besides, he's out of town on business for the next few days. So, it's girls' night out." She grinned at her girlfriend.

"Oh, where are my manners? I've not introduced myself," he said. "I'm Truman Thibadaux."

"I'm Trudy Ramsey. And just where does that accent come from?"

"New Orleans. I live all by my lonesome in the Garden District."

Ignoring the baited comment, Trudy said, "One of our favorite places to visit. My husband and I love spending time in the Quarter and the Garden District. Especially taking one of those trolley cars out to the district."

"How did you lose that southern accent?"

"I had to go to speech school when I was a flight attendant and worked out of New York. Can you just picture a New Yorker trying to understand my deep accent?"

"I can just imagine."

"That's where I met my husband. He was, and still is, so debonair. Let me introduce my girlfriend."

Turning to her friend on the barstool next to her, she began the introduction, but her friend jumped in and introduced herself. "I'm Jannie and I'm available—so don't waste your time on her."

"Jannie, don't be so forward," Trudy chided her short, 70-year-old girlfriend.

"Trudy, send him my way," Jannie hinted unabashedly. "Ole Mustang Jannie here will take him for a ride in her golf cart! It looks like a Mustang convertible!"

"You'd kill him, and I don't mean with your driving," Trudy grinned back and turned to face Thibadaux. "Don't let my friend bother you. She's just overly friendly," Trudy explained.

"No problem." Looking over his shoulder, he saw that his buddies were engrossed in a conversation with three other ladies. "Besides, it looks like my friends have abandoned me."

Trudy peered around his back and saw them conversing. "That kind of happens up here on the island. Everyone is sociable here."

As the music started playing, Thibadaux leaned toward Trudy. "Care to dance?"

Trudy flashed a big smile as she answered, "I'd love to dance, but I only dance with my husband. It's just something that the two of us do together. Sorry."

Thibadaux put aside the rebuff and stared at her winning smile. His mind was racing as to how he would be able to take advantage of this beautiful woman. Finishing his drink, he asked, "Can I buy you ladies another round?"

"Oh why not?" Trudy asked. She was enjoying the attention and felt safe. All of the locals watched out for each other.

"Behave yourself," Jannie warned good-naturedly. "Of course, at my age, I don't need to!"

Lowering her voice, Trudy responded, "Jannie! You're reading too much into this."

"Maybe, but not as much as he's reading into it."

"And baby, it's all fiction!" Trudy made a face at her girlfriend and turned to continue talking with the gentleman. After an hour had passed, Jannie excused herself to go home. Trudy decided to leave shortly thereafter.

"Thank you for the drinks. I enjoyed our conversation. I'm sorry that my friend had to leave early," Trudy said as she stood to leave.

"No problem. It just gave us more time to talk," Thibadaux grinned. "I'll walk you home," he offered.

Trudy's radar went to full alert. "Thank you, but that's not necessary. I drove my golf cart tonight."

"Then, I'll walk you to your golf cart," he said. He realized that he had too many drinks when he stood from the barstool.

"Suit yourself, but I'm really quite capable of walking myself to my golf cart," said as she walked toward the door and opened it, stepping out to the cool night air. She sensed him moving closer to her and felt him put his arms around her. "That is not a smart thing to do, buster!" she said as she began to wiggle out of his grasp.

"I was just being friendly," he retorted as he pulled her tight against him. He began to lean his head closer to hers.

"Trudy, everything okay here?" a voice called behind Thibadaux.

"Not really," Trudy said as Thibadaux released her and spun around to see a young, thin man with scraggly hair standing before him. "Truman, I would like you to meet a dear friend of my husband and mine. This is Bahama Joe. He lives on a small sailboat over at Oak Point."

Thibadaux didn't shake Bahama Joe's extended hand. He just nodded with a face filled with annoyance at the interruption in his plans.

Speaking to Trudy, Bahama Joe observed, "It didn't look like things were going too well. Thought you might need a little help, Trudy."

Thibadaux began to raise his clenched fist in preparation of striking Bahama Joe.

"There you are, Truman!" Schenk called as he and the other two crewmembers walked out of Tippers. "We wondered where you got off to." Schenk realized that he had interrupted a confrontation of some sort and saw the inebriated state of his guest. "Looks like it's time we escort you back to our boat."

Thibadaux grumbled under his breath.

"Hope there wasn't any inconvenience caused," Schenk said to Trudy.

"No harm done," she replied.

"You might want to keep him on a tight leash!" Bahama Joe teased.

Thibadaux glared at Bahama Joe and then took a threatening step toward him. He didn't get far as Schenk jerked his arm back. "I think you're done for tonight, Truman." Schenk said as he forcibly led Thibadaux away.

"Thanks, Joe."

"Good thing that I was walking around the corner," Bahama Joe retorted.

"Yes, it was a good thing. Well, I'm off to home. Have a nice night, Joe," Trudy called as she stepped into her golf cart and started it. "See you around," Trudy said as she pulled onto Catawba Avenue for the short ride home.

Ashley's Island House
Catawba Avenue

~

Frustrated by the unwanted advances from Thibadaux, Trudy had driven through the moonlit night the few short blocks to her bed and breakfast. A brisk wind was blowing and caused a chill to run up her spine as she parked her golf cart.

She mounted the steps to the front porch and picked up an empty wine bottle and a couple of used plastic cups on the porch, which had been left by some of her more rowdy guests. Entering the house, she allowed the front door to shut behind her as she flew down the hallway to a trashcan in the dining room. She didn't notice that the front door didn't close all the way and lock shut.

Tossing the trash, she returned to the front of the house and peeked into the parlor to be sure that it was orderly, then climbed the stairs to the second floor. When she topped the stairs, she entered one of the guest bedrooms to drop off an extra set of fresh towels, which one of the guests had requested earlier in the afternoon. She busied herself with freshening the bathrooms on the second floor as she made her way to the rear of the house.

Downstairs, the front door opened ominously, and a figure sneaked into the front hallway. Trudy wasn't in a position to hear the front door open and realize that an intruder had just walked into the house.

Creeping into the front parlor, the intruder saw that it was empty. He returned to the hall and began to check the individual room doors, finding each one locked. The only rooms off the long hallway, which he found to be unlocked, were the bathrooms. Making his way through the large, but empty dining room, he entered the massive kitchen and found it also empty. He checked the laundry room with its commercial washers and dryers and found it also to be empty.

Returning to the kitchen, his eyes focused on the sign on one door. The sign read "owners' quarters." An evil smile crossed his face as his hand slowly reached for the doorknob and turned it. The door opened easily on its well-oiled hinges and the intruder entered the owners' small kitchen. Slowly and quietly he walked into the owners' office and work area and found them to be empty. Advancing quietly to the master bedroom door, he stealthily twisted the doorknob only to feel it stick. He applied more pressure and swung open the door. As he burst into the bedroom, his eyes swept the room and saw that it was unoccupied.

On the other side of the room was a glass-paned door, which he opened. He walked into the house's parlor, closing the French door behind him. Remembering the stairway in the hallway, he walked to it and began to quietly smile to himself as he closed in on his prey on the second floor.

Slipping down the rear stairs from the second floor to the first floor, Trudy was unaware that an intruder had invaded her home. She walked through the kitchen and into the owner's quarters to their bedroom, where she began to undress and change into her nightgown.

The phone's ring interrupted her activity.

"Hi, Honey," the deep voice said on the other end of the line.

"Hi, Sweetie," Trudy replied to her husband.

"And how are things going with you today?" he asked. He was anxious to return home to his beautiful wife. He enjoyed being with her and still gave her a hard time about the long six weeks that she had been away last summer when their daughter's baby was born. The way he told the story, it sounded like his wife had abandoned him for six months rather than just six weeks.

"Fine," she said. "We're sold out for the weekend."

"Good."

"Nice group staying here, but none of them are in yet for the night. Must still be downtown having a good time." She hesitated in telling him about the incident at Tippers and decided to wait until he returned. She didn't want to worry him. *Besides,* she thought, *he was used to guys trying to hit on her and knew that he was the only one who had her heart. He had had it for 27 years.*

Upstairs, the intruder had also responded to the ringing phone. He had walked furtively toward the front of the house and began to slowly descend the front stairs to the main floor.

"Good. Things are going well here. I've found some interesting crystals that I'll bring home to show you. Is the island busy today?"

"Yes, the harbor looked full and the streets are filled. It should be a good weekend for everyone."

"That's good. Well, I'm going to let you go. See you in a few days, Honey."

"Bye, Sweetie," Trudy said as she hung up.

She set the phone down and quickly unbuttoned her blouse as started getting ready for bed. A few minutes later as she slipped her blue nightgown over her head, the phone rang. She smiled to herself as she approached. *I bet Rob forgot to tell me something*, she thought, *and he's calling me back.* She picked up the phone and answered. "Hi, Sweetie!"

"Hi, Beautiful!" the voice in the other end responded flirtatiously. "And how did you know it was me calling?"

Trudy froze as she recognized the voice. It wasn't her husband.

Off Rampart Street
New Orleans

~

"What do we have here, Morris?" slender and attractive Detective Melaudra Drencheau asked, as she and her overweight partner, Harry Elms, walked over to the surveillance vehicle after parking their car behind it.

Based on a tip from an informant, the surveillance team had been operating in shifts for the last two days.

"We've got limited floor plan intelligence. The front door might be barricaded. We've been told that there're handguns and shotguns on the premises. Not sure how many, though," Jon Morris replied with machine gun precision. The red-haired, lanky Morris was known for his quick assessments and also for his untamed, smart mouth.

"They using lookouts?" Melaudra asked.

"Yeah. We spotted him in a second floor window. He routinely looks out about every ten minutes, almost like clockwork. When a buyer appears, he stays at the window, watching up and down the street."

"Are all the sales taking place inside?" Melaudra asked.

"Yep."

"How many inside?" Elms questioned.

"Three. All drug users. You've got the skinny lookout upstairs. Somewhere in the house, you've got the suspect's 400-pound boyfriend. He goes by the name of Tank! Isn't that appropriate?" Morris chuckled.

Ignoring him, Elms continued. "Is she there now?"

"Snow White?"

Elms nodded.

"Yeah. She's the third."

Morris was referring to Lavonia "Snow White" Helton. She had been able to evade arrest over the years so often that she had picked up the nickname "Snow White" for allegedly being as clean as the snow. She was always one step ahead of the New Orleans law enforcement officials and had never been caught. The police were hoping to change their track record since they had found a reliable informant who turned against her for selling his son bad crack. The son had been found dead of an overdose in his apartment by the father.

"When are we going to rock and roll?" Melaudra asked.

"Carlson said around two in the morning," Morris replied, referring to the head of the special unit assigned to bring in Snow White.

"Yeah, we'll be back just before that," yawned Morris' partner, Scully Jones, who was seated in the passenger seat. The slightly built Jones had a penchant for wearing brightly-colored Hawaiian shirts.

"You guys rolling now?" Elms asked as he eyed the tired Jones.

"I think so. What do you think, Morris?"

"Sounds good to me, especially since the Lone Ranger and Tonto are here," he said sarcastically as he looked enviously at his two fellow officers. The two had a stellar reputation for crimesolving and moving quickly into action, sometimes contrary to orders. Morris was jealous of their accomplishments.

"Careful, white boy," Melaudra, a Creole, said quietly as she glared at Morris.

"Easy now," Elms cautioned her as he sensed the friction. Friction between Morris and Melaudra wasn't anything new. It dated back to earlier in their careers when Morris' sexual advances to Melaudra were rebuffed. He hadn't quite got over the formal complaint Melaudra filed or the disciplinary action warranted by internal affairs.

Morris decided to let it go and started the car. "We'll be back in time to make sure the raid is a success," he said pompously as he shifted the car in gear and they drove away.

"He'll get his," Melaudra said knowingly. "What goes around comes around." She walked over to their parked car and got in the driver's side, sliding low in the seat.

Elms sat in the passenger's side as they prepared for the vigil. "Morris is the poster boy for corruption," Elms said as he settled into his seat.

"It's funny how that very few of his cases go the distance. It seems that whoever he busts knows how to beat the system. They know which bail bondsman and attorney to get. Then, the judge reduces bond. And if they are convicted, somehow, a lot of those convictions are expunged," Melaudra groused.

"The guy should have a motto. With every bust, get an 'out of jail free' card!" Elms mused.

"Easy to do when this parish has the lowest drug conviction rate in the entire state," Melaudra added sardonically.

"Mel, that's why they call it the Big Easy," Elms grinned.

Melaudra didn't respond. She knew that Elms hit the nail squarely on the head.

Two hours later, they watched as a car parked near the front of the house. The driver turned off the lights and the engine and then sat there.

"That's interesting," Melaudra observed. "Wonder what he's up to?"

Elms sat up higher in his seat as he peered through the dark night.

The car door opened, and the occupant emerged with a cell phone to his ear. He looked up and down the street, then leaned against his car.

Momentarily, a second vehicle turned on to the street and began to crawl slowly towards the first vehicle. As it passed the detective's vehicle, the occupants scanned the car and saw a couple making out. Ignoring them, the car pulled to a halt behind the second car.

The driver from the first car approached the second car and began to open the door.

Meanwhile, Melaudra pulled herself away from the clenches of Elms. "Okay, okay. That's enough!"

"I don't think so. Looks like they're coming this way again, Mel," Elms said weakly, hoping that they would resume their amorous activities.

Melaudra glanced at the parked cars and saw no one was even looking at them, let alone approaching their vehicle. "Fat chance! What I do for this department!" Melaudra muttered softly.

"And you do it quite well!" Elms grinned as he began to extend his arms to embrace her again.

"Harry, that's enough! Oh, and next time, just remember that our deal does not include real kissing," she admonished her partner.

"Did I do that? I wouldn't cross the line. How could you say that about me?" he asked, feigning hurt feelings. As much as he would enjoy it, he knew not to push the issue with his drop-dead, gorgeous partner.

"I don't know. I could feel your hot breath on my neck," she teased in response. "Besides, what would your wife say if I told her you tried to kiss me?"

"She wouldn't be surprised!"

Calling his bluff, Melaudra very slowly said, "Then, maybe I'll tell her the next time I see her."

"Okay, okay. I'll try to restrain myself."

Seeing someone beginning to get out of the newly arrived car, she warned, "Looks like activity is picking up."

"You ready again?" Elms asked jokingly with his arms extended.

"Elmo," she said using his nickname, "I'm referring to the activity out there."

Smiling sheepishly, Elms replied, "I knew it." He looked toward the parked vehicles as a rough-looking black man emerged from the car and began striding briskly toward the drug house.

"Do you see who I see?" Melaudra asked as she pulled herself up in her seat to observe the figure walking to the house.

"Yep. Toma." Elm's heart began to beat faster as he watched their target enter the building.

"I can't believe he would be here to buy drugs. He wouldn't expose himself this way. Maybe he's dating Snow White or collecting a bad debt," Melaudra guessed wildly.

Toma had been a target of federal, state, and local law enforcement officials for years. No one had been able to catch the crafty kingpin in drug trafficking, prostitution, loan sharking, and all sorts of violence.

Melaudra and Elms were salivating at their opportunity to nab Toma.

"They're moving," Elms noticed as he directed Melaudra's attention toward the two previously parked vehicles as they headed down the street and turned the corner at the first intersection.

"Probably don't want to make it obvious to anyone like us that there's an important visitor in the house." After a few minutes passed, Melaudra had grown edgy. "What do you think?"

Elms knew what Melaudra was thinking. They had been partners for too long, but he wanted to hear her say it. "What do you mean what do I think?" Elms asked in response.

"You know."

"No, I don't know.

Melaudra emitted a big sigh of frustration. "You know exactly what I'm thinking. Let's go get him."

"Without back-up?"

"Yeah, the odds are in our favor."

"Yeah, in our favor all right. There are four of them and two of us," he replied, knowing that they had been in similar predicaments and always came out on top.

Turning on her womanly charm, she looked at Elms with raised eyebrows. "I'll let you tickle me, Elmo," she teased.

Elms mouth broke into a wide smile. "Promises, promises. You've said that before, but never let me." They knew that there would never be shenanigans between them. Elms was happily married and the father of two daughters, one of whom had Melaudra as her godmother. Elms' wife, Angela, and Melaudra were close friends, and Angela had tried fixing up Melaudra with couple of single men whom she knew.

The bantering back and forth between the two partners was evidence of the close relationship the two had. They would take a bullet for each other without hesitation.

"Let's go," Melaudra said as she opened the car door.

"Just a second, Mel. I'm calling for back-up," he said as he reached for the radio to call in.

"Be quick about it."

"I am. I am."

Elms placed the call and joined Melaudra who was standing behind the car and its opened trunk. She had slipped on her body armor and was holding out one for Elms to wear.

As Elms struggled to put on his vest and fasten it, Melaudra produced a shotgun from the trunk. Seeing Elms out of breath, she offered some advice. "Better quit eating all of those beignets," she said, thinking about the French Quarter's doughnuts covered with powdered sugar for which Elms had an addiction. "You must be cutting back. I didn't notice any powdered sugar on your shirt tonight."

Ignoring her comments and seeing her begin to walk toward the house, Elms asked, "Aren't we waiting for back-up?"

"And let Toma get away? No way!"

Elms hustled to catch up to her. "You're going to be the death of me yet!"

"But not tonight, Elmo," she cooed.

"As long as you promise," he teased.

"I promise," she said as she walked and watched the second floor window for the lookout's head to appear.

Ashley's Island House
Put-in-Bay

~

"Yes, I do know who this is," Trudy responded cautiously. "I thought it was my husband calling back," Trudy added nervously.

The intruder's eyes lit up as she innocently confirmed that her husband had not returned. "I didn't think that he returned."

Thinking quickly, Trudy replied, "Oh, no. He's just getting off the Miller Ferry. He should be here any minute now."

"Nice try, Trudy. I don't believe you." He paused, and then asked, "What are you doing now?"

Without thinking she replied, "I'm getting ready for bed." As soon as she said it she grimaced to herself for answering so quickly.

"Need any help?" he said as his heartbeat quickened and his mouth formed into a wicked smile.

Ignoring his question, Trudy asked, "How did you get my number?"

Thibadaux looked down at the brochure in his hand. "From the brochure describing your bed and breakfast."

Trying to change the subject and cool his jets, Trudy asked, "And where did you find the brochure?"

"On the table in your hall."

Trudy froze. She knew that he had never been in her bed and breakfast. Beginning to panic, she asked, "Where are you calling from?"

"I'm standing in your front parlor," he said in a husky voice.

A cold chill ran through Trudy's body as she looked toward the curtained French doors that separated her bedroom from the front parlor. As quietly as she could, she eased herself across the sanctuary of her bedroom to the French doors. She raised her shaking hand to the lock and carefully locked it. Then, she breathed a small sigh of relief.

"Was that a breath of passionate anticipation I just heard?" Thibadaux asked.

"No. Definitely not," Trudy replied as she silently traversed to the other side of her bedroom and locked the door to her bedroom.

"Trudy, I want you to know how much I'm attracted to you," Thibadaux said seductively.

"Thank you for the compliment," Trudy responded as her mind raced with ideas on controlling the situation. She had never been in a situation like this before and found that all logical thinking was beginning to flee her.

"Have you sensed the chemistry between us?"

"No. Not for one moment."

"You're suppressing your true emotions, my dear. The electricity between us is overwhelming."

Trudy didn't comment.

"I'd like to make love to you."

Trudy's eyebrows lifted in response to the panicked look on her face. Cautiously she said, "Listen Truman, I am really quite flattered, but . . ."

"You should be flattered," he interrupted. "This is the first time that I've felt this way about a woman," he lied.

"I'm sure it is," Trudy responded although she knew better. "I love my husband, and I'm not interested."

"But I'm interested," Thibadaux's slurred voice growled back. He was becoming inpatient with his beautiful prey. The cat-and-mouse game over the phone was growing old. He began to creep out of the parlor and down the long, narrow hallway to the rear of the bed and breakfast. "I was attracted to you from the first moment I laid eyes on you."

"Thank you, but I'm still not interested," Trudy replied graciously as she searched her numbed brain for a way to deter Thibadaux's intentions and get him to leave the house.

Thibadaux had passed through the communal dining room and entered the large kitchen at the building's rear. "Trudy, I'm going to take you to a place you've never been before," he salaciously teased as he placed his hand on the door to the owner's quarters.

"Trudy! Trudy!" the voices yelled from the open front door.

Trudy crossed the bedroom quickly, unlocked the parlor door, and walked into the parlor. There in the front hallway, she found two couples who had rented rooms for the weekend. They had just returned from partying downtown.

Trudy asked, "Could you four come with me down into the back. I may need all of you to help me with an uninvited guest."

The taller of the two husbands said, "Sure, whatever you need."

The five of them walked down the hallway and through the dining room into the kitchen. There, they were greeted by a wide-open back door.

"Looks like he heard us coming and ran off," the lead husband said with feigned disappointment.

Trudy thought for a moment. "Maybe and maybe not. Could you follow me into my quarters to be sure that he's not hiding there?"

"Sure," the husband replied.

They searched her quarters and then the entire bed and breakfast room-by-room to make sure that no one was hiding. After securing the front and back doors, the couples went to their rooms for the night—quite excited about the unexpected drama they encountered when they walked in.

Returning to her bedroom, Trudy picked up the phone and called her husband. She began to cry as her emotions took control. Rob answered the phone and listened quietly to his wife's explanation. When she finished, he began to ask questions.

"Trudy, what happened to your common sense? We live across from the EMS station and two blocks from the police station. You should have just hung up on the guy and called one of them to come over," he said with exasperation. "This is very unlike you. You're a smart woman, Sweetie."

"My mind just went blank," Trudy answered. "I don't know what came over me, but one thing for sure, I wasn't able to think clearly."

"I want you to call the police right now and file a report on this guy," Rob said.

"I really don't want to stir things up. Let's just let it go. I'm sure he'll be off island tomorrow."

"No, I want you to get the police there, right now."

She knew how persistent Rob could be. "Okay, I'll call them," she agreed reluctantly.

"Then, you call me back after you've met with them and let me know what happened."

"Okay."

"Honey, I love you."

"I know."

"Call me."

"I will."

Trudy hung up and dialed the police department.

Five Minutes Later
Bayview and Catawba Avenue
≈

Through a quickly settling mist that was invading Put-in-Bay, a lone figure could be seen near the corner of Bayview and Catawba Street, near Mossback's Pub. It was leaning against a tree and taking deep breaths. Thibadaux seethed with anger and frustration at having his pursuit of Trudy interrupted. His rage was boiling, and he felt the need for a release. Fate played a hand as it presented him with an unsuspecting target.

Whistling as he walked, Bahama Joe was returning from a late pizza party with friends at Cameo Pizza. He stopped whistling for a moment to release a huge belch. *Onions,* he thought as he resumed his whistling and his trek to his sailboat, which was docked at Oak Point. He was deep in concentration and failed to notice that he was being followed at a distance.

Keeping Bahama Joe in sight, Thibadaux's adrenaline surged as he followed his prey to his sailboat. He watched as Bahama Joe noisily clumped along one of the docks to his sailboat and boarded it for the night. A plan began to formulate in his mind as an evil smile crossed his face.

He looked at his watch. It was close to one in the morning. Thibadaux decided to return to the *Cutting Edge* where he would put his plan into action. As he turned, he walked into an impenetrable wall and fell backwards on to the ground. He glared up at the figure standing over him.

"Ho Bruddah! Try watch where you goin," Lanny the Boardwalk cook said with a big smile. He extended his hand to assist Thibadaux to his feet and took note of the letters stenciled on the front of his T-shirt.

Ignoring the proffered hand, Thibadaux bounded to his feet. "Village idiot," he spit out the words disdainfully and walked briskly toward town.

"Tourist!" Lanny shouted back at the quickly departing Thibadaux. He then began to guffaw with his deep laughter. He had dealt with them in Hawaii and now at Put-in-Bay. Tourists were a strange breed, but he enjoyed watching them and their antics.

Lanny looked down the dock through the light fog where he saw the cabin lights go out on Bahama Joe's boat. He then looked at the departing figure. "Dat guy trouble," he said aloud.

He shrugged his shoulders and started walking towards his small apartment on Peach Point. For a guy of Lanny's size, almost any-sized apartment was considered small.

Outside of Snow White's House
New Orleans

~

"Freeze! NOPD!" Melaudra shouted as she aimed the shotgun at the lookout who poked his head out of the window.

The lookout withdrew his head and yelled into the house, "Cops!" When he reappeared, he was pointing a .45 at Melaudra.

"Drop it!" she yelled as he fired, narrowly missing her. Her shotgun blast caught him in the face and knocked him back into the room where he died, alone.

Racking the shotgun as she ran up on the porch to rejoin her partner, she yelled to Elms, "One down, three to go!"

Elms had approached the point of entry, the front door, without incident. He ripped open the dilapidated screen door and threw his shoulder at the exterior, hollow-core door. As he bounced off the door, he yelled at Melaudra, "Deadbolt!"

Without hesitation, Melaudra discharged her shotgun into the lock, disintegrating it. Elms pushed open the door. He then threw a distraction device and stepped back as it detonated in the front room with an explosion, followed by a brilliant, blinding flash of light.

They deployed into the front room, a sparsely decorated living room with an open dining area. Sweeping through the front room without suspect contact, they observed no one in the kitchen area and proceeded to the foot of the stairs to the second floor. With weapons pointed, they raced up the stairs where they encountered a metal gate. It ran from the ceiling to the floor and blocked access to the second floor. Melaudra pointed the shotgun down the short hallway as she looked for suspects while Elms affixed a breaching device to the locked gate. Stepping back a few feet, the officers detonated the explosive charge, and the gate swung open.

They charged into the hallway and began to enter one of the bedrooms, which had a semi-closed door. As they began to shoulder open the door, they encountered resistance and found the door being pushed shut from the other side. The source of the resistance was the 400-pounder nicknamed Tank.

Melaudra and Elms shouldered the door together and were able to push the door open wide enough that Elms began to sweep the room with his Glock in his right hand. As Elms' hand holding the Glock came into view, Tank grabbed for the gun and its owner's arm. He threw his weight to the floor and dragged Elms to the floor where they wrestled for control of the weapon.

Tank rolled on top of Elms, pinning him to the floor and virtually suffocating him with his weight. As he moved his hands to a choke grip on Elms' neck, Tank felt the cold steel of Melaudra's weapon pressed against his skull.

"I wouldn't do that if I were you," Melaudra warned. "Release him and roll over here on your stomach," she commanded authoritatively as her eyes darted around the room for the other two suspects.

Tank released his grip on Elms' neck and obediently rolled onto his stomach, where a gasping Elms pulled Tank's arms behind his back and handcuffed him.

At that moment, the door to a small bathroom off the bedroom burst open and first one, then a second shot echoed in the small bedroom. Elms dropped to the floor where he quickly assumed a prone defensive posture, using Tank's body as protection. The second round had passed through Tank's tibia and fragmented it into three sections, subsequently lodging in his left calf.

Melaudra turned her attention toward the now open bathroom and observed a naked female suspect seated on the bathroom floor. Her knees were drawn up, and her arms were resting on her knees in a two-handed, gun hold position. As she fired each shot, her hands jerked forward as the .357 Taurus Magnum discharged its jacketed, hollow-point bullets. It was the blonde-headed Snow White, and she—they would confirm later—was high on cocaine. She began screaming expletives at the detectives as she continued firing from the bathroom floor.

Melaudra stepped behind the limited protection offered by the hollow core bedroom door and began to return fire. She was using a Colt Combat Elite and 230-grain, Hydroshock rounds. She'd recall later that it was as if everything was happening in slow motion—from her muzzle blast, the slide moving forward and back, to the ejection of each casing.

She felt as if she could have reached out and grasped each ejected casing as it fell.

Elms opened up fire from his position behind Tank. Without realizing what she was doing, Snow White's fire at Elms ended up hitting Tank, wounding him. Tank shrieked obscenities at Snow White when the rounds entered his portly body.

Hitting the transmitting button on her radio, Melaudra called for assistance as she returned fire, "Officer down! Where in the hell is our back-up?" she screamed as a couple of misdirected rounds from the female shooter embedded themselves in the woodwork over her head.

After a matter of 15 seconds, Snow White ceased firing and so did Melaudra and Elms. They carefully peered from their defensive positions and saw that Snow White had dropped her weapon and was bleeding profusely. A later analysis of the shooting would show that 16 rounds were discharged: six rounds by the suspect, four by Elms, and six by Melaudra. Emergency room physicians would later document 10 entry wounds and 41 exit wounds on the shooting suspect who would survive her wounds.

Two of the entry wounds caught her in each of her forearms, causing her to drop the weapon and cease firing. Lucky shots from the two detectives.

Melaudra began to ease herself around the door to enter the bedroom and secure Snow White. A floorboard squeaked behind her, and she turned her head. She was looking into the dangerous end of a gun barrel.

Crew's Nest Docks
Put-in-Bay Harbor

∼

It was nearing three in the morning. Music and shouting from the public docks drifted over the boats at the Crew's Nest docks. There was little activity on board most of the boats as their owners and crews had settled in for the night. On board the *Cutting Edge,* Thibadaux listened to the snoring of his shipmates. He smiled to himself as he recognized that they were slumbering deeply.

Quietly, he slipped from his berth and padded out of the cabin and to the stern. Peering through the growing mist settling over the harbor like a veil, he eased himself over the side.

For a brief moment, he allowed himself to enjoy the water's warmth as it enveloped his body, as he thought about his cold-blooded plan. He rubbed the water from his eyes and began swimming quietly through the warm water toward Oak Point and Bahama Joe's boat.

Just before clearing the last of the docked boats, he stopped and slid close to the stern of a Hunter sailboat, seeking concealment. Someone had sworn when they stumbled in the stern. Thibadaux treaded water quietly as the drunken sailor peered through his bloodshot eyes around the harbor. Thibadaux was hoping that the sailor wouldn't look down and see him.

Above him, Thibadaux heard a zipper being pulled down and then a stream of urine begin to shoot into the water near him. He swore softly to himself, took a deep breath, and slowly sank below the water. He swam underwater for about 30 seconds, and then carefully raised his head to take a reading on his position. He glanced back at the sailboat, which he had just fled, and didn't see any more movement on board. He then resumed swimming toward Bahama Joe's boat.

Minutes later he found himself at the stern. He smiled to himself as he read the name of the boat. It read "*Shark Bait.*" *How prophetic,* Thibadaux thought as he carefully crawled aboard with his eyes scanning the nearby boats for any activity. There wasn't any. It was a typically quiet night at the Oak Point docks.

Crouching, he walked across the deck and down into the cabin. He paused in the doorway to allow his eyes to adjust and to listen. From the small cabin below, he could hear Bahama

Joe snoring. Carefully, Thibadaux walked through the cluttered cabin and to the berth. He stood over his sleeping victim. Bahama Joe's breath reeked of alcohol, and an empty rum bottle lay nearby.

This was going to be too easy, Thibadaux grinned evilly. He moved to the head of the berth and positioned himself above Bahama Joe's head. Slowly he extended his hands through Bahama Joe's beard and began to press firmly on both sides of his neck. The pressure on his neck cut off the blood flow to his brain. In his drunken state, Bahama Joe didn't react and within minutes, he was dead.

Thibadaux's eyes lit up as Bahama Joe's body breathed its last breath. Anyone trying to find the cause of death would assume that it was of natural causes. There wouldn't be any idea that Bahama Joe had been murdered since his beard would hide any marks.

With his vengeance taken, Thibadaux quickly left the boat and swam back to the *Cutting Edge.* He grabbed a nearby towel and dried himself before returning below deck.

As he entered the cabin, he could hear his shipmates still snoring. He smiled to himself as he entered his cabin and crawled into berth. As he lay down, his mind raced back to Trudy and how she had rejected him. He wasn't finished with her yet. He was still turning over ideas when he fell asleep a few minutes later.

Snow White's House
New Orleans' Ninth Ward
~

Looking from the gun barrel to its holder, Melaudra cracked, "It's about time you got here!"

Morris greeted her with a sardonic grin. "This is probably one of the few times in your life in which you were actually glad to see me!"

"Dream on, Morris."

"Sure, sweetheart!" Morris replied. "Elmo take a hit?" he asked as he saw Elms on the ground and Jones, his partner, entered to take custody of the handcuffed Tank.

"Yeah, don't think it's too serious," Melaudra replied.

"Maybe you're going to need a new partner while he recovers," Morris said with his eyebrows arched.

Knowing what he was thinking, Melaudra responded, "It would be a cold day in hell when I'd consider you as a partner. Besides, you already have one."

"Yeah, but not as sexy as you," Morris grinned.

"Being sexy hasn't anything to do with being partners."

"It does with me."

Morris' eyes scanned the room and focused on the nude shooter whose body was splattered with blood from her wounds. She was whimpering in pain. Morris noted that her weapon had fallen to the floor and was not within her reach.

"Who's the Playboy centerfold?" Morris asked as he approached the naked suspect to get a better look and to carefully retrieve the Magnum.

"Why don't you take a picture?' Melaudra asked as she looked from Morris to Elms.

"That's not a bad idea," Morris said as he whipped out his cell phone and snapped a picture. "I'll take it back to the station for evidence."

"Right! For evidence, I'm sure," Melaudra said skeptically.

"Hey, anyone call me a medic?" Elms cried out as he held a towel he found on the floor to his shoulder, stemming the blood flow.

"Someone call us?" asked an ambulance attendant as three attendants walked into the room with two uniformed police officers. One of the attendants dropped to work on Tank and then, with Jones, assisted in taking the wounded Tank out of the room.

"We're taking him outside," Jones said to Morris as he passed.

"Yes, he could use your help," Melaudra said as she nodded her head in the direction of the fallen Elms. Turning to Morris, she noted, "We need to find Toma."

"Toma's here?" Morris asked incredulously as he began to look around the room.

"Somewhere," Melaudra said as she began to walk out of the bedroom.

Morris assisted Melaudra in searching the remaining bedrooms. The third bedroom had an opened window that drew Melaudra's attention. She slowly approached the window and saw that the screen had been pulled from the window and laid askew on the floor. Melaudra slowly eased her head out of the window and looked down onto the porch at the back of the house. "Looks like he may have gotten away."

She didn't know how right she was. When the lookout yelled, the lean and muscled Toma had raced to this room. He dropped through the window onto the porch and then to the ground. He ran through the small fenced backyard, jumped over the fence at the rear of the yard, and cut through the adjoining yard to the street one block away. There, he had called his driver to meet him two blocks over so that he could complete his getaway.

Melaudra and Morris swept the rest of the house to make sure it was secure and then walked into the backyard where they looked into the neighboring yards for any signs of Toma. There were none.

When they returned to the front of the house, they saw Elms sitting in the rear of a waiting ambulance. They walked over to the ambulance where Morris was the first to speak and then it was sarcastically, "I've told you that you need to take lessons from me, Elms. When you're in situations like this, you breach the door and start firing."

"Yeah, sure. And what if there're kids in there? And like I've told you before, you've got to follow procedures." Elms winced from the pain shooting up his shoulder.

"Cut him some slack, Morris," Melaudra cautioned Morris. "Can't you see the poor guy's in pain?"

"Only because he didn't go in with guns blazing!" Morris said angrily. "It's just a flesh wound, you big baby!"

"Step back, Folks," the white-coated attendant said as he began to swing the ambulance's rear doors shut.

"Where you taking him?" Melaudra asked.

"St. Albans."

"I'll catch up to you there, Elmo," Melaudra called out. She watched momentarily as the ambulance with its siren screeching disappeared around the corner. She turned her head and approached the watch commander to assist in investigating the site.

"You and Elms should have waited for back-up," Carlson, the watch commander, lectured.

"We saw an opportunity and decided to move fast. We couldn't take time to wait. Toma was inside."

Carlson looked up and down the street and toward the house, then back to Melaudra. "And where is he then?" he asked in a condescending tone.

Sheepishly, Melaudra replied. "He got away."

"If you had the appropriate back-up, the house would have been surrounded, and we would have had him. But no, you had to play cowboy, err, should I say 'cowgirl,' and enter the house without a warrant."

Melaudra was quiet.

"You two were lucky that neither of you was killed. Based on what we've been able to determine so far, your shooter was a 43-year-old who had been smoking crack. We found this .380 caliber semi-automatic handgun on the floor near the male suspect, the big boy."

"His name is Tank, Sir," Morris sucked up.

"Thank you, Morris," Carlson replied. "There were two .20-gauge sawed-off shotguns in a corner of the room."

"Who fired first?"

"The woman."

"And what did you do?"

"When she opened up, we returned suppressive fire until she stopped her aggression, Sir." She watched as the gurney containing the shooter, whose nude body was covered by a sheet, was carried down the front porch steps, and wheeled to a waiting ambulance. The EMS team had worked quickly to stem the bleeding and was taking her to the hospital. "Which hospital?" Melaudra called.

"St. Albans," the attendant responded as a uniformed officer assisted in placing the gurney in the ambulance and climbed in to accompany the suspect to the hospital.

Seeing the commander's attention diverted, Morris whispered quietly, "Maybe she and Elmo will end up in the same room, and Elmo can arrest Toma when he comes to visit her."

Melaudra didn't say anything. She didn't need to. Her narrowed eyes carried a clear message to Morris. She began to walk away and then stopped. "Morris," she called.

Morris turned to look at her. "Yeah?"

"You're such a frigging suck up!"

Ashley's Island House
Later The Next Morning

⌒

"Wasn't that terrible about Bahama Joe dying last night?"

"Yes," Trudy said as she served the lemonade to Father Maloney, who was seated in a white wicker chair on the private wooden deck. The wooden deck was trimmed in white and had white latticework on three sides. There were two doors—one to the house and one to the rear of the deck. The entire deck was screened although there wasn't a roof. The screening served as a means to keep her declawed house cat, Ignatz, from escaping.

As she set her glass on the table, she thought briefly of how Bahama Joe had come to her rescue outside of the Wrinkle Room the previous night. "That came out of the blue! He was so healthy. Did they find out what he died of?" Trudy had withheld discussing with the priest her prior night's incident and her late night report to the police.

"No. The coroner from Port Clinton is doing the autopsy to determine the cause of death."

"I didn't hear who found his body."

"Lanny the Hawaiian did."

"Sure. I know Lanny," Trudy had dropped into a white wicker chair. "He's such a sweetheart."

"It seems that the two of them had a morning ritual of cooking breakfast together on Bahama Joe's boat. When Lanny showed up to cook, he found Joe in his berth. I heard he had been drinking," the priest frowned. "There was an empty bottle next to his berth."

"He liked his booze."

"The ruination of many a man," the priest warned.

Trudy glanced at her watch.

"Am I keeping you from something?" the priest asked.

"Oh, no. I have some guests scheduled to arrive earlier this morning. I wonder what's keeping them?"

"Maybe they missed the early ferry. Tell me now, how is your daughter, Ashley, getting along? I haven't seen her this summer. Has she been up for a visit?"

"Just fine. She and Aidan. You remember her son?"

"Yes."

"They plan to be in here next week. Aidan is getting so big! They usually stay in the carriage house," she said, referring to the two-story structure behind the bed and breakfast.

The first floor of the bright-yellow carriage house, which was painted to match the main house, was used as a storage area and contained garden tools, mowers, and other outdoor accessories. The second floor was reached by a set of exterior stairs at the building's side and led to a small apartment. Trudy reserved its use for family members and close friends, including a certain local island novelist who found its solitude inspiring.

Before she could go further, the front doorbell rang, announcing arriving guests. "Looks like I've got guests ready to check in. Would you like to come in for a second? It's been a while since you've been inside."

"Sure." Father Maloney rose from his chair and followed Trudy into the house.

A figure, who was hiding in the nearby shrubs, stepped out and surveyed the deck where Trudy and her visitor had been meeting. He looked at his watch and guessed that he had two minutes in which to disrupt her life. He quickly looked around and spotted the two-story carriage house that had one of its doors partially opened. He could see a gasoline can just inside the door. The idea of torching the house crossed his mind, but he put it aside. Then, through the open door, he spotted a container of antifreeze. Ethylene glycol is poisonous when ingested, but death would take awhile, and he wasn't sure that he wanted to give someone a chance for medical care.

He then remembered that he had a container of pills in his pocket, which would be deadly if taken in a large quantity and not detected easily. He reached into his pocket and pulled out the small container. Dropping six of the small pills into his hand, he looked at the deck area, and saw that no one had returned.

His heart was racing as he opened the screened door to the deck and walked briskly to the table. Carefully he dropped the six pills into Trudy's lemonade glass and stirred the mixture to make them dissolve faster. He stood back to take a last look at the lethal drink and was greeted by a scream.

When he looked around, he saw that he had stepped on the cat's tail and quickly moved his foot. He then ran out off the deck and behind the carriage house. He cut through a couple of backyards until he reached the Episcopal Church, where he slowed and began to casually walk down Lakeview Avenue to Victory Avenue to the Crew's Nest docks where he'd rejoin his friends for their scheduled departure from the Put-in-Bay.

Ignoring the throbbing pain in its tail, the cat jumped on the table where it found Trudy's lemonade glass. Seeing that Trudy had not returned, the cat leaned its head over the lemonade glass and tentatively licked the sweet drink. It raised its head one more time in the direction of the closed door. Seeing no one returning from the house, the cat turned back to the drink. The little bandit allowed its tongue to lap up more of the cool drink before it returned to a corner of the deck where it curled into a ball for another snooze.

Moments later, the door to the house opened, and Father Maloney walked onto the deck. "Trudy, I'll be out here," Father Maloney called. Thirsty for a cold drink, he picked up his empty lemonade glass and looked at it. He set it down and looked over at Trudy's. He started for the door and then decided against it. Instead he picked up Trudy's glass and sipped it. *Tastes sweeter than mine,* he thought. He threw the contents of the glass down his throat and smiled to himself as it quenched his taste. He then sat in his chair to await Trudy's return.

Five minutes later, Trudy returned to the porch where she found Father Maloney slumped in his chair. She noticed that his eyes had bulged out and that his chest wasn't moving.

"Father?" she called.

There was no response. With growing concern, she walked over to him. "Father, are you okay?" she asked as she placed her hand on his shoulder and shook him. When she didn't get a response, she ran into the house and called the paramedics from across the street.

Thirty Minutes Later
Aboard the Cutting Edge

~

The *Cutting Edge* moved slowly through the harbor.

"Did you enjoy your visit?" Schenk asked his guests.

Inman was the first to respond. "Yes. This was just great! I enjoyed the music the best. The Menus cracked me up with their antics." Inman was referring to a popular show band, which had played the previous night at the Beer Barrel.

"Yeah, I liked them, too. And that Pat Dailey singer was absolutely outstanding!" Wildman added. Turning to Thibadaux, Wildman added, "Too bad you weren't with us for the whole evening. You must have had a hot date!"

Thibadaux didn't respond.

The *Cutting Edge* was coming about the east end of Gibraltar Island and began to pick up speed as Schenk pushed the throttle forward. "You're the quiet one this morning. Something bothering you?" Schenk asked.

Thibadaux wanted to tell them about his escapade in chasing the elusive Trudy, but knew better. He had been staring blankly as Put-in-Bay began to fade from their sight. He had been thinking about the deaths he had caused. Gone were Bahama Joe and the woman who had rejected his advances. He smiled softly to himself as he thought about Trudy's death. He looked at Schenk and responded. "Sorry, Guys. Didn't mean to be in a funk. I've just been weighed down by concern for a couple of patients. I'm not sure that either one of them is going to pull through," he lied.

Schenk agreed, "It doesn't matter how many years you practice, it's always tough when you lose a patient."

"I think I just lost one who I wanted to save," Thibadaux replied.

The *Cutting Edge* flew past Gibraltar Island and rounded South Bass Island's Peach Point. From there it was virtually a straight run to the Catawba Peninsula and the Catawba Island Club.

Ashley's Island House
Catawba Avenue

~

Seeing the police cars and ambulance at the bed and breakfast, Emerson swerved his golf cart onto its front lawn. Quickly parking, he sped to the owner's deck where EMT personnel were pushing a gurney toward the ambulance's open rear doors. On the gurney was a body covered with a white sheet.

A police officer was stringing yellow police tape around the wood deck to prevent onlookers from trampling on any evidence. Toward the rear of the house, Trudy was standing with her friend, Joan. Joan had her arm around her and was comforting the stressed Trudy. Her face was drawn from what had transpired.

Emerson spotted Barry Hayen and his wife, Sybil. They owned the *Put-in-Bay Gazette* and had become friends with Emerson a few years ago. Emerson approached them as they talked with Put-in-Bay Chief of Police, Chet Wilkens.

"Was that Rob they just carried out of here?" Emerson asked, referring to Trudy's husband, as he turned to look at the gurney being loaded into the ambulance.

"No. It's Father Maloney," Sybil answered.

"Really! He just died here? Was it a heart attack?" Emerson fired off the questions.

"Don't know yet. We're trying to figure out just what happened here," the police chief said stoically. "The body is on its way to the coroner. So is the cat."

"The cat?" Emerson asked.

"Funny thing. Trudy's cat is dead, too," Barry added.

"Coincidence or foul play?" Emerson probed.

"Don't know," the chief said.

"All I know it's been one hell of a 24 hours," Trudy said. They hadn't seen her approach them from behind.

"Well, let's see what the autopsies reveal," the chief said with a worried look. This was unusual. Two deaths on the island. Three if you count the cat, and all within 24 hours. *Suspicious,* thought the chief. He didn't believe in coincidence.

Two Days Later
Put-in-Bay

~

The cream-colored 1929 Model A Ford with deep green fenders moved quickly down Bayview as Emerson kept its 289 cubic inch V8 engine in check. There was nothing more that he would have enjoyed than opening it up, but he knew how strictly the speed limit was maintained on the island.

As he drove past the Boardwalk, he tooted at Lanny the Hawaiian, who was helping unload a truck. Lanny threw Emerson a large Hawaiian smile and made the hang loose gesture with his hand.

Slowing the vehicle, Emerson turned left and climbed the slight grade to the home of *Put-in-Bay Gazette* publisher, Barry Hayen. Parking the little truck, he walked up the three steps onto the porch and knocked. While he waited, he looked at the bay toward Gibraltar Island.

"Ready to go?" Hayen asked as he emerged from the house.

"Yes," Emerson replied. Hayen had called him two hours earlier and invited him to accompany him as a witness to Mother of Sorrows' church and the parsonage. Hayen indicated that he was the executor of Maloney's will and that the police had notified Hayen that he could go through the priest's belongings to begin to work on the estate.

"Barry, how did Gibraltar Island get its name? After the Rock of Gibraltar?" Emerson asked as the two stepped aboard the truck, and Emerson began to back it down onto Bayview for the short ride to the church.

"We had a story in the *Gazette* about that back in the 1980s," Hayen said as he ran his fingers through his hair. "You've heard about the Battle of Trafalgar?"

"Yes. That's the one where Nelson was killed."

"Right. Nelson had a young lieutenant serving aboard the *Swiftsure*. His name was Robert Barclay, and he had just been promoted by Nelson about a week before Nelson was killed."

Emerson nodded as he turned right onto Catawba and headed for the church.

"Two years after the Battle of Trafalgar, Barclay lost his left arm in another battle with the French. He was later assigned to the British fleet stationed at Fort Malden, better known today as Amherstburg, Ontario. Barclay ended up here in the Battle of Lake Erie, and the poor guy had his other arm shattered.

"After the British defeat, Barclay was befriended by his captor, Commodore Perry. While Barclay was recovering here in Put-in-Bay, he and Perry discussed naval strategy and past battles. During one of those discussions, Barclay mentioned that the rocky cliff of the small island protecting Put-in-Bay reminded him of the Rock of Gibraltar and their victory at Trafalgar. Perry then decided to name the small island Gibraltar in honor of Barclay."

"That's something how events tie together," Emerson mused as pulled into the church parking lot. They stepped out of the truck and walked toward the entrance.

Built in 1927, the church was constructed of limestone, quarried from nearby Kelley's Island, and is a smaller version of a Romanesque-style church in Lombardy, Italy. To the left of the entrance was a statue of Our Mother of Sorrows, which had been carved from Indiana limestone.

Hayen paused to point out a plaque to the right of the doors. "Thought you'd be interested in this, Emerson."

"What is it? Looks like Noah's Ark."

"Very good. It is. It's a symbol of the universal church, buffeted by the waves of adversity."

Emerson nodded his head as Hayen continued. "It's truly symbolic for us on the island. We depend so much on the surrounding water for transportation, food, and our livelihood."

"What's that?" Emerson was pointing at a stained design set in the stone and above the doorway. "At first glance, it looks like the petals of a flower."

"You're close. The 14 petals are grape vines, symbolizing the wine used during mass and one of the key agricultural products on the island. The stained glass was made in Germany. When the first Catholic Church on the island was built in 1883, they had so many Germans on the island that the services were held in German. They didn't switch to English services until 1910."

"What happened to the original church?"

"It was over on Put-in-Bay Road. They razed it and sold the property after they built this one." He placed his hand on one of the massive oak doors and swung it open. "Let's go in."

"It's unlocked?" Emerson asked, amazed.

"Yes. Father Maloney was a giving guy. He really felt that this church was an island sanctuary. He didn't lock it at night so it could be a refuge for some of our Saturday night partyers and an errant husband or two here on the island."

"Interesting," mused Emerson as he allowed his mind to race and guess which islanders Hayen was referring to. "Is this the only Catholic church on the islands?" he asked as he followed Barry through the doorway.

"No, there's one on Kelley's Island. Father Maloney flew there to hold services each week."

To their left, as they entered, was a small sacristy where the priest would put on his robe for mass. To their right was a set of stairs, leading to a small balcony. Both sides of the church had four large, stained-glass windows.

"I've always thought stained-glass windows were beautiful," Emerson said as he admired the workmanship as they walked toward the altar. "They always tell a story."

Pointing toward the window partially hidden by the sacristy, Hayen commented, "I find that one to be of particular interest. It's a Jesuit priest who was sent on a mission. He was to live with the Huron Indians and teach them about Christianity. However, the Mohawks, who were the Huron's enemies, captured him. They tortured and killed him."

They stopped in front of the sanctuary where the main altar stood. It was carved out of a single piece of Italian Florentine marble and weighed 10 tons. The entire rear wall was dominated by a 12-foot-high crucifix carved from gray Italian marble.

Emerson's eyes were drawn to the ceiling where a painted fresco represented the Blessed Trinity. A triangle symbolized the triune God and a dove represented God the Holy Spirit. An angel held a crown in his hands to signify Christ as King of Kings.

"I can't imagine the patience it took to paint that—or to even design it," Emerson commented as he admired the detailed fresco.

"The guy who painted it used real gold foil to decorate the ceiling and other parts of the church. The funny thing about it was that kids used to come over to the church after school and search the floor for pieces of gold. They hoped it would fall from the ceiling."

"They find any?"

"Never heard that they did, but it was an adventure for the kids. Let's go next door," Hayen said as he walked to a door to the left of the sanctuary. Opening the door, they walked into the attached parish house, which was also constructed out of the same limestone as the church.

After walking down a narrow hallway, they entered a small kitchen area from where you could see into an equally small living room in the front of the small house. Two open doors, on the other side of the kitchen, opened into a small bathroom and another room where Emerson could see a desk and bookcase. The plainness of the living quarters was a sharp contrast to the richness of the church.

"Spartan quarters," Emerson observed. "Is that the bedroom?" he asked as he pointed to the room with the desk.

"No, that's his study. It was a bedroom at one time, but he moved his bedroom back to the church basement."

"The church basement?"

"Yeah, it's been years since I've been down there. When the church was first built, they didn't have enough money to build a parish house. So the first priests who resided here lived in the basement with the boilers, furnace, and coal chute. I understand that Father Maloney kept the basement bedroom locked. Even his housekeeper couldn't get in there."

Housekeeper, Emerson thought. *That would explain the home's cleanliness and probably the flowers in a small vase on the kitchen table.* Emerson's natural instinct began to grow suspicious. "Why didn't he want anyone in his bedroom?"

"Don't know. Maybe he just enjoyed the solitude down there. There're no windows down there. If there was a fire, his only routes of escape would be the stairs or the coal chute, if he could climb up it."

They peeked into the quaint living room and entered the study. The study was lined with books. Loving research the way he did, Emerson walked over to the bookcases and scanned their titles. What he saw surprised him. "Interesting combination," he observed. "Books about the Vatican on one shelf and books about the early history of the United States on the other."

"Part of that comes from Father Maloney's early days in the priesthood. You'd be surprised to learn that he was a Rhodes scholar in history. While studying in England, he was drawn to early church history. When the call was placed on his life, he traveled to Rome and entered the priesthood. He spent time in a number of universities and conducted archeological research. He was called back to the Vatican and put on some top-secret, special project. He wouldn't talk about it, although one night, he started to tell me, and then abruptly changed the topic. He didn't like to talk much about his days at the Vatican."

"Why?"

"Don't know. There was something that came up though, because the next thing that you knew, he was reassigned to our little island. My sense of it was that he got a raw deal."

"Interesting," Emerson's interest was piqued. "Think he saw something that he shouldn't have?"

"Don't know. I tried to broach the topic several times. If you started asking him questions, he usually changed the subject. We did a story about him coming to the island a number of years ago. Probably the most information that anyone pulled out of him—and that was quite limited and cryptic at that." Barry sat in the chair at the very organized desk. "Guess I better get started with sorting through his paperwork," Hayen sighed as he pulled open a drawer and extracted a handful of files.

"Did Father Maloney have any family members still alive?"

"No, he was an only child and his parents passed away some time ago."

Emerson turned to the bookcase and began to study the books. He always thought that the books which people owned were windows into their personality. "Here's a section on treaties of the world and international politics. It looks like he has accumulated some old books," Emerson said as he carefully pulled an aged book from the shelf and began to gingerly leaf through its pages. "Was he a collector?"

"Don't think so. Probably just a hobby," Hayen said as he replaced the original file folders into the desk drawer and extracted another handful.

Emerson delicately replaced the aged book and looked through the other shelves of books, but they were basic theology books and books on self-help and counseling parishioners. Emerson found himself drawn back to the shelves filled with books about the Vatican and U.S. history.

"My gut tells me that there's something here. But I don't know what it is."

"That's what being a good reporter is all about," Hayen teased. "It's that instinct stuff."

Hayen worked diligently through the files as Emerson opened one of the books he had extracted from the bookshelf. It talked about secret societies in the Vatican and their efforts to control and influence the workings of the Catholic Church. Emerson lost all track of time as he absorbed the material. Putting it down, he stood and removed another book from the shelf. Reading the foreword, he saw that it was written by a banished priest. He alleged that there were certain forces at work in the Vatican, which were destined to manipulate world power and control governments. Emerson noted that the book was originally written in the 1700s.

Emerson began going through the books on the second shelf. As he reached for the last book, Hayen's voice broke through his thoughts. "We've been here about three hours. Where did the time go?"

Emerson looked at his watch and shook his head. "Amazing how time flies when you're having fun."

"Did you find anything interesting? You seemed pretty focused on what you were looking through."

"Strange thing. Each book on this shelf was written by a former priest or a priest who was banished from the Vatican."

"And what is that telling you?"

"Not sure. Think Maloney was banished?"

Hayen thought for a moment before answering. "Interesting thought. Might have been one of the reasons he didn't want to talk about the Vatican. It does seem strange that a man as well-educated as Father Maloney would go from Rome to here. Must be because we're such a cultural and learning center," Barry teased.

"Think we should check the bedroom in the basement? You've got my curiosity up," Emerson said.

"Sure, I need to take a break anyhow. I'll come back tomorrow to finish going through his files." Hayen stood and walked out of the room, closely followed by Emerson.

Halfway through the narrow hallway, which connected the parish house to the church, they paused at the top of a stairwell leading to the basement. "Watch your head as you go down. It's tight quarters," Hayen cautioned Emerson.

They descended the stairs and emerged into a room with an earthen floor and shelves on one side. More than half of the room was dominated by a limestone rock outcropping that protruded from the floor.

"The basement was hand-dug, and they ran into that rock. They could have dynamited it, but they didn't want to take a chance of damaging the church next door."

Emerson nodded his head as he quickly scanned the storage area.

"Follow me," Hayen said as he stepped to his left and entered the furnace room. The bare room was dominated by the old coal-burning furnace, which had been retrofitted for propane. On the far wall, they could see the non-functional coal chute. "This was the living quarters for the first priests at the church."

"To live down here, you had to be called to the priesthood," Emerson observed.

"There's the door to the bedroom." Hayen was pointing at a wooden green door, which was secured by a padlock. "It's locked."

"Strange that for someone as trusting as you say Father Maloney was, he'd lock his bedroom door."

"Don't know why," Hayen replied as he approached the door and reached his hand above the doorframe, feeling for a hidden key. "Nope. No key up there."

Both men walked around the furnace room, vigilantly searching for a hidden key.

After a few minutes of futile searching, Hayen announced, "I give up. He probably has it in his wallet. We can get it when they turn over his personal effects."

Emerson wasn't ready to give up. "You'd think that he would have an extra key somewhere." Emerson eyes returned to the giant furnace, and he stared at it. "Maybe he hid the key in purgatory. Wouldn't that be fitting?" Emerson approached the massive hunk of steel and pulled open the door through which coal used to be fed into the fiery Hades. He bent over and peered inside. Just inside the open door and to the left, he spotted a black object affixed to the wall. He reached in, pulled at it, and withdrew his hand that clutched a small magnetic key holder. "I think we have the key to our mystery," he kidded Hayen as he handed the box to him.

As he opened the box and withdrew the extra key to the bedroom, Hayen commented, "Nice going, detective."

"Got lucky on that one," Emerson grinned as Hayen inserted the key into the padlock and unlocked it. He pulled off the padlock and twisted the doorknob. The door emitted a loud, ominous screech as it opened.

"Needs oiling," Emerson noted as the door stopped halfway, and they peered into the bedroom.

The windowless bedroom had poured concrete walls and an unfinished ceiling with one bare light bulb. Hayen felt along the wall near the doorway and found the light switch. When he flicked it on, the solitary light highlighted the room's sparseness. With its headboard against the wall directly across from the open door was a worn narrow bed with sagging springs. Next to the bed was a small metal nightstand with a small lamp and alarm clock.

"Spartan is an understatement," Emerson commented as he began to enter the room. Hearing his voice echo in the semi-circle shaped room, Emerson said, "Reminds me of a monk's cell in a monastery. This would be the perfect place to seek solitude and do penance. Think there's anything to that?"

Hayen didn't respond. He had walked to the right of the open door and was staring at his discovery.

"Barry?" Emerson asked when he didn't hear a response.

"Look at this," Hayen said in disbelief.

Emerson turned and looked to where Hayen was staring. In front of him were a bookcase filled with old worn books, a couple of stacks of files, a worktable, and the latest in computer technology with a Hewlett Packard laser printer/fax/copier/scanner.

"What do we have here?" Hayen mused as he approached the computer and sat at the lone chair. He reached down and turned on the computer. "Let's see what we have here."

Emerson was already standing next to the bookcase and scanning the book titles. They all dealt with treaties. Most focused on European treaties from 1600 through 1900.

"Look at this." Emerson was holding up two faded files. "These two files have labels on them."

"And the labels read?"

"They read, 'Property of the Vatican. Not to be removed from the Secret Archives.' It's written in English and, I'd guess, Italian. What do you think these are doing here?"

Hayen arched his eyebrows as he looked at the labels. "It certainly does seem like something is amiss here." He watched as Emerson opened the files and began to leaf through them. "What does it say?"

"I don't have the slightest idea. It's all written in Italian, and I don't know the language."

"You know Gino, who works on the Miller Ferry?"

"Sure. He's the guy that anyone would love to have as a grandfather for their kids!" Emerson responded as he thought about the warm and kind ferryboat deckhand.

"We can have him take a look at the files and tell us what they're about. Then, we can arrange to have them returned to the Vatican," the publisher suggested as he turned back to the computer screen. "Looks like this is password protected. We can't get in."

Holding the files in his hand, Emerson approached Hayen to look at the screen, which was requesting a password. "Sometimes, people use very simple passwords that you can figure out like 'secret' and even 'password.'"

"You're kidding!"

"Nope. Others use family member names, nicknames, or the names of something important to them like God, sex, or money. I had a friend from Taiwan, and all he used to talk about was Taiwan. We were talking one day about passwords, and I suggested to him that his password was Taiwan. He was shocked."

"You guessed right?"

"Right on the button. And you as executor probably have a responsibility to see what's on his computer in the event that it affects the value of his estate. He may have some bank accounts listed or other financial data," Emerson pushed.

"I'm not sure how comfortable I am about trying to break into his computer," Hayen said with concern.

"You've got a responsibility," Emerson urged as he hoped whatever was there wasn't also written in Italian. "Let's give it a try. Now, what was important to him?"

"God, Jesus, Virgin Mary, and the Vatican, just to name a few," Hayen said thoughtfully.

"Let's try them."

Each time they tried to access the computer, their attempts were thwarted with invalid password messages.

"Did he have a pet?" Emerson asked. "Sometimes, people will use their pet's name as a password."

"No."

"Try entering Sunday."

Hayen tried and saw invalid password greet him.

Exasperated, Emerson allowed his eyes to scan the room, hoping to find a clue to a possible password. A study that he had read said that some people left clues about their password in their computer areas. He noticed a small framed painting of the Virgin Mary. It had a faded red cast to it. "Try Bloody Mary!"

Hayen's fingers flew over the keyboard and a message flashed on the screen. It read, "Password accepted."

"How about that? He had a sense of humor when it came to selecting his password."

Emerson looked over Hayen's shoulder as he opened a number of Word files, which contained normal correspondence to the diocese office. There were a number of files that were password protected and to which they could not gain access even though they tried guessing. They tried to crack his e-mail password too, but couldn't access it.

Hayen pushed his chair back from the computer monitor and stretched. "I don't think we're going to get anywhere with this. And it's probably not something that we even need to worry about. I will have Gino take a look at the items that may belong to the Vatican and try to see what we have there."

"Could you let me know? I'm curious."

"Now, why doesn't that surprise me?" Hayen asked good-naturedly.

Emerson grinned. "Did you find his Will?"

"Yes, although I already had a copy of it. And I found his listing of checking, savings, and investment accounts so I can start to work my way through them." Hayen was holding up a handful of files that he had found upstairs.

Looking at the files in Hayen's hand, Emerson watched as Hayen pulled one file out of the group and held it in his other hand. "This is interesting. I found it here on the computer desk. It says, 'In case of my death, please hand-deliver this envelope to Father Alsandi in New Orleans.' The church's name is noted here. It's St. Louis Cathedral."

"Know it well. It's right on Jackson Square in the French Quarter. It's absolutely beautiful with its white spire reaching skyward," Emerson smiled as he recalled his visits to the French Quarter and some of his favorite haunts there.

"You've been there?"

"First time was a number of years ago to do a story about the river boat, *Natchez*. President Clinton was planning a visit to New Orleans, and I was sent down to cover some of the security precautions that were put in place."

"Oh, to protect the women of the French Quarter from him?" Hayen asked with a grin.

"Nice try. It was interesting working with the Secret Service and seeing the detailed work they go through. One of them had to dive under the *Natchez* where Clinton was going to speak. He had to sweep the bottom of the boat for explosives. He said it was one of the most difficult dives he ever did."

"Why's that?"

"He had dived all over the world, but he said that the current in the Mississippi was the strongest that he encountered and, to make matters worse, the visibility was very poor because of the muddy water."

"Probably a lot of mud on the river bottom, too."

"Layers of mud. If you dropped something in it you might as well as give up finding it. That's why they call the river, 'Big Muddy.'"

"Since you apparently love the city so much, would you like to deliver this envelope?"

"Would I? You betcha!" Emerson was pleased with the opportunity. He had a series of questions beginning to surface in the back of his mind concerning the contents of the priest's library. He was sure that something was amiss and he wanted to get to the bottom of it.

They wrapped up their visit to the church and Emerson drove Barry home. A few minutes later, Emerson parked the Model A truck next to the Chamber of Commerce building at the corner of Delaware Avenue and Toledo Avenue. He waved at Maggie and Linda, two of his good island friends at the Chamber, as he walked next door to the Village Bakery & Sandwich Shoppe.

The screen door swung open easily at the combination bakery and deli. "Pauline," he shouted as he greeted the 55-year-old vivacious owner, who was making sandwiches for customers.

"Turkey on whole wheat?" Pauline smiled back as she guessed that Emerson was there to pick up one of his favorite sandwiches.

"Not today. But I do want to pick up one of your peach pies."

"They're extra good today, Emerson," she grinned as she slid one of her tasty pies out from the display counter. "You just bought the last peach pie of the day."

Emerson enjoyed visiting with the bubbly Pauline as well as grabbing a piece of her famous pies. He didn't think anyone on the island made pies as good as hers although his aunt felt that her pies were the best. He didn't have the heart to tell his aunt that she ranked second to Pauline's pies.

Emerson paid for the pies and walked out of the bakery. As he turned the corner, he caught a movement out of the corner of his eye and at the same time heard tires screeching. Jumping off the sidewalk and into the flowerbed, Emerson avoided a collision with two bikers and almost dropped the peach pie.

"Sorry, Mr. Moore," 11-year-old Riley said while straddling his blue BMX stunt bike.

"I'm sorry, too," nine-year-old Elyse apologized as she sat on the seat of her purple bike, which had a white basket attached to the handlebars.

Both of the dark-haired island children joined Emerson in looking at Emerson's feet. He was ankle deep in mud in the freshly-watered flowerbed. Seeing the mud on his shoes, the children's eyes widened, and they looked up at Emerson. "We are really sorry," they said in unison.

Stepping out of the mud, Emerson stomped on the sidewalk, trying to shake the mud off his shoes. He then scraped his shoes against the wooden border surrounding the flowerbed. "It's no problem," he grinned. "How many speeding tickets have the island police given you?" he asked.

Elyse was the first to answer. "None," she giggled.

"We're picking up a pie for dinner," Riley volunteered.

"I hope it's not peach because I just bought the last one."

"Nope. My dad likes apple," Riley replied as he parked his bike and began to walk into the bakery.

Emerson resumed walking to the truck as he thought about how much he liked Elyse and Riley. He had interviewed them earlier that summer for a story about island life from a children's perspective. He opened the door of the truck and slid the peach pie across the seat. Looking down at his muddy shoes, he decided to slip them off and tossed them in the back of the truck for the short drive to his aunt's house.

Jimmy's Café
Cuyahoga Falls, Ohio

∽

"Jimmy, the phone's for you," Carla, Jimmy's attractive slender wife, called from the kitchen where she was finishing up a batch of jambalaya for the dinner crowd.

While he waited on the other end of the phone, Emerson pictured the unique coffee house just north of Akron, which he had visited on several occasions two years ago in connection with a story he wrote on the Fallsview Tire takeover battle. He recalled the building's, green artsy exterior that seemed to be more of a fit for Greenwich Village, Haight Asbury, or New Orleans rather than a conservative community such as Cuyahoga Falls. Emerson had established a bond with the artistic owner of the café, who previously ran a restaurant in the French Quarter of New Orleans.

In front of the café, a tall, 59-year-old man wearing black rectangular glasses and who had a thick shock of white hair separated himself from talking to a couple of patrons and walked to the phone. He didn't hear the two ladies comment about his movie star good looks.

"This is Jimmy."

"Jimmy, it's Emerson Moore. How are you doing?"

"Wonderful, man. Just wonderful. It's been awhile since I've seen you. When you coming to see me and have a Jimmy's Special?"

For a moment Emerson could taste the flavorful coffee drink piled high with whipped cream and drenched with chocolate and caramel syrup. "Oh, you're killing me. I wish I had one right now."

"Come on down, We're only an hour-and-a-half away," Jimmy entreated.

"I really can't. I'm heading out of town."

"Somewhere exciting I trust?"

"That's part of the reason I'm calling you. I'm heading to New Orleans."

"Now, I'm envious. Wish I was going."

"I wanted to know if you knew anyone at St. Louis Cathedral."

"Nope. That's not a place I'd hang out. Now, if you need to meet any one on Bourbon Street, I can rattle off a ton of names."

Emerson paused. He had hoped that Jimmy might be able to connect him with some other priests in the event he saw a story developing there and needed additional information. "I may take you up on that and call you. I never know where events may lead me."

"If you get a chance, stop at the River's Edge. It's at the corner of Decatur and St. Anne, across from the Café du Monde. Look up Chellie and Tricia Smith. They own the place and several others in the Quarter. You'll like them. They're good people."

"I ate there once, and the food was outstanding. I'll make a point of stopping in and introducing myself. Tell Kylia, Heather, and Tim that I said hello." He was referring to two of the waitresses and one of the regulars whom he had met on his previous visits.

"I'll do that." And they ended their call.

French Quarter
New Orleans

~

After the plane slowly descended over Lake Pontchartrain and landed at Louis Armstrong International Airport, Emerson claimed his luggage and stepped out of the baggage claim area into the covered arrival area. The humidity hit him as though he had walked full stride into a wall. The heat hung over the city like a heavy shroud, sucking the breath right out of people.

He settled into the old cab he had hailed and the brief respite it tried to provide from the outside humidity. Its weary air conditioner was long overdue for service and did little to provide any retreat from the humidity. It was going to be an uncomfortable drive into the Big Easy, as the city was often called. Emerson had made several trips over his career to this saucy and tantalizing bastion of the South. To Emerson, the city itself reminded him of a cultural gumbo. Its recipe was a concoction of Spanish, French, Italian, Caribbean, Canadian, and African influences with dashes of Southern Protestantism and Haitian voodoo and a hearty helping of Catholicism. From the Garden District's upscale formality and lavish homes to the lively and festive French Quarter with its sumptuous food and Bourbon Street decadence and rich jazz, the Crescent City was a gumbo of varying personalities and a laid-back lifestyle.

During the mid-1500s La Salle had sailed the Mississippi from the Great Lakes to the Gulf of Mexico and had claimed all of the territory for France, naming the territory Louisiana in honor of Louis XIV and his wife, Queen Anne. In 1718, two French Canadian brothers, Pierre Le Moyne, Sieur d'Iberville, and Jean Baptiste le Moyne, Sieur de Bienville, founded New Orleans.

In 1762, Louis XV gave Louisiana to his cousin, Charles III of Spain, which extended Spanish control from Florida westward. In 1803, the Spanish ceded Louisiana to France, who promptly sold it to the United States. Even though the Spanish rule over Louisiana was for a short period of time, they had a significant impact on the architecture. This was due to a massive fire, which devastated the Quarter in 1794. The rebuilding reflected the Spanish influence with the buildings rebuilt close to the curb and adjacent to each other to create a firewall. Wooden siding was banned and, in its place, residents used stucco, which was gaily painted in varying pastel hues. Many of the buildings were rebuilt with elaborately decorated ironwork balconies and galleries—balconies with a roof over them.

The Quarter's varying styles of architecture never seemed to stop fascinating Emerson when he visited. The mixture of Creole cottages, Greek and Renaissance Revival, and Victorian styles created their own special ambiance to the Quarter which runs 12 blocks from Canal Street to Esplanade Avenue and from the banks of the Mississippi and Decatur Street to Rampart Street, a distance of seven blocks.

Exiting I-10 at the Orleans Avenue/Vieux Carre exit and after a couple of turns onto North Rampart and St. Anne, the cab made its way carefully through the crowded and narrow streets. It stopped in front of 625 St. Anne Street at the Place d'Armes Hotel. Emerson stepped out of the cab onto the sidewalk and breathed deeply of the French Quarter's unique aroma. He paid the cabbie, took his suitcase and laptop, and entered the French Provincial lobby of one of his favorite hotels. He had found the hotel several trips ago and fell in love with its distinctive architecture and rooms.

It was conveniently located near to St. Louis Cathedral and Jackson Square and within a few blocks of Café du Monde, Bourbon Street jazz, and his favorite antique weapon shop, Cohen's on Royal Street. Besides having the best location in the Quarter, Emerson enjoyed the hotel's secluded lush garden courtyard with its fountains and inviting pool. The intimate garden was surrounded by the brick townhouses, which housed the hotel's 83 guest rooms.

Behind the desk was a stunning woman in her late 30s with dark hair and a slim figure. When she looked up, Emerson saw bright blue eyes and a smile emanating from her full lips. "May I help you, Sir?' she asked with her southern drawl.

Her drawl teased Emerson's ears. He had always loved the drawls from southerners. There was something about it that was a cross between politeness and warmth, with a touch of sensuality.

"Yes, Candy," Emerson returned the smile as he read the name on her tag. "I have reservations for Moore. Emerson Moore."

"You've stayed with us before, haven't you?"

"Yes, how kind of you to remember." Emerson thought that he remembered her, too. This time, he noticed, she wasn't wearing a wedding band.

Her fingers flew over the keyboard as she searched their database. "Yes, Sir. Mr. Moore, if you'll complete this registration form. We have you upstairs, almost right above us with a balconied room as you requested."

"Thank you. Thank you very much." Emerson began to walk around the corner as he carried his bags to the set of stairs behind the lobby.

"I hope you enjoy your stay with us," she called.

So do I. So do I, Emerson thought as he began to turn his head. He should have been watching where he was walking as he didn't quite get his head turned completely around when he bumped into a man, who stepped out of his office behind the lobby.

"I'm sorry," Emerson began.

"No problem," the man responded.

Emerson recognized the man as Bubby Valentino, the hotel's general manager and owner. The Valentino family were longtime French Quarter residents and owned several hotels in the Quarter. Emerson had met the dapper, high-energy general manager on his last visit, and they had enjoyed conversing together.

"Moore, isn't it?" Valentino was impeccably attired in a crisp white shirt, blue and gold striped tie, dark-blue sport coat, and tan slacks. His graying hair was combed back. He looked like he belonged in the movies.

"Good memory. Emerson Moore."

"Yes yes. We talked in the courtyard the last time you were here. You're the newspaper reporter?"

"Right."

"How many days are you staying?"

"Two or three, although it could be more."

"Good. I'm late for a meeting, but I'll catch up with you." Valentino excused himself and walked briskly out the door to attend his meeting.

Emerson went up the steps to his room on the second floor. Opening the door, he smiled as his eyes took in the rich appointments of his elegant room. One wall was exposed antique brick with a French Provincial, king-sized bed. The other walls were wallpapered with a gold tone and contained subdued stripes. He set down his belongings and walked to the French doors, which he opened, and then he stepped onto the gallery overlooking St. Anne Street. A metal table and two chairs were the only furnishings on the gallery.

Emerson leaned on the railing and took in the sights and sounds from the narrow street below.

Jackson Square
The French Quarter

~

Walking slowly toward St. Louis Cathedral, which was across from Jackson Square, Emerson found the ambiance of the area energizing. The city block-sized square was surrounded by artists displaying their artwork for sale by hanging the paintings on the fence, which surrounded Jackson Square. The artisans were selling jewelry, and there were mimes, caricaturists, fortune tellers, and tarot card readers. There was a carnival-like sense of excitement in the area.

An oasis in the middle of the French Quarter, Jackson Square was surrounded by ironwork and filled with lush tropical plantings and trees. The center of the square was dominated by a statue of Andrew Jackson on a horse to commemorate his victory over the British during the Battle of New Orleans on January 8, 1815. The statue reminded Emerson of another battle, considered the greatest naval battle of the War of 1812. It was the Battle of Lake Erie on September 10, 1813, during which Commodore Oliver Hazard Perry led his fleet of nine ships from South Bass Island's Put-in-Bay to defeat the British fleet of six ships.

Turning his head to his right, Emerson saw St Louis Cathedral, its triple spires reaching to the heavens. Its façade was painted a brilliant white and contrasted sharply against a bright blue sky. It was flanked on both sides by two buildings. The Calbildo, on its left, was the old city hall where the Louisiana Purchase was signed. It was now a museum. On the right was the Presbytere, which was built to match the Calbildo and used as housing for the priests. It was later a courthouse and then a museum.

Entering the cathedral's open doors, Emerson was at once drawn to the numerous Renaissance style paintings and murals of scenes from the life of Christ. Emerson casually looked around the cathedral and through a brochure about the cathedral, which he had picked up when first entering the massive building.

His eyes were drawn to the description of the 4,500 pipe organ that towered 51 feet above the choir loft. He noted that it had been built by the Holtkamp Organ Company in Cleveland, Ohio. *Small world,* Emerson thought, as his concentration turned toward the city located an hour east of his island home.

Emerson was beginning to walk toward the altar when he sensed someone approaching.

"Do you have any questions that I can answer for you?" the voice asked from behind Emerson.

Turning, Emerson saw a young priest. "Yes, you can. I'm looking for Father Alsandi."

"I can find him for you. Who should I say is inquiring, and what is the nature of your visit?" the young priest asked politely.

"My name is Emerson Moore. I'm here on the behalf of a friend of his who passed away."

"Oh dear," the young priest fretted. "Let me take you into the garden. It may be better for you to talk with him in the peace that the garden offers."

"Thank you." Emerson followed the priest through the cathedral to St. Anthony's Garden. Within minutes they walked through the church and into the private garden behind the cathedral.

"You may wait here while I find him." The priest left Emerson to enjoy the lush garden's tranquility.

The garden was filled with towering oak, sycamore, and magnolia trees. It contained a marble statue of Jesus Christ with his arms outstretched, which, at night, cast a large shadow on the rear of the cathedral. Emerson leisurely walked to the garden's far end, which bordered on Royal Street, and walked halfway back.

A slim priest with white hair entered the garden and walked toward Emerson. As the priest neared him, Emerson guessed his age to be in his late 50s.

"I'm Father Alsandi, Mr. Moore. You wanted to see me about one of my friends?" The priest had stopped three feet in front of Emerson and was looking inquisitively at him.

"Yes, Father. I'm from Put-in-Bay. It's on one of the islands in Lake Erie."

Alsandi couldn't hide the look of concern that flashed across his face when he heard Put-in-Bay. He shuddered involuntarily as his mind raced to fathom what might be amiss.

"Yes?"

"It's about a friend of yours, Father Maloney."

"Yes, I know Father Maloney." What Alsandi didn't say was that the two of them had been inseparable during their days doing archival research at the Vatican.

"I'm sorry to tell you that he has passed away," Emerson spoke slowly and compassionately.

"No!" Alsandi was shocked to hear the news.

Emerson nodded his head. "I'm sorry."

He sat down in disbelief on a nearby chair. "How did he die?"

Taking a vacant chair, Emerson sat down. "We don't know yet. An autopsy is being conducted."

"Are you the police? Why are you coming to me with this?" the priest's questions tumbled forth rapidly.

Deciding not to tell him of his background, Emerson responded, "I live on the island and my friend, Barry Hayen who runs the *Put-in-Bay Gazette,* is the executor of Father Maloney's estate. When he was going through Father Maloney's belongings, he found this envelope with a note to please hand deliver this envelope to Father Alsandi in New Orleans at St. Louis Cathedral. Barry couldn't get away and asked me to deliver it. And it didn't hurt that Barry knew that the French Quarter is one of my favorite places to visit." Emerson held out the large manila envelope, which he had been carrying in his left hand. "So, here it is."

Gingerly, the priest took the large envelope and turned it over to look at the handwriting on the front. The familiar handwriting belonged to Maloney. He would have recognized it anywhere.

Standing, Emerson spoke, "I'm not sure what more I can say. He had a great reputation on the island and everyone always had kind words to say about him."

Holding the envelope tightly, Alsandi also stood. His eyes had reddened. "Thank you." As Emerson turned to leave, Alsandi asked, "Are you flying out today?"

"No. I'll be in town for a few days. Would you like to get together over coffee to talk?"

Pausing before answering, Alsandi looked at the messenger standing in front of him. "That would be nice. Where are you staying?"

"Place d'Armes."

"Let me," he started, "let me get over this shock a bit. Then, I'll call you and we can talk." He raised the envelope and clutched it to his chest. "If you'll excuse me, I want to read this."

Emerson nodded his head and left while the priest began to walk to his apartment.

Alsandi's Apartment
The French Quarter
~

Stunned by the unexpected news, Alsandi sat in his large overstuffed chair and stared at the large photo on the opposite wall. It was a bird's-eye view of the Vatican with its daunting medieval towers, Renaissance statues, domes, fountains, and expansive jumbled network of buildings, apartments, offices, and archives dominated by the centerpiece created by St. Peter's Basilica and the nearby Sistine Chapel with its Michelangelo artwork. It was as if time was frozen by these symbols of stability and permanence.

He allowed his mind to drift back to the time he spent there so many years ago as a young up-and-coming priest. Days were filled with the excitement of the crowds in St. Peter's Square when Pope John Paul appeared in the balcony of his papal apartment on the north side of the square. Standing on his balcony, between the open metal shutters of his window, Pope John Paul would say his noonday prayers on Sundays and Holy Days to the crowds sandwiched together on the square below.

From his apartment's balcony on the top floor of the Apostolic Palace, Pope John Paul could look to his right and enjoy an unobstructed view of St. Peter's Basilica. Pope John Paul was a huge fan of Michelangelo and knew quite a bit about the painter.

Alsandi had been in the papal apartment on several occasions as the Pope saw him as a rising star in the church's hierarchy. He was familiar with the Pope's study and chapel and had dined with him privately on several occasions to discuss his research in the archives. Pope John Paul had a keen interest in the influence that the Vatican had had on world events. Down the hall from the Pope's quarters were apartments for his secretary, chauffeur, valet, and a number of Polish nuns who cooked and cleaned for the Polish Pope.

When he had moved into his apartment, he had the old papal collections, furniture, and busts replaced with comfortable antique chairs and tables and seventeenth-century oil paintings. The walls were repainted cream, and the black-and-white marble floor was livened up with a few bright rugs.

Each morning, the Pope would start his day at 5:00 a.m., after sleeping five hours, by praying by himself, while he held his rosary in his hands. Alsandi's hand reached to grip his own rosary, the one that had been given to him by Pope John Paul.

At 7:00 a.m., the Pope would say mass in his private chapel with its white marble walls and light piercing through the stained-glass windows. Here, he was joined by his secretary and the Polish nuns. Following a Polish-style breakfast, he would retreat to his office to complete his morning readings before he conducted his first audience at 11:00 a.m. Some visitors would be invited to join him for lunch, which usually consisted of Italian and Polish food.

Following an afternoon of audiences with visitors the Pope would adjourn to his quarters for dinner. It was here that Alsandi had been invited to join him. Over meals of Polish and Italian food, the Pope would listen attentively with his head cocked to one side or sunk in his hands as he pondered their discussions. Pope John Paul was intensely keen on the progress that Alsandi was making in his studies in the archives.

After dinner, they would often take the stairs to the rooftop where the Pope had a private trellised garden of walks, fountains, and shrubs. There, the highly energetic Pope donned tennis shoes and would walk briskly as he took his daily exercise. Alsandi had been surprised how fast he could walk, while holding detailed discussions.

At times, they would adjourn to the Pope's private library where he would sit with his back to a rich Perugino painting flanked by two sixteenth-century bookcases, while Alsandi would sit across from him. Often the Pope's face was set in contemplative repose.

The Pope was conscious of his responsibility to continue the long papal tradition of influencing worldwide politics and religious issues. His ability to ignite change was significant. He supported the diplomatic aims of the Holy See, tactically and strategically, and was intrigued by the Machiavellian machinations of past Popes. He and many of the Popes before him felt a spiritual responsibility for the human race, which transcended country sovereignties.

Over the centuries, the Papacy had played a vital role with its envoys and mission to influence national and international politics. It had set up diplomatic offices in many countries with relations with the fledgling United States starting in 1784.

Alsandi had been assigned to research work in the Secret Archives over which the Pope had absolute authority as far as its management and use. No one could be admitted to the Secret Archives without the written approval of the Pope and taking a sacred vow of silence. Breaking the vow would result in excommunication from the church.

Since the fifth century, the Vatican had been accumulating documents for the archives and the Apostolic Library, which was started at the same time. There are thousands of volumes of papal letters, briefs, written material, letters from rulers, international treaties, and Papal declarations. It also contains the excommunication documents of Luther and Queen Elizabeth I, and letters signed by Michelangelo, Erasmus, and Lucrezia Borgia.

There are other documents there—documents meant to be hidden from the public's eye on the more than 30 miles of shelving. These documents contain scandals, secrets, and revelations. Some of which Alsandi and Maloney had reviewed— and that's what had got them in trouble. If only Maloney had listened to him, they might still be at the Vatican and Maloney would be alive.

Even with the high level of security in the archives, over the centuries documents would go missing from time-to-time. It was as if some of them disappeared into thin air. Alsandi suspected that some disconcerting documents were burned, but he couldn't prove it.

Alsandi turned his attention to the large envelope. He held it carefully in both hands and began to slowly open it as he wondered what message Maloney wanted to leave him. He pulled out the three-page letter. It was dated three months earlier. Alsandi began to read.

After reading through the salutations and opening comments about their lives at the Vatican, he came to Maloney's apology for involving Alsandi in the scandal. They were discovered in the act of smuggling several documents from the archives and were banished after returning the documents. He had suspected that Maloney had taken other documents from the Secret Archives without telling him, but he wasn't sure where Maloney had hidden them. When their apartments at the Vatican had been searched, no documents had been discovered. Somehow, Maloney must have stashed the files off-site so he could have evidence of what he had seen.

Alsandi reread the last paragraph several times and wondered what action he should morally be compelled to take. He sat back in his chair and thought about potential alternatives. Maloney's letter detailed his discovery of a confidential one-page document from Pope Pius VII to a senior staff member in 1805. It directed the dispatch of a special envoy on a highly secret mission to U.S. President Thomas Jefferson to inform him about a treaty violation that would have grave consequences for Napoleon and the United States.

Alsandi recalled the difficulties that Pius had from the very beginning with Napoleon and the French. When Pius VII was crowned on March 21, 1800, a paper-mache tiara was used. Previously, Napoleon had seized the jeweled papal tiara and kidnapped the prior Pope, Pius VI, who died in Napoleon's prison.

The conflict between the Vatican and Napoleon continued when Pius VII was elected. Napoleon expected the Pope to comply with all of his demands, while the Pope argued for the return of the Papal States and seized ecclesiastical property as well as the release of a number of imprisoned clergymen and nuns.

The Church—and Pius in particular—suffered additional humiliation in 1804 when Pius was ordered to Paris by Napoleon to consecrate Napoleon as emperor. At the last minute, Napoleon demeaned Pius by taking the crown from Pius' hands and crowning himself.

Pius took a brave stand when he excommunicated Napoleon from the Catholic Church in 1808. Napoleon had

had enough and ordered French cannons pointed at his papal bedroom. He then ordered Pius kidnapped and held in French captivity like his predecessor. Pius was eventually freed by the British in 1814.

Alsandi fretted about consequences to himself, even though Maloney was dead. He feared that the Vatican would take repercussions on him for Maloney stealing documents from the Secret Archives. He didn't want any undue attention cast upon himself. He had other demons torturing him and didn't need any additional pressure.

Knowing that one of the ways he relieved stress was nearby, he stripped to his boxers as he walked to his bedroom where he admired his well-chiseled body in the full mirror attached to his closet door. He slipped on a pair of jogging shorts, seated himself in his Nautilus, and began a heavy workout. Keeping his body in shape was one way in which he could focus on other things. He picked up the pace, and sweat began to pour out of his pores as he seemed to try to purge himself of any evil thoughts.

James H. Cohen & Sons, Inc.
437 Royal Street
~

Across from the Louisiana State Supreme Courthouse on Royal Street sat Emerson's favorite antique gun, sword, and coin shop, James H. Cohen & Sons. It was between Conti and St. Louis Streets. The sign over the store's door and large front windows read *James H. Cohen & Sons—Rare Coins*.

Pushing the gated door open, Emerson entered the three-story building, which had a balcony overlooking Royal Street. It was a store, which he had visited every time he was in New Orleans—and every time he walked in, a chill ran down his spine. It was the store's magical ability to transport customers back in time as imaginations were unleashed to think about the person who might have handled the various muskets, dueling pistols, rifles, cutlasses, swords, and gold and silver coins.

Before him were two walls lined with Kentucky long rifles, Civil War carbines, shotguns, British Enfield rifles, cutlasses, and sabers. The display cases were filled with rare coins and handguns, some more than 200 years old.

The store dated to 1898 when James Cohen's grandfather started it. He lived in an apartment over the store where he and his wife raised seven children. His grandson, Jimmie, who was the current owner and always Mr. Cohen to Emerson, showed interest in the business at an early age and traveled with his grandfather around the country and internationally as he learned the business. His wife, Beverly, and his sons, Jerry and Steve, as well as his grandson, Barry, worked with him at the store now.

The gray-haired gregarious Mr. Cohen greeted Emerson warmly when he saw him walk in. "Mr. Emerson Moore, me thinks you have not darkened my door lately," he teased as he shook Emerson's hand. Mr. Cohen was the epitome of a gracious southern gentleman. He was a person that Emerson held in the highest regard.

"It's been maybe two years," Emerson responded.

"Way too long!" Mr. Cohen replied. "Barry, come here," he called to his grandson. "See how tall he has grown since you were last here," he said as he beamed with pride at his own grandson's involvement with the business.

"A fine-looking young man," Emerson said as he shook Barry's hand. "You're stepping right into your grandfather's shoes."

"Yes, sir," Barry stated warmly.

Emerson had admired the family-like atmosphere in the small store. Turning to Mr. Cohen, Emerson asked, "Anything new since I was last here?"

"'Anything new?' he asks. Not a thing. I only carry things old!" the wily storeowner teased. "Step over here," he urged

Emerson to a display case in the middle of the store. Pulling out a revolver from the top shelf, he laid it on top of the display case. "It's an 1863 LeMat. It was manufactured in France primarily for Confederate officers. They fought to get their hands on one of these." He passed the weapon to Emerson who held the weapon carefully as he examined it.

"It looks like two barrels," he observed.

"Exactly! The top barrel is a .42 caliber percussion with a nine-shot cylinder. Below it is a .63 caliber percussion shotgun."

"Two guns in one," Emerson commented in awe.

"Exactly! The hammer has a pivoting striker so that you could fire either barrel."

"Ten deadly shots."

"Yes, for a handgun, it packed a lot of firepower," Mr. Cohen said as he took the gun from Emerson and placed it back in the display cabinet. Emerson noted the price was $22,500. He knew he wouldn't be buying that one today.

Mr. Cohen pulled out a mahogany box and set it on the display case. "Open it," he said to Emerson.

Emerson's eyes took in the fine mahogany wood as he slowly opened the box to reveal two flintlock pistols. "Beautiful!"

"They're Irish flintlocks from 1800. They were manufactured in Dublin by Thomas Fowler. They have .50 caliber octagon barrels and are inset with gold at the barrel breech. They've got silver initial trigger guards, locks, hammers, and throats." He picked up one of the pistols and turned it so Emerson could easily see the stock. "They've checkered walnut stocks, too."

He passed the pistol to Emerson who held it carefully as he felt its weight. Handing it back to Mr. Cohen, he asked, "What's in the box?"

"This is the original mahogany box. It holds a screwdriver, a combination Sykes flask, cap box, and ball holder," he said as he opened the box and displayed its contents.

"This is exquisite," Emerson murmured as he looked at the well-preserved pieces. "I just love your place," he said, looking around the quaint store. "It is so full of history!"

"There's a piece of history that was actually birthed in this store," Mr. Cohen said with a twinkle in his eye.

"Oh?"

"You'd never guess it, but the cocktail originated here!" he stated proudly.

Emerson looked perplexed. "In an antique weapon shop? How's that?"

Cohen's face broke into a warm smile as he began to tell his story. "In 1793, a French planter and pharmacist by the name of Peychaud fled Santo Domingo and opened an apothecary shop here. One of the things that he brought along with him was an old family recipe for bitters. He added a few drops of the bitters to brandy toddies that he prepared for Creole gentleman. The drink became the rage of New Orleans and his business boomed. Peychaud, for some reason or another, served his drink in a double-end eggcup called a coquetier (kah-kuh-TYAY).

"After Louisiana was purchased from France, a large number of Americans moved to New Orleans and began to enjoy his drink, which had spread by then to a number of New Orleans establishments. After a few drinks, people would slur the pronunciation and began calling it cocktail."

"And it all started here!"

Beaming, Mr. Cohen nodded his head.

"I'll be in town for few days and I'll plan to stop back for another visit."

"Good. We enjoy seeing you."

Emerson left the store and walked the two blocks to one of his favorite restaurants in the Quarter, The Court of Two Sisters. The restaurant was named after the two Creole sisters who had owned the notions store that originally was run on the site and served the Creole aristocracy. Entering it from the Royal Street entrance, he walked past its large ornate bar in the Carriageway Bar. The sign on its Charm Gate read, *"Touch the Gate! Will Give You Charm!"* Emerson couldn't resist and reached out to touch it as he walked past.

He approached the waiting hostess and requested a seat in the picturesque courtyard with its flagstones, ornate metal chairs, white tablecloths and flowing fountains. At night, the courtyard was softly illuminated by gaslights, and a strolling trio played jazz to the delight of the restaurant's patrons.

When the waiter appeared, Emerson ordered a glass of wine and the Creole Seafood Gumbo and Lobster Etouffee, which was gulf lobster sautéed in a rich etouffee sauce laced with seasonings and spices and served with white rice. He had already made up his mind for dessert. It would be crème brulee.

Jumping Jay's Blues Café
Bourbon Street

~

A dense cloud of cigarette smoke blurred the vision of the patrons in the crowded Bourbon Street bar. The patrons were a kaleidoscope of residents and visitors to the Quarter. Sultry jazz music gently filled the café as each of the patrons pursued their own dreams. Some were talking. Others were huddled together planning their evening's opportunities. Some sat back and sipped their drinks as they listened to the soulful music.

A tall white-haired man wearing black sunglasses, despite the evening's darkness, and tight trousers entered the bar and paused inside the doorway where the light showcased his chiseled face. His black shirt's buttons strained to contain his well-developed and muscled chest. Knowing that he had captured virtually everyone's attention, he smiled slowly and then walked confidently across the room to a table secluded in a dark corner. Its only light came from a solitary candle whose flame flickered slowly as the air from the overhead fan's blades teased it. After ordering a chardonnay, he settled back in the chair to wait and see what type of opportunity the evening would present him.

He didn't have to wait long before he spotted his prey entering the bar. It was an overweight man in his early 50s with graying thick hair. His attire signaled that he was a tourist or attendee at the week's convention.

Edison Fordham had given his friends a flimsy excuse about turning in early and escaped from the boring chatter about the day's speakers. He was looking for some excitement and escaped to the depravity of Bourbon Street where this somewhat wealthy entrepreneur would seek companionship.

He looked around the room and spied the handsome man seated alone in the corner. Their eyes locked momentarily, and he thought he saw a welcoming smile cross the man's face for a moment. That was the only invitation that he needed. Throwing caution to the wind, he walked over to the stranger.

"May I join you?" Fordham asked.

The stranger looked up at him and then around him toward the doorway. "I was actually waiting for someone," he responded, then looked toward the open doorway again as he lied to his unsuspecting target. It was all a part of the charade, which he was playing.

Fordham began to turn. "I won't trouble you then."

"No trouble. You might as well as sit. It looks like my friend is running late."

"Thank you," Fordham replied as he dropped his heavy frame into the chair and loosened his tie. "Warm in here," he commented.

"Yes, it is."

The waiter appeared with his wine and looked at Fordham. "May I get you something to drink, Sir?'

Fordham looked at the stranger's drink and back to the waiter. "Sure, why not. I'll try a Hurricane!"

"Strong drink!" the stranger commented as the waiter scurried off to the bar.

"I like 'em strong and powerful like hurricanes," he said cryptically.

"Be careful for what you wish," the stranger cautioned. "Hurricanes can be very dangerous."

"Nothing that I can't handle!" Fordham responded.

Just then the ringing of the stranger's phone clamored for attention. "Might be my friend," the stranger suggested as he reached into his right pocket for his cell phone and withdrew it. "Hello," he answered as he placed the phone to his ear. "You can't? Why not? Okay, I understand. I'll give you a call later this week . . . Sure, that sounds delightful. I'll see you all on Saturday for dinner at eight." Switching off the cell phone, he placed it back in his right pants pocket and leaned forward in his chair. "Damn. Stood up for tonight. And she was a good-looking Cajun," he said with all of his southern charm.

"I couldn't help overhearing, but it sounds like it may work out for you later in the week," Fordham responded as he wiped a few drops of sweat from his face. Even though the bar was air-conditioned, the unit was old and was straining to cool the room in the night filled with high humidity. He picked up a napkin from the worn table and wiped his wet brow.

"Yes, it will. And she's a tall glass of cool water," the stranger lied as he slipped his hand into his left pants pocket and switched off his other cell phone, the one he had used to dial the cell phone that he had answered and held the fictitious conversation with.

Closing his eyes momentarily, Fordham tried to picture in his mind how this woman must look. A smile crossed his face as a vivid picture formed. He smiled as this vision of beauty stepped out of the recesses of his mind.

The smile was not lost on the stranger. "Guess I'll have to implement my back up plan," he said as he set the bait.

"Back up plan?"

"Oh yes. I know quite a few women in town who enjoy associating with me, if you know what I mean?" he said with a sly grin.

Noticing the grin, Fordham responded as he lifted his second Hurricane. "Yeah. Any of them got a friend?" he asked hopefully and then sat back suddenly as he grimaced and a look of pain crossed his face.

"You all right?" the stranger asked.

Gripping the small table with one hand as the other set the Hurricane back on the table, Fordham grimaced again. "It's my back. Threw it out, and the pain killers aren't working!"

"What happened?"

"Just reached for my razor, and it went out."

"Taking anything for it?"

"Skelaxin and Naproxen. A muscle relaxant and anti-inflammatory."

"Should you be drinking if you're taking drugs?"

"Probably not. Maybe that's why I'm starting to get a little woozy."

The stranger smiled to himself. "I think I have the answer for your back."

"You do?"

"Yes, her name is Star, and she'll put you out of this world."

It was Fordham's turn to smile as his imagination ran wild. "I like stars. And I could use an out-of-this-world experience."

The stranger retracted the cell phone in his right pocket and quickly dialed a number. As he put the phone to his ear, he looked at his tablemate. "Let's see if she's available." A moment later, the stranger began talking into his phone. "Hello, Star. Is your star rising tonight?" he chuckled softly at his quip. "I have a friend with me who could use your ministrations. Are you available?" The stranger looked across the table at his newly made friend.

Fordham returned the look as more sweat pooled on his chubby face. He was smiling, and his chubby fingers thumped the table top in eager anticipation.

"Good then. Where shall we meet you?" he paused as he waited for an answer. "Sure, we can walk on over to your place. I know where the key is." He paused again, and then continued, "We'll be waiting." He disconnected the call and placed the cell phone into his right pocket.

"What did she say? Is she busy?" Fordham flooded the stranger with questions as his excitement raced.

"She's working now, but will meet us at her apartment within the hour. So why don't you finish your drink, and we'll walk over."

"She's really good with her hands?" Fordham asked as he downed the Hurricane quickly. He couldn't believe his luck and how this stranger was helping him.

"There's no comparison," the stranger said cryptically. "Ready to go?"

"Yeah. Do we need to call a cab?" he asked as he stood, wobbled, and grabbed the table for balance. The combination of the drugs and the alcohol were taking effect on him—and the stranger noticed it.

"No, we can walk from here."

Fordham groaned when another spasm of pain surged through his lower back.

"Here, let me help you," the stranger said as he walked next to Fordham and placed his arm delicately around his waist to help support him.

"Thank you," he said, and then offered, "My name is Edison Fordham."

"It is an absolute delight to make your acquaintance. I'm William Woods," the stranger lied again.

"It certainly is nice of you to go out of your way to help me this evening."

"The pleasure is all mine. I'm what you might call an angel of mercy," he replied as the two began to exit the bar.

"Faggots!" one of the men at the bar called as the two walked by.

"Coon ass redneck!" Woods yelled back.

The man at the bar stood from his stool and began to take a step towards the muscular white-haired Woods and Fordham. His friend grabbed his arm. "Let them be, Morris. You don't need any trouble."

The detective pulled his arm away abruptly and turned to his partner. "Listen here, Jonesy. If I want to have fun every once in a while, I'm going to."

"Count the cost," Jones said.

"Ahhh! I was just scaring them anyway," Morris said as he returned to his bar stool.

Outside the two men wobbled through a light rain along Bourbon Street. One in pain and anticipation of a rendezvous with a woman named Star. The other plotting his next steps to an enjoyable evening, which was set by the fictitious call to a woman named Star, a woman who didn't exist.

The Apartment
Above The River's Edge Restaurant
The Lower Pontalba

~

"Make yourself at home," Woods said as he replaced the key to its hiding place in a cutout above the entrance doorframe. While it wasn't Woods' apartment, he had been a guest there on two occasions and remembered where the owner hid the key. He also knew that the owner was working late that night and decided to take the chance that the apartment would be vacant. It had been a relatively short walk from Jumping Jay's Blues Café to the small second-floor apartment above the River's Edge Restaurant and overlooking Decatur Street and Café Du Monde.

Fordham stumbled into the opulent entranceway, which was lined by expensive paintings of women and into an overstuffed red-velvet chair. Fordham smiled and adjusted his glasses as Woods walked over to a sideboard, which was filled with an array of alcoholic beverages. The various cuts of glass sparkled in the low light of the room. It was a small apartment dominated by a large fireplace and mantel. There was a small sofa, also finished in red velvet, and heavy red velvet drapes covered the French doors, which led to the balcony.

"My own version of a Hurricane," Woods said as he walked over to Fordham who was stretched uncomfortably in the chair. Fordham licked his lips as his grubby little hands reached for the strong drink. He raised his glass in a toast to Woods. "To a mutually beneficial friendship," he said before downing the glassful of strong liquor.

"Cheers," Woods' voice said softly as, unnoticed, he set his glass down without tasting it and watched Fordham gulping his drink.

Placing the glass on the ornate cherry end table next to his chair, Fordham looked through his pain-filled eyes at Woods. He was getting dizzier and having second thoughts about the amount of alcohol he had consumed that evening, starting with the wine at dinner with his friends. "Where's Star?" His voice was slurred.

"She should be along shortly," Woods said as he began to quietly approach Fordham. "Let's get you in the bedroom where she can work her magic on you."

"Yeah yeah. Don't want to keep her waiting when she arrives," he said as he began to slowly lift his pudgy body from the chair. Wincing in pain, he asked as Woods put his arm around him to steady him, "Why are you still wearing those sunglasses? Don't you want to take them off?"

It wasn't the first time that Woods had been asked that question. "It's my eyes. They're very sensitive to light."

"But there's hardly any light on," Fordham gasped as his body spasmed from its back pain.

"I know, but they're still sensitive," he responded in an icy calm tone.

Fordham stood awkwardly and leaned against Woods.

Café du Monde
Decatur Street

~

Following dinner, Emerson strolled through the Quarter toward Decatur Street as a light rain fell. He ended up at one of his favorite haunts in the Quarter, Café du Monde with its chicory coffee and French beignets, doughnuts covered with powdered sugar.

The chicory coffee flowed down his throat like slippery mud, but with an edge that gave it its distinct flavor. Protected by the green-and-white awning from the gentle rain, Emerson reached for his sugar-coated beignet. Lifting it to his mouth, he paused to breathe in its sweet aroma, allowing it to fill his nostrils, before sinking his teeth into the hot delicacy. He bit into the savory pastry and quickly reached for the glass of water. Hot from the oven was an understatement as he drenched his tortured tongue with the cool water. It happened every time, but it was a part of his routine when he visited the Quarter.

Emerson sat back in his chair, which was located next to the sidewalk. He swept his eyes along Decatur Street and down St. Anne and observed pedestrians scurrying through the light rain. The rain had little cooling effect on the late-night heat. It just seemed to add to the steamy evening. Laughter from the patrons at the River's Edge Restaurant carried across the street to where Emerson was seated. The River's Edge was located at the corner of St. Anne and Decatur, the 27th busiest intersection in the world.

Behind him and from the top of the levee on the banks of the Mississippi, the music from a lone saxophone filled the damp air as it wafted through the quarter. Across the street from where Emerson sat, a lone mule-drawn carriage made its way along the street. The slow but steady clippity-clop of the mule's hooves added to the sounds of the late night.

Looking toward Jackson Square, Emerson saw the white spire of Saint Louis Cathedral bathed in light. The entire front of the brilliant white cathedral stood out in contrast to the muted tones of the nearby buildings. The park itself contrasted to the surrounding buildings. It was a green oasis, offering locals and visitors a respite from the busy streets and alleys.

Emerson sipped his coffee and tentatively took a small bite out of the cooling beignet. Its sweet doughy richness touched his taste buds and a smile crossed his face.

Looking again down cobble stoned St. Anne Street, Emerson noticed the dark pools of rainwater that had accumulated in depressed areas. They reflected the warm inviting lights from the stores in the lower Pontalba building and served as beacons to weary travelers. Farther down St. Anne Street, a rotund figure in a clown suit was leaning against the wall. *Probably had a little too much to drink*, Emerson thought.

Finishing off his beignets and coffee, Emerson stood.

A gunshot, followed by breaking glass and a scream, pierced the evening's quiet tranquility. The Café du Monde broke into a sudden silence as everyone's attention was drawn to the balcony above River's Edge Restaurant. A chunky disheveled man in his 50s staggered to his feet on the balcony. Blood was oozing from his body and from the multiple cuts he'd suffered by the broken glass and the gunshot wound.

"No," Fordham screamed. "I promise. I won't tell anyone!"

It was then that the watchers from the street and Café du Monde saw a man with thick white hair and wearing dark sunglasses standing inside the second-floor apartment. He was holding an object in his hand, a handgun.

"Too late for that," he said softly as his finger began to curl around the trigger.

"No! No!" the wounded man cried out as his eyes darted for an escape route. They didn't have a chance to dart for more than a few seconds as he lost his balance and plummeted backwards over the balcony's scrolled ironworks onto the Decatur Street sidewalk. The figure in the doorway retreated into the apartment and out of sight of the spectators below.

Emerson had raced from the restaurant as he realized what was happening. He had been halfway across the street when Fordham tumbled over the railing. He ran to the victim's side and checked his pulse. Picking up the limp hand, he wasn't surprised when he couldn't locate one.

Looking into the River's Edge Restaurant, he shouted to one of the waiters, "Call the police," and raced around the corner to find an entrance to the second-floor apartments.

He wasted precious minutes until he found the stairway. It was down a small alley and led to the apartments on the second and third floors of the structure. He took the stairs two at a time to the second floor. Arriving at the door, which opened into the second-floor hallway, he cautiously eased the door open. Looking up and down the narrow hallway, which was lit at both ends by a low wattage bulb, he stepped into the hallway. He slowly walked to the end of the hallway where the door to the apartment facing Decatur Street was ajar.

Careful not to touch the knob, he gently pushed the door open. When the door squeaked, Emerson shuddered. In reaction, he stepped back suddenly and into someone who had walked quietly behind him.

"Don't move!" the feminine voice commanded. "I'm a police officer."

Emerson relaxed. He turned and his eyes moved from the gun's barrel to the feminine hand holding it. It looked feminine, but it had the strength of a man's hand. He saw the fingernail polish and looked up at the face of an attractive dark-haired Creole. It was Detective Melaudra Drencheau. Before either one could speak, a voice called out from the other end of the hallway.

"Nothing here," the rotund figure in a clown suit huffed as he walked down the hallway toward them.

"Elmo, you'd be in better shape if you cut a few dozen of those beignets you eat every day!"

"Down to two dozen a day, now," he chortled.

Emerson couldn't resist. He had to ask, "Who's the clown?"

"Not funny, Son," the other detective fumed. "Detective Harry Elms on undercover duty!" he said smartly.

Turning her attention back to Emerson, the female detective appraised him with her large brown eyes. He felt as if she was undressing him. Her wide and inviting mouth broke into a smile as she began to speak.

"And just who do you think you are? Running up here and unarmed at that?" She asked as she looked at his clenched hands. "What would you do if you found the shooter? Ask him politely to give you his gun?" she asked sarcastically.

"I was just trying to spot him and tell you guys where he went."

"Lucky for you that he fled. I wouldn't expect any killer in his right mind would be hanging around."

"Yeah, Mel, but what killer is in his right mind?" Elms retorted with a grin.

Ignoring her partner, Melaudra asked Emerson, "So, you're one of the witnesses?"

"Yes."

"Okay then, you stand back now while we check the apartment to be absolutely sure he's gone."

Emerson stepped to the other side of the hall as the two police officers with their guns drawn entered the small apartment.

Emerson waited a moment and then stepped into the apartment. Broken glass from the shattered French door was scattered on the highly polished wooden floors and the balcony floor.

"All clear. Must have fled down the back stairway in there," Melaudra reported when they rejoined Emerson at the apartment's doorway. "Let's go check on our victim," Melaudra suggested as they left the apartment. Two uniformed officers ran past them on their way to the apartment. "It's clear," she told them as they continued on their way to secure the premises for the crime investigation unit. When they returned to the street, an ambulance was pulling away.

"To the morgue?" Drenchau asked a nearby uniformed officer.

"No, to St. Albans. They found a pulse," the officer replied.

"They found a pulse?" Melaudra asked.

"Yeah," the officer answered.

Melaudra turned to Elms. "This might be our break."

Standing nearby and hearing her comment, Emerson asked, "Big break?"

Melaudra paused and looked at him. "You. Who are you?"

"Emerson Moore. I work for the *Washington Post*," he explained.

Melaudra and Elms groaned.

"A reporter? Just what we don't need! We can't talk to you!" Elms moaned.

"Why not?"

"It's got to be cleared through the community relations department. Send your written request to community relations."

"Like I have time to do that and follow up on this story!" Emerson fumed.

"It doesn't matter anyway, Pal. They don't respond to written requests anyway!" Elms commented sardonically.

"So, what do you want me to do about it?" Melaudra asked.

"Take me along with you to the hospital. That's where you were going, right?" Emerson pleaded.

"No can do," Elms answered. "We'd be in big trouble for breaking the rules."

"I'm not asking you to break them, just bend them a bit. Come on, what do you say?"

Neither of the two detectives responded.

"Okay then, I'll just have to write my own version of what's transpired here tonight. I'm not sure that it's going to show the police in a positive light, since I'd have to draw my own conclusions due to limited access and missing facts."

Elms looked at Melaudra. "What do you think, Mel?" He was worried about any more bad press for the department. There had been a rash of negative stories over the last few months about the department.

"The department certainly doesn't need any more negative stories. The stories lately all have had a negative slant," Elms said warily.

"Good point," Melaudra said as she appraised Emerson carefully. "How do we know that you're not setting us up?"

"Not my style. I do my best to be fair and accurate. Besides, I'm from out of town. I don't have any axes to grind."

"If we let you come along, you'd contact community relations in the morning?" Melaudra asked.

"First thing!" Emerson answered eagerly.

Melaudra eyed the reporter. He was kind of cute, and there was an edginess about him that she liked. "Oh, what the hell. Come along. I'm Detective Melaudra Drenchau and you've already met my partner, Harry Elms."

"Charmed," Elms beamed a large smile through his clown make-up.

"Thank you!" Emerson replied. "Now, what were you saying about a break?"

"You don't miss anything do you?" Melaudra asked as she smiled.

"Not too much!"

"Harry, you tell him."

"Okay. Over the last few months, there have been a series of unsolved murders in the Quarter that appear to be related."

"How do you know they're related?" Emerson asked.

"There's a common thread that runs through each one of them. They're usually murdered somewhere else, then their bodies show up in one of the alleys the next morning. All of the victims have a cross drawn on their forehead. It's drawn in their own blood."

"How do you know this one is related?"

"Actually, we don't for sure. This one is different. It involved gunshot wounds. The others didn't."

"So?"

Melaudra responded to Emerson's question, "Forensics should be here any second. If they find a white hair sample that matches the samples found on the other bodies, we know we're on the right trail."

"The guy who pulled the trigger had white hair," Emerson volunteered.

The two detectives looked at each other and arched their eyebrows.

"Hmm. There's one big difference this time," Melaudra said confidently.

"And that is?"

"We've got a survivor. If he lives, he can help us identify the killer," Melaudra explained.

"Don't you think the killer is concerned?"

"Yep. That's why we're headed for St. Albans. It's only a five-minute drive. You coming?"

"Sure, I'd like that," Emerson replied.

Emerson followed the leggy Melaudra and the chubby Elms as they walked through the small crowd, huddled under a sea of umbrellas, watching the police at work. Two of the uniformed police officers were ordering the gawking spectators to disperse.

They wove their way through the maze of police and emergency vehicles and past the raucous chatter blaring from the police radios. The flashing blue lights of the parked police cars punctuated the rainy night.

Emerson slid into the back seat of the detective's car, which was parked on Decatur Street. Melaudra sat on the driver's side, and Emerson noticed that she slumped in her seat, homeboy style. They drove slowly through the Quarter on their way to North Rampart and the hospital.

"One nice thing about the hospital," Melaudra commented as she drove.

"What's that?" Emerson queried.

"It's located across from the police station."

"Convenient," Emerson replied.

St. Alban's Hospital
North Rampart Street

~

Opening ominously, the emergency room doors revealed two EMTs wheeling a gurney with a young black man, who was moaning from a knife stabbing in the right chest.

"Is this the knife wound?" the emergency room administrator asked as they approached her station.

"Yep, we called it in a few minutes ago. It was a gang fight."

"Take him to bed three in the trauma bay," the emergency room administrator urged.

The EMTs rolled the gurney as instructed to bed three where they were met by a team of ER professionals. Together, they lifted the sheets and transferred the wounded man to bed three.

One of the EMTs commented as they shifted the young man from the gurney to the trauma bay bed, "Low blood pressure. He's been going in and out of consciousness. Some difficulty in breathing and an elevated heartbeat."

The ER doctor began ordering procedures. "I want a chest x-ray on him now!"

Before the technicians arrived, nurses were hooking up the heart monitor, pulse oximetry, and IV, which contained fluids to sedate the young man who had a tendency to thrash about. They fastened restraints to him to keep him still until the medication could calm him.

Technicians scurried into the room with the portable x-ray equipment and quickly took x-rays of the young man's chest. Within minutes, they handed the results to the ER doctor on duty. He quickly reviewed them and ordered a chest tube for decompression. "Looks like a hemothorax and a collapsed lung," he said, referring to blood accumulating in the cavity between the deflated lung and the chest wall.

Bed Six
Trauma Bay
St. Albans Hospital

~

"How's he doing, Doc?" Melaudra asked as she, Elms, and Emerson stood at the foot of Fordham's bed and watched the team of medical practioners scurrying to attend to their patient.

"It's going to be touch and go. We just got the x-rays back, and it looks like the bullet is lodged in his abdomen. We're going to take him to surgery," the ER doctor said hurriedly.

"What about other injuries?" Elms probed.

"We're still assessing. It looks like a concussion. He's got multiple broken ribs, head trauma, and probable back injuries. But folks, you've got to excuse me. I need to work with the trauma team."

"Sure, Doc. We'll check back tomorrow," Melaudra replied as the doctor pulled the curtain shut to block off further conversation.

As they began to walk away, Emerson commented, "Guess it would be safe to say that he didn't want to talk any more." Emerson didn't see a white-coated doctor rushing toward them and almost bumped into him. "Excuse me," Emerson apologized as he dodged him at the last second, and the doctor threw a stern glance at him.

"Truman, I didn't know that a cardiologist of your stature would be on call here this late at night," Melaudra said in surprise.

Turning his head, the doctor saw Melaudra, and his demeanor changed immediately. "And how did I not see such a beautiful woman in my presence? Good evening, Melaudra. What a pleasure it is to feast my eyes on you!" An evil grin came over his face as he spoke in a lecherous manner.

"Give it up, Truman," she responded to his ignominious comment. "Emerson, meet Truman Thibadaux. He's the head of cardiology here."

"Emerson Moore, *Washington Post* investigative reporter." Emerson said as he extended his hand to Thibadaux.

"Welcome to New Orleans. And what brings a reporter like you from Washington to here?"

"Actually, I'm from Put-in-Bay. It's a . . ."

"Yes, I know. It's on Lake Erie," Thibadaux interrupted.

"You've been there?"

"Yes. Recently I had a chance to visit it with some colleagues of mine. What a coincidence that I should meet someone from the islands," Thibadaux commented. He wanted to ask about Trudy's death, but knew it would be unwise to ask.

"Yes, our world just keeps getting smaller," Emerson responded.

"Well, I must attend to our new patient," Thibadaux said urgently as he reluctantly pulled his eyes away from Melaudra and toward Fordham's bed. "If you'll excuse me." Thibadaux took two steps then paused. "Melaudra, the invitation is still open. Any time that you would like to go out for a nice romantic dinner with one of New Orleans' most eligible bachelors, just call me," Thibadaux said invitingly as he arched his eyebrows. He didn't wait for a response, just turned and walked to Fordham's curtained area.

Emerson had watched the exchange between the two. "You two have a thing going?"

"There's no way in hell!" she answered without hesitation. "I'd be on my deathbed, and I still wouldn't let him touch me. He is so full of himself, having his photo in every newspaper possible."

Looking at Elms, Emerson asked, "Do I detect a little hostility there?"

"Long story short, he wanted to take her out, she wasn't interested, but he doesn't give up," Elms responded. "He's got women in this town falling all over him."

They reached the emergency room parking lot and the detective's car where Melaudra regained her composure and posed a question. "Okay Mr. Investigative Reporter, what's your angle here? What are you writing about tonight?"

"Nothing. If you're worried that I'm here to do a crime series, forget it."

"Then, why are you here?" Melaudra questioned.

"I had a meeting with one of the priests at St. Louis Cathedral today. A friend of his, who was also a priest, died suddenly on our island. I was asked to deliver an envelope concerning the estate to him," Emerson explained. "That's the only reason that I'm here."

"I see," Melaudra said. "So, you're not going to write anything about our little escapade tonight, are you?"

"Don't have any reason to."

"Good. It's getting late," she said as she looked at her watch. "Why don't you stop by our office tomorrow, and we can take your statements."

"My statements?"

"Sure, you're a witness," she replied.

They agreed on a time, and Emerson turned to walk back into the Quarter.

"Do you need a ride back to your hotel?" Melaudra asked.

"No. It's only a few blocks, and it'll give me a chance to sort through the evening events."

"Okay, but don't say that I didn't offer," her voice replied warmly. *He's kind of cute,* Melaudra thought again as she eased herself into the car and slouched behind the wheel.

Emerson waved and began to cross the street.

"Nice guy," Elms observed as he watched Emerson leave. "For a reporter," he added.

Melaudra didn't reply. She was analyzing the night's events, although most of her analysis centered on Emerson.

Ten Minutes Later
Emergency Room Lobby

The emergency room administrator was focused on entering patient data into her computer and didn't notice the harried young black man walk briskly into the emergency room's waiting area. He had a wild look in his eyes as he nervously looked around the waiting area and then approached the administrator seated behind the admitting window.

"Excuse me," the man stammered.

"Yes. May I help you?" she asked as she looked up at the agitated visitor.

"Yeah. My brother. He was stabbed. I need to see him," the man answered as he looked around the waiting room again.

"His name?"

"Jackson Jenkins."

"Sir, do you know why he was brought here?" she asked as she looked at her records.

"He was knifed in a gang fight. Our mama got a call and she's on her way down here."

The administrator's fingers flew over the keyboard as she looked up his name. "Sure, here he is. They just brought him in, and he is stabilized. You can go through that door to the trauma bay. He's in bed three."

"Thank you very much," the wild-eyed youth responded anxiously as he followed her instructions and walked down the hallway. Finding bed three, he pulled back the curtain and entered the room. He saw that Jackson's eyes were closed, and he looked around the room at the medical equipment.

With an evil grin, he walked over to his supposed brother. He raised one hand and clamped it over the brother's mouth, awakening him. When Jackson's eyes opened and he saw who was standing over him, he gasped and began to contort his body wildly in bed as he tried to break the restraints to escape. The man who had stabbed him was standing over him.

"These honkies thought you was my brother, and they let me in to see you. I bet you thought you were done with me, Baby."

The patient tried to scream, but nothing came out as the intruder clamped harder on his mouth.

"You and I's got some unfinished business. And I'm finishing it now," he said as he produced a knife from under his shirt and plunged it deep into Jackson's heart, killing him.

The monitor's alarm began to ring, and the killer ran out of the room, nearly knocking over the approaching nurse. "It's my brother. He started moving all about, and then he quit breathing!" he yelled as he ran toward the door to the emergency room lobby. "I can't stand the sight of blood," he called as he went into the waiting room, and the doors swung shut behind him. He ran to a waiting car and escaped into the rainy night.

The Next Morning
St. Albans Hospital

~

It was nearing 7:00 a.m., and someone entered Edison Fordham's room in intensive care. Fordham was unconscious and on a ventilator which was breathing for him. He was in serious condition after his surgery.

The visitor had brought Fordham's medical chart into the room, reviewed it, and then replaced it in the holder outside of the entrance. Re-entering the room, the visitor walked over to the various devices and turned off the alarms on the heart monitor, pulse oximetry, and the ventilator. Then he pulled the ventilator's plug from the socket, shutting it off, as well as the oxygen supply to Fordham. Within minutes, Fordham was dead and so was a witness who could identify his assailant.

The visitor allowed a smile to cross his face as he walked to the doorway and looked out to make sure that no one was watching closely. Not seeing anyone coming, he walked out of the room and down the hall.

A few minutes late, a nurse at the nurse's station sensed someone approaching her. She looked up in surprise and into the eyes of a priest who seemed on edge. "Good morning, Father," the nurse said.

"Good morning," he replied with a nervous yawn.

"Making your rounds a little earlier than usual today, aren't you?"

The priest paused and ran his fingers through his thick white hair. "Yes, I am. I've got an appointment today that is throwing off my entire schedule. But, such is life," the priest said.

"Could you kindly direct me to Mrs. Pucelli's room? It looks like they've moved her."

The nurse's fingers flew swiftly over her keyboard. "Here it is. They moved her late yesterday from the private room to semi-private room. I did hear that it had something to do with her medical insurance coverage. It didn't pay for a private room, so she insisted that she be moved to save her money. It's room 325."

"That would be the Mrs. Pucelli I know. A very thrifty lady," he said as he began to walk to the room to pray with her. "Other than when it's time to contribute to the church," he added.

The detectives' office was located on the third floor of the police department and could be reached by taking the slow-moving elevator or the stairs. It seemed that, on most days, there was no choice. The elevator was usually down for repairs.

The offices were laid out in an open floor plan with each partners' worn desk lined up across from the other so that they could easily talk to each other as they worked. Most of the desks were littered with stacks of files and notepads. Each desk had a phone and desktop computer. Here and there, a laptop computer could be seen on a desk. A number of detectives had switched over to the more mobile laptops complete with wireless connections, making it easier to e-mail from the field into the department or other city offices.

Overhead, a slow-moving fan struggled to help the feeble air conditioning in cooling the humid summer day. Many of the desks had small desktop fans to augment moving the hot tepid air.

From the stairwell, a woman's voice was growing closer as she ascended the stairs. Morris and Jones had been leaning back in their chairs and swiveled around to face the stair top. They recognized the voice as belonging to Melaudra.

"We'll grab Elms and have him join us," she said as she stepped onto the third floor.

A tall dark-haired gentleman was following her and wiping his sweaty brow from the climb from the first floor, which housed the main lobby and a small parking garage. As he watched Melaudra's lithe figure, Morris thought that he would have loved to follow her as she climbed the stairs.

"Elmo, could you join us in the conference room?" she called as she began walking down the narrow corridor to one of the multi-purpose rooms. Morris watched the sway of her hips as she walked.

"Sure, be right there," he called as he grabbed two more beignets and his cup of chicory coffee.

"You got sugar on your mouth, you stupid coon ass," Morris sneered sarcastically as Elms walked past him.

Elms didn't reply. It wasn't worth the effort. He hurriedly wiped the area around his mouth and hoped that he had eliminated the sugar. He was already on his fourth beignet for the day.

"Morning, Emerson," he said as he entered the room and saw Melaudra handing Emerson a cold bottled water from the small fridge.

"Hello, Harry," Emerson replied as he looked at the plate of beignets.

Looking from Melaudra to Emerson, Elms asked, "And to what do we owe the pleasure of your visit today, Mr. Pulitzer Prize winner?"

"You've been busy," Emerson observed.

"We have," Melaudra responded before Elms could answer. "We did a little background checking on you since we met during last night's mayhem. Pretty impressive, right, Elmo?"

"Yes. Based on my review of some of your online stories, it looks like you have a knack for going for the jugular," Elms observed.

"Only when necessary," Emerson replied.

"And that appears to be often," Elms said as he watched Emerson for a reaction.

Emerson didn't comment. He gave them a warm smile.

Elms continued as he looked longingly at his beignets. "I did like your story about Hurricane Ivan hitting Pensacola. I can't imagine what it would be like."

"That was a tough assignment. I had left Key West and headed to Pensacola for some R and R. I had finished a story about the heist of Mel Fisher's treasure during Hurricane Charley. It seemed like I wasn't there long and Ivan hit. You can never tell about those hurricanes."

"That's for sure. We've been pretty fortunate here. We've had some damage, but no direct hits. That would be devastating since most of the city is below sea level," Melaudra added. "I think Betsy was the last one that damaged us."

"That's right," Elms agreed. "So what brings you to see us, today?" he asked as he bit into the sugar-coated beignet, which he had picked up and raised to his mouth.

"Last night, you folks indicated that you wanted to take my statement, plus I want to see where this all is going."

"You do?" Elms replied.

"I can't leave things hanging."

"You're a lot like us, I'd guess," Elms commented as Melaudra looked at her pudgy partner curiously.

"How's that?" Emerson quizzed.

"You're driven to get the facts and expose the truth," Elms said.

Emerson smiled. "Must be why I usually get along with you folks in law enforcement. But then again, I've written exposes on cops gone bad, too."

Before answering, Elms thought about passing along his suspicions regarding Morris, but then decided otherwise. "You do run into bad cops once in a while," he responded as he looked toward Melaudra and lifted his right eyebrow. Melaudra knew that Elms was thinking about Morris and just smiled in return.

The exchange was not lost on Emerson. "Is there something I should know?" he probed.

"No," Melaudra said to close the direction in which Emerson was now trying to take the conversation.

"Nothing like a little razzle-dazzle play, huh, Melaudra?" She ginned at Elms.

"Razzle-dazzle?" Emerson asked.

"Yeah. It was a con worked here that the two of us busted," Elms beamed with pride. "There were several locations over on Bourbon Street that ran gambling. They worked the tourists' angle. The tourist would be wooed into these gambling dens and fleeced."

"I still don't get the razzle-dazzle."

"That came into play when the tourist would call into the police. Gambling calls for the Quarter were routed to the officer in charge of gambling issues in District Eight. He'd arrange for the tourist to meet with a police officer in front of the gambling den to file a complaint. When he met the officer, the officer would tell the tourist that if he filed the complaint, he be sent to jail too for illegal gambling."

"So they didn't file their complaints?"

"Right. The tourists were razzle-dazzled out of filing complaints and left town a few dollars less in their pockets."

"There's more to it," Melaudra said as she uncrossed her long legs and stood. "The police officers, with whom the tourists met, worked part-time as security guards for the gambling dens. Talk about conflict of interest, let alone allowing illegal gambling."

Emerson shook his head in disbelief. "And you two busted this?"

Elms and Melaudra nodded their heads.

"That was nothing compared to the stolen car scam," Melaudra said.

Emerson looked at her quizzically and she continued. "Over in one of the other districts, they were supposed to try to locate the owners of stolen cars and tell them to come down to the impound lot. If they didn't come down to get their cars, the cars normally were assigned to the narcotics unit for surveillance use."

"That would sound usual," Emerson commented.

"Everywhere, but in New Orleans. We got a tip that we should check out the vehicles some of the detectives were driving home. So Harry and I checked it out."

"And?" Emerson asked.

"Some of them were driving home high-end SUVs and Cadillacs as their 'take home cars.' So one day, Harry and I took a walk through the police department's parking lot and wrote down the vehicle identification numbers from below the windshields. We then searched the motor vehicle records to determine who the actual owners were." She paused and looked directly into Emerson's eyes. "None of the vehicles were registered to any of the detectives."

"What did you do?" Emerson probed.

"We called the owners to see if they had been made aware that their stolen vehicles had been recovered. None of them had been called by the department."

It was Elms' turn to comment, and he did so with a big grin. "The funniest thing was that one of the vehicles they were driving was a stolen undercover FBI surveillance vehicle!"

"What happened?"

"It's not so much what we did as what the crime-story writer at the *Times-Picayune* did," Melaudra smiled.

Emerson raised his eyebrows.

"Somehow," she was grinning ear-to-ear, "he got wind of the story and reported it. All hell broke loose in that district! Everyone suddenly got their stolen vehicles back!"

"Yeah," Elms started. "When the FBI went to pick up their car, the engine was running with the air conditioner on. The car had been washed and waxed and had a full tank of gas," he chortled.

Turning to the matter at hand, Emerson asked, "How's our friend from last night doing?"

"We have to check this morning," Melaudra said.

"I'll do that now," Elms volunteered as he stood and reached for the plate of beignets.

"Leave the beignets here, Elmo," Melaudra advised.

Elms looked at her in mock horror, then turned and left the meeting room.

"I got up early this morning and did some online research on your string of unsolved serial murders here. And your investigation appears to be moving at a glacial pace."

Nursing Station
St. Albans Hospital

~

Flipping through Fordham's chart, Thibadaux reviewed the patient's vitals. "How's our patient doing this morning?" he asked the nearby nurse.

"Resting well," she answered. "I'm due to check him again." She began to walk to Fordham's room with Thibadaux following closely.

"I'll come along," he said.

They walked into the room and saw the lifeless body of Fordham. His eyes were closed, and his cool skin was a pasty white.

"Oh no!" the nurse said as she dialed for assistance on the nearby phone while Thibadaux raced to Fordham's side. He quickly checked for vitals and found none.

"What in the hell is going on here?" Thibadaux fumed as he saw the unplugged ventilator and turned-off alarms. "I want an investigation as to what happened here!"

"It's too late," he said as the approaching footsteps of the emergency reaction team were heard racing down the hallway. Thibadaux walked out of the room. "I'm expecting a full autopsy. I want to get to the bottom of this."

As he walked out of the room, he saw the elevator doors closing and glimpsed its sole occupant. It was a white-haired priest headed to the lobby level.

Police Station District One
Ramparts Street

~

"Yes, that's correct," Melaudra agreed.

"The newspapers were silent as to whether or not you had any suspects."

"Yes, they were," Melaudra said coyly. She wasn't sure where Emerson was going and didn't like him trying to sniff out a story.

"And so are you," he cracked as he realized that she wasn't volunteering information.

Melaudra grinned. "And what did you expect? Did you think I'd offer you a list of suspects? I don't think so."

Emerson ignored her dodge. "So you do have suspects?"

"Are you going to give it up?"

"Nope. Not when you've had a string of 13 unsolved murders in the Quarter in the last six months. That's basically two a month. Aren't you concerned?"

"Of course, we're concerned. We don't publish the status of investigations in the paper. That's all."

"Has there been any pattern to the murders?"

She saw that he was going to be persistent and decided to talk around the edges of the investigation. "Nothing more than what I'm sure you read in your research. They appear to happen randomly whenever the murderer is stimulated into killing. We're not sure what the motive is for driving the killer, but I'm sure you're reading about the symbolic nature of the murders."

"The cross on the victim's forehead, drawn in their own blood?"

"Yes. Psychologically, there's some linkage, but we haven't figured that one out yet. It's part of this killer's ritual."

"Maybe the killer was abused emotionally or physically by a priest," Emerson suggested.

"We're ahead of you on that one. We're looking at all of the angles. As you can guess, the police psychologist is working the case and constructed a psychological profile. But again, these killers are skilled at concealing their true selves behind a façade." She took a swallow of her coffee. "Serial killers usually target victims who are weaker than themselves so that they can dominate and control the person."

"Have all of the victims been tourists?"

"All but one. That one may have been a mistake."

"And they've all been in the Quarter?"

"Yes. We think the killer hunts for prey in the Quarter and then lures them into his trap by manipulating them to gain their trust. He must be wearing some sort of mask of normalcy. Some of his enjoyment may come from hunting down the victim."

"I hear you saying 'he.' Does that mean the killer is a man?"

"That's our suspicion. Most serial killers are. They're responding to a variety of psychological urges, primarily power and sexual compulsion."

"Any evidence of sexual compulsion here? I didn't see anything written in the *Times-Picayune*."

She thought for a second before answering. "I'd think you could safely assume that there was no evidence of it. Sometimes, serial killers come from dysfunctional families where they were humiliated and abused. They were powerless in their situations. For some strange reason, later in their adulthood, the right trigger is pulled, and they get delusional visions or stimuli which drive them to kill."

Emerson nodded his head as he listened.

"The facades of normalcy make them difficult to spot. They could be from any level in society, from the lowest to the highest. That's why they are difficult to track. They're usually highly intelligent and know how to play on others' sympathy. Ted Bundy, for instance, would place his arm in a fake plaster cast and appeal to his victim's sympathy to help him. Then he'd whip off the cast and dominate them."

"I read in the paper that the victims' bodies are usually found on the street, thrown in the morning garbage pick up," Emerson observed.

"Yeah. We believe the victims are killed in one place and then discarded along the street curbs. At least, that has been the pattern."

"Any clues on what the killer looks like?"

Melaudra knew that nothing had been disclosed to the media and was certainly not going to disclose anything to this reporter, including the sample of white hair, which had been found on several of the corpses. "No," she answered.

"But I told you last night that the killer had white hair."

"I would say that was a breaking development since you saw the killer."

"You know, there could be a story here for me," Emerson mused out loud.

"And how do I convince you that there isn't?" she asked demurely.

Her brown eyes seemed to melt Emerson. "Maybe there's a way. Maybe . . ."

Their conversation was interrupted when Elms burst into the room. "We've got trouble, right here in river city."

Melaudra and Emerson turned to face Elms who had white-powdered sugar on his face, evidence that he had found beignets in the department and downed one or two.

"I just talked to St. Albans. Fordham's dead."

"What?" Melaudra asked in shock.

"Yeah, dead. They're trying to figure out what happened to him. Someone apparently unplugged his ventilator. He was murdered."

Emerson looked at Melaudra. "Fourteen murders, now."

"And that's not all. Apparently a kid who was brought in last night with wounds from a gang fight was killed last night. Somebody, posing as his brother, penetrated security and finished the job. The kid is dead, too."

Emerson arched his eyebrows as he looked at Melaudra. "Is it always like this around here?"

"You better go now, and we better go over there."

Emerson allowed himself to be escorted to the top of the stairwell where Melaudra said, "We'll resume our conversation later."

Starting to take the first step, Emerson replied, "I was hoping that we would." He gave the attractive detective a warm smile.

Melaudra heard his comment, but was already heading to her desk where Elms was placing a phone call. Emerson decided to head over to the French Market and look around before returning to his hotel.

Seeing Emerson walking down the stairs, Elms covered the phone's receiver. "Mel?"

"Yes?"

"I didn't want to say anything in front of the reporter, but there was something else."

"Yes?"

"There was a cross drawn on Fordham's forehead."

"With his blood?"

"No, in ink."

Melaudra's eyes widened at the brazenness of the killer to track its prey into the hospital. "Did they get anything on the security cameras?"

"I'm checking now."

St. Louis Cathedral
French Quarter

~

The door slammed abruptly behind him due to the unusual amount of force he applied in closing it. The noise did little to interrupt the tormented thoughts racing through Alsandi's mind. His morning mission to St. Albans had proved as stressful as the meeting with the reporter the day before.

It was unusual for Alsandi to miss morning mass, but this morning was different. His anguish continued when it was his turn to confess his own sins and he wasn't completely forthcoming. He held back on a number of secrets that had tortured his mind. He knew that there were things that he needed help with, but felt powerless to confront. Revealing the truth would shock not only members of the church, but the inhabitants of New Orleans. He would have to continue wrestling with the devils in his personal hell. And he was losing the battle.

He dropped to his knees and tried to pray, but he felt an emptiness. He thought back several years ago when Pope John Paul had visited New Orleans. To the public, it was a visit to the Cathedral to bless it and the city. In reality, it was to confront and warn Alsandi.

Alsandi could clearly recall that day. It had been a typical hot, sultry New Orleans day in the Quarter. He had been given a note that the Pope wanted a private audience with him in one of the Cathedral's offices. In some ways, he was surprised. In other ways, he was not surprised, but worried about why the Pope would want a private meeting with him.

When Alsandi entered the office, he was astonished to see the Pope dismiss his personal secretary. He wanted no witnesses to their conversation. The secretary was bewildered by the unusual request, but scurried from the room, closing the door behind him.

The room was filled with silence as the Polish Pope looked at Alsandi with eyes filled with sadness. After a few minutes he spoke. "It's been a long time since I've seen you."

"Yes, it has."

"I've missed our evening conversations."

"They were very invigorating and challenging," Alsandi replied thoughtfully as he reflected on those moments.

Pope John Paul's eyes scanned the priest in front of him. He still felt the pain from what had transpired in the Vatican with Alsandi and Maloney years ago. "If things had gone in a different direction, you would have been a cardinal. You were such a rising star among our Vatican priesthood."

Nodding his head slowly, Alsandi replied quietly. "I had always felt that there was a higher calling for my life."

"There still may be. It's not so much what big things we accomplish in our life that God cares about. It's also some of the little things. Not everyone will be a pope or a cardinal. God needs people to serve the poor and all levels of life. To those to whom much is given, much is expected. What has He given you, my dear Alsandi? Where does He want you to serve?"

"I was fortunate to be sent here. It is my home."

"I knew that. That's why I sent you here."

"But it would be easier to serve somewhere else."

"That's why you were sent here. Because it is difficult to serve where people know you, where you were raised. Maybe this is somewhere you wanted to escape from, and there are unresolved issues confronting you here." Pope John Paul peered intently at Alsandi. "There are two reasons why I wanted to see you."

"Yes?"

"First, I wanted to see an old friend."

"Thank you," Alsandi said with his eyes cast downward.

"Second, I wanted to remind you of the oath you took with Father Maloney that you would never reveal what you two discovered."

"I took an oath. I would never do that."

"I am told that some files have been discovered to be missing," Pope John Paul said as he leaned forward.

"I didn't take anything," Alsandi said as he looked straight into the Pope's eyes.

"I wouldn't think you would," the Pope answered reassuredly. "But, I'm not sure about Maloney. I'm having someone follow-up with him." The Pope paused and stared at Alsandi before posing a question. "You have not talked with Father Maloney since you were sent away, have you?"

"No." Alsandi wasn't entirely truthful. They had exchanged letters on several occasions.

"Good. I suspected that you would follow our edict." Pope John Paul relaxed in his chair. "Come here beside me so that I can bless you and pray with you, my friend."

As he had approached the Pope, Alsandi thought he saw the Pope's eyes fill with tears. He knelt next to the Pope for his blessing and prayer.

French Market
Decatur Street

～

Lively jazz music filled the air, as the crowd pushed forward into the covered French Market located on a triangle of land between Peters and Decatur Streets. The French market, which dated back to the late 1790s, had the distinction of being the country's oldest public market.

Visitors were first greeted by vendors with a wide variety of accents hawking meat, gulf and lake fish, fresh vegetables, and fruit. The next section of the market resembled a flea market where vendors sold alligator heads, clothing, belts, hats, sunglasses, etc. At one booth, a Vietnamese vendor was trying to interest Emerson into purchasing a watch or necklace even though it was apparent that Emerson had stopped to admire one of the wooden encased gel pens, which were on display.

Ignoring vendor attempts to interest him in other merchandise, Emerson paid for the pen and continued his walk through the crowded market. He enjoyed visiting the market and experiencing the aromatic smells from the items cooking as well as the variety of items for sale. He purchased gator on a stick and devoured it quickly. *It tastes like chicken,* he thought as he grinned to himself.

He spent an hour slowly strolling through the crowd and the midday heat before purchasing a vanilla ice-cream cone and returning to his hotel to make travel arrangements for his return to Put-in-Bay. His plans were interrupted when he was given a message by the receptionist.

Carrying the unopened note in his hand, he climbed the stairs to his ice-cold room, which was a haven from the steamy heat outside. Kicking off his shoes, he sat at the desk and opened the note. As, he read it, his eyes widened at its contents. It looked like he wouldn't be leaving town as soon as he thought.

His thoughts were interrupted by the ring of his cell phone. "Hello," he said, answering.

"Emerson, what are you doing?" the enthusiastic voice of Barry Hayen asked.

"Taking a break from this August heat. How are things in the islands?"

"Good. Good weather, and that's bringing a lot of tourists to the islands."

"Glad to hear that."

"I'll just take a few minutes, but something came up that I wanted to make you aware of."

"Yes?"

"I was over at the police department, and the chief got a call from Dr. Jim Crawford. He's the county coroner, and it was about Father Maloney's death."

Sitting straight up, Emerson listened closely. "Yes, go on."

"He overdosed on digitalis."

"What's that?"

"Heart medication. He had enough in him to kill an elephant."

"You think he did it on purpose?"

"Nope. He didn't even have a heart condition." The publisher paused a moment, then continued. "And another thing."

"Yes?"

"The cat that died."

"Yeah?"

"Overdosed on digitalis, too!"

"Suspicious."

"That's an understatement. Chief says that we're working on a double homicide."

"Maloney and the cat?"

"No, Maloney and Bahama Joe! At first Doc Crawford and his staff were stymied in determining Bahama Joe's cause of death. It looked like a stroke caused by excessive alcohol. You know Joe liked his bottle."

"Yeah, I heard that."

"Doc Crawford is a pessimist. He thought it was strange that there would be two deaths—three if you include the cat—in 24 hours on the island. So he kept digging."

"And he found?"

"Marks under Joe's beard. Apparently someone decided to cut the blood flow to the brain by pressing on his artery. The resulting appearance would have been just a stroke, but Doc Crawford kept on investigating until he found the marks."

"Any leads?"

"A couple from what I can gather. They've been checking the docks, hotels, and bed and breakfasts to see who was registered. The Crew's Nest had a group of doctors aboard a Michigan boat called the *Cutting Edge*. You probably didn't know this, but one of the guys on the *Cutting Edge* is alleged to have walked into Ashley's Island House and stalked Trudy. They've got his name and are trying to track him down in Michigan for questioning."

"I wasn't aware," Emerson responded. "Any tie into Maloney's murder at her place?"

"Don't know yet. They're running them down to see what they can find. Lanny, the Hawaiian cook at the Boardwalk, saw something interesting on the night that Bahama Joe was killed."

"What was that?"

"It was foggy, and he was out late. He bumped into a tourist not too far from Joe's dock."

"Hmmm."

"Yeah, the tourist was wearing a T-shirt. It had something lettered in white, but Lanny isn't sure what it said. He thought it was something that started with a 'C,' but he's not sure."

"Think he'd recognize the guy if he saw him again?"

"He's not sure, but I'll call you back when I have more."

"Did Gino get a chance to translate the files we found in Maloney's basement?" Emerson wondered.

"I showed them to him, but his Italian is too rusty. I'm just planning on shipping them back to the Vatican since it appears to be their property. Well, I've got to go. Have a beignet for me and one of those Hand Grenade drinks."

Emerson grinned. "I may pass on the Hand Grenade, but I'll certainly have another one of the beignets."

They ended their call, and Emerson sat back to think about the developments with the deaths on the island. After a few minutes, he sat at his laptop and began to outline his thoughts in case he decided to do a story.

Two hours later, Emerson was walking down St. Anne Street towards Decatur. He had decided to have dinner at the River's Edge and see what he could learn about who owned the apartment where the murder had taken place.

Arriving at the restaurant, he walked through the tall French doors and inside. He allowed his eyes to sweep the room, taking in the huge mural of the Mississippi River, which dominated the wall on his left and the six ceiling fans, which were spinning just below an ornate tin ceiling to cool the restaurant.

"May I seat you?" the hostess asked.

Emerson was stunned by the 39-year-old beautiful woman with streaked blonde hair and a leopardskin cowboy hat perched atop her head. *Her deep-brown eyes and tanned complexion would make her stand out in any crowd,* Emerson thought. She was wearing a short dark-brown jacket over a black bustier and a leopardskin-style full skirt. She was drop-dead gorgeous.

"I said, may I seat you?"

"Cat got your tongue, Son?" a deep voice asked from behind Emerson.

Emerson turned around to face a six-foot-three, well-built man in his late 50s with graying hair. "My wife has that sort of effect on men," he chuckled. "Tricia, why don't I take him to the bar and see if I can get him loosened up a bit?"

Tricia smiled at Emerson and then said to her husband, "Okay, Honey. I'll stop back a little later and see how the two of you are doing."

Putting his arm around Emerson, the man began to guide him across the uneven brick floor and past a five-foot-tall statue of jazz legend Louis Armstrong into the adjoining bar area. "I'm Chellie Smith. That's spelled with a C not an S. I'm no sissy, Son." The gregarious owner of the restaurant laughed at his comment.

"I'm Emerson Moore, and you're just the guy I was looking for."

"I am?"

"Yes. A mutual friend of ours told me to look you up when I got to town. His name is Jimmy Van Hoose."

Chellie's face broke into an even larger smile. "How is he doing? I haven't talked with him in a couple of years. Give me a beer," he said to the barmaid as they sat on bar stools at one end of the long bar. "What will you have?"

"Seven and Seven," Emerson said and then filled Chellie in on how he had met Jimmy Van Hoose and how well his coffee house was doing.

"We miss Jimmy being around here. I first met him when he played wide receiver for the Saints." Watching his wife seat patrons, Chellie commented, "She's beautiful, isn't she?"

Emerson swung around on his stool and spied Tricia seating another couple and laughing with them. "Yes, she is quite beautiful."

"Got guys chasing her all the time, but she stays true to me. She's a good woman, Emerson. I met her when she came to see me dance."

"You were a Chippendale dancer?" Emerson asked in surprise.

A wide grin filled Chellie's face. "More like a Clydesdale dancer. At that time, I had bulked up pretty good. I had just won the Mr. Pensacola Body Building contest. I mean to tell you, I was massive."

Emerson couldn't imagine. The guy was well-built as it was.

Teddy the bartender spoke up. "That's not the way it happened. He used to come in here almost every day to see her. He was here so much that we wondered if he had a key to the place!"

Chellie smiled and leaned toward Emerson. "When you find someone that special, you bet your bottom dollar that I was here chasing her. Teddy here is the guy who actually introduced the two of us." Changing the topic, he asked, "Did you see the painting above the bar?"

Emerson looked behind the bar at the large painting of a Mississippi steamboat, which dominated the wall. It seemed to capture every detail of a steamboat as Emerson thought back to his trips on the *Natchez*.

"See the name on the side of her?" Chellie asked.

Painted on the side of the steamboat was the boat's name in large letters. It read, "Smith." Chellie beamed with pride. "That boat's named after my family."

Thinking for a second, Emerson commented, "I don't think I've ever heard of a steamboat named that way."

"That's because it was so special. People just whispered her name," Chellie laughed. "Really, I just had it painted on there that way. Nothing like having a little fun now and then. After all, I'm nothing more than a Mississippi redneck and darn proud of it!"

"I thought I'd better come over here and rescue you from my husband," Tricia said as she walked around from behind Emerson and placed her hand lovingly on her husband's shoulder. "Has my man been telling you tall tales?"

Emerson just grinned and changed the topic. "Have you folks any idea about who owns the apartment upstairs where that incident took place last night?"

"Sure," Tricia responded. "That's our apartment."

"Yeah, the nerve of that murderer, he apparently found the hidden key and broke into our apartment," Chellie muttered angrily.

"Any ideas who it might be?" Emerson queried, hoping for a lead.

"No. The police were here and asked all kinds of questions. But we don't have any ideas," Tricia responded.

"Emerson, they are running down previous apartment owners to see if they can tie anything in," Chellie volunteered.

"You two were lucky that you weren't in the apartment at the time."

"Yes, we were. We actually were out of town last night and just got back. So all of this was a big surprise to us," Tricia commented.

"We've got a place on the other side of town. The apartment is just for our weekend use," Chellie explained.

The three of them continued to talk about life in the Quarter and the other three restaurants they owned—Pere Antoine on St. Anne and Royal, The Oyster Bar and Grill on the far side of Jackson Square and along Decatur Street, and the Louisiana Heritage Restaurant.

The Funeral
First Baptist Church
The Ninth Ward

~

"Jackson wasn't a bad boy, but he got caught up running with bad boys. He grew up in this church. His grandmother was on the ladies auxiliary and baked for the church bake sales for years." The minister stopped for a moment and looked toward Jackson's grandmother who was seated next to Jackson's mother in the front pew. He smiled briefly and continued with his funeral sermon.

"What we have here is a good boy who got caught up with bad people. You know what I mean. Jackson knew the Lord at one time in his life. He wasn't walking with the Lord when he was kilt. So where is he now? I can look you in the eyes and tell you I don't know. But more important is where are you now? Have you made peace with your Maker? Have you accepted Jesus Christ as you savior? Well, I'm a good person, you're saying to yourself. I don't need any of this churchy stuff. I just came here today to pay my respects to a boy who was kilt.

"Well, let me tell you that the wages of sin are death. But the key to everlasting life is through Jesus Christ. We all have sin in our lives, don't you think? Let me just review a few of the Ten Commandments with you to see if any of us have violated any of these. And let me remind you that these are God's Ten Commandments, not God's 'ten suggestions.' Thou shalt not kill." The minister stopped for a moment and peered over the tops of his glasses as he looked at his audience. "Hopefully, that wouldn't be an issue for most of us in here."

Emerson looked at Melaudra with a raised eyebrow. She saw him and shrugged her shoulders. That was one commandment that she had violated in her police work. She tilted her head as the minister continued.

Emerson had been surprised to receive the note from her two days ago. It had invited him to join her in attending the funeral of the boy who had been murdered at the hospital. It turned out that she was a friend of the boy's mother and wanted to attend. According to the note, she had invited Emerson so that he could taste another side of the city. He had gladly accepted.

The previous day, he had spent visiting with Bubby Valentino at his hotel and at the offices of the *Times-Picayune* newspaper where he had researched the recent spate of unsolved murders in the Quarter. He also squeezed in time to visit some of the antique stores on Royal Street and had dinner at Antoine's, one of the Quarter's top restaurants.

"Thou shall not steal. Now listen closely. It doesn't say just big things. It implies all things. So just because you didn't knock off the 7-Eleven on your way to church today so that you'd have something to put in the offering plate doesn't mean you are innocent. It applies to stealing anything!" he paused for effect. "Like a pad of paper from the supply room here or scotch tape at Christmas time. It don't matter. Thou shall not steal! It's just plain and simple!

"Let's look at the next one. Thou shall not bear false witness! You and I know what it means. We are commanded not to lie!" He lowered his head and peered over the top of his glasses again. "I'm not sure that I need to go on. I don't think any one of us is free on that one, even if it's a small white lie or should I say, in most of our cases, a small black lie?"

He paused and allowed a sly grin cross his face as the crowd tittered at his remark.

"We are all guilty of sin. There was a young man who was blind. His name was Blind Willie Johnson. The boy lost his eyesight when he was seven-years-old, and his stepmother was fighting with his father. She threw lye in his face and blinded him. But the boy didn't let it get him down. He went on to write quite a few successful songs and never complained about his plight in life. From his youth, he sang gospel songs for donations and sang his way from Dallas, Texas, through Atlanta.

"He even recorded a couple of songs at a small studio on Canal Street, above Werlein's Music Store. He recorded 30 songs by 1930 and became a Baptist minister. He always said that he was accountable and that it was nobody's fault but his. When it came time to step through them pearly gates, he'd be looking at the Lord and saying that it was nobody's fault but his.

"I'm going to sing Blind Willie's song that he wrote about it being nobody's fault but his. I want you all to close your eyes and listen closely to the words. If you don't get to those pearly gates, it's nobody's fault but yours for not accepting Jesus into your heart."

The minister's deep baritone voice broke out in song, accompanied by the pianist. When he finished singing, the minister looked over the crowd once again. "It is nobody's fault but mine. What are you going to say when your time comes? Folks, the decision is in your hands. I'd like you to bow your heads and pray with me a simple prayer. It's as easy as praying 'Jesus, please forgive me for my sins and I accept you into my heart as my savior. Amen.' It's that simple, folks."

Melaudra nudged Emerson in the side as the minister continued preaching. "Did you?"

Emerson wrinkled his forehead. "Did I what?"

"Did you do what the preacher asked?"

Emerson smiled and didn't respond for a moment. "It's a private matter for me."

"Okay, tough guy." She stopped as the minister was calling for people to take a final walk by the casket. "You ain't seen nothing yet," she said as they rose with the rest of the row to follow the people walking past the casket.

"What do you mean?" he asked.

"Wait until we're outside," she said. "You'll see a New Orleans funeral procession."

"I've seen those before. It's like a small jazz parade, isn't it?"

"Shhh," she replied as they neared the open casket.

They walked by the casket and then toward the door at the rear of the church. Once outside, she began to explain as the musicians began to line up. "For the less affluent of us, neighborhoods would band together in social clubs and help pay the costs of a funeral. Nobody had much insurance, and it was a way that we could afford to bury our loved ones and celebrate their ascension to a better afterlife."

Emerson was listening closely.

"The tradition of having a procession dates back to our African culture and was used by slaves. Originally, they had drums and a tambourine-like instrument, but that changed over to brass instruments. On the way to the cemetery, they'd play slowly and mournfully, but on the way back from the cemetery, they'd step it up. They'd play something lively like

'When the Saints Go Marching In.' We're celebrating the soul leaving this hard life on earth."

"You folks in New Orleans sure do like to celebrate a lot," Emerson observed as he gained insight into a side of Melaudra, which he hadn't realized existed.

"New Orleans is known for its celebrations. We're happy people, for the most part," she explained. "We are always looking for an opportunity to celebrate." She turned toward the church as the casket was carried out.

"Who's the guy all dressed up?" Emerson asked as he looked at a distinguished-looking tall black man wearing a solemn expression and a black tuxedo. His white-gloved hands held a black top hat.

"He's the grand marshal. His job is to lead the procession in a dignified manner to the cemetery. It's only a few blocks from here. They may walk past Jackson's mother's home. If they do, there'll be a black wreath hanging on her front door. At least, they've had them in processions that I've walked in.

"Once they inter Jackson and they march a respective distance from the interment, it will be the grand marshal's job to signal the lead trumpeter to sound it's celebration time with a blast from his horn. Then the drummer begins, the music picks up, and out come the umbrellas."

"Yeah," Emerson agreed. "I've seen those umbrellas. Why do they use them?"

"Styling, Emerson. Styling," she answered. "They decorate them in fun colors and open them up as part of the celebration. And one other thing about our celebrations that you may have noticed." She paused.

"What's that?"

"When we celebrate, we do a little strutting and a little booty bounce." She illustrated both to a surprised Emerson as she strutted a few steps and shook her hips provocatively in front of him.

Watching the booty bounce, Emerson couldn't recall seeing anything quite like it before. He remembered seeing the strutting. He commented quietly, "Nice bounce!"

"What did you say?" she asked although she had heard him clearly.

"Oh, nothing important," he replied.

Melaudra smiled warmly at the handsome reporter.

The solemn procession began to form and the band started playing "Nearer My God to Thee." Slowly they began to walk away and Melaudra and Emerson headed for the car.

As they drove toward Emerson's hotel, Melaudra slouched low in her seat while she drove. Her left leg was lifted slightly higher against the driver's door and caused her skirt to rise up daringly on her thighs.

"Melaudra?"

"Yes?"

"I've got to ask you. How do you see over the steering wheel? You're sitting so low while you drive."

She laughed. "It's something I picked up from my days living in Chicago. Sometimes, I do run into things, and the guys teasingly call me 'Crash'." She giggled after she made the comment. Then, she posed a question. "Tonight, I've got to go to a dressy fund-raising charity event on the *Natchez*. Harry was going to go with me, but can't." Pausing for a moment, she turned her face toward him and asked, "Think you might be interested in subbing for him?"

Emerson didn't have to think one nanosecond about his answer to the attractive detective's invitation. "Sure, I'd like that very much. I don't have a suit with me to wear to a dressy affair. Sport coat okay?"

"That would be fine." The car pulled to a stop in front of his hotel. As he got out, she told him, "I'll meet you in the lobby at eight. We can walk since it's just a few blocks."

"Fine with me."

Putting the car in gear, she gave him an inviting smile. "See you then," and pulled away.

Outside of the Hotel Lobby
Place d'Armes
~

The early evening air did little to relieve the humidity of the day. Mopping his brow with his handkerchief, Emerson contemplated stepping back into the air-conditioned comfort of the hotel's lobby versus standing outside and taking in the smells and sounds of life in the Quarter. He never tired of the Quarter's special ambiance. He couldn't explain it to anyone, you just had to be there and experience it yourself. He watched as a couple walked on the sidewalk across from him and toward Jackson Square. They were loaded down like packhorses with bags of souvenirs and paintings, which they had purchased during their walk. Emerson had been through that. He had a painting in his bedroom of Jackson Square with St. Louis Cathedral looming over it.

"Looking for a date?" the feminine voice asked sensually.

Emerson whirled around in surprise to identify its source. Seeing cocoa-skinned Melaudra wearing a plunging black cocktail dress with spaghetti straps, Emerson was speechless. She was a vision of beauty. His eyes quickly took in the small diamond earrings affixed delicately to each ear and the high heels she wore. He couldn't help himself. He moaned aloud as he momentarily lost control of his senses.

"You okay?" Melaudra asked hurriedly.

"Hmmm," was the only response that Emerson could utter as a flush of crimson began creeping up his face.

Realizing that her attire was causing this strange reaction from Emerson, Melaudra teased, "Maybe I better go back to my apartment and change into something else. Something that doesn't make you go deaf and dumb!"

"Oh no, don't do that," Emerson responded hurriedly. "Just give me a second to catch my breath. You just took it away from me!"

"Think you need mouth-to-mouth?"

"That might help!" Emerson teased back.

"Okay then," she said as she turned and spotted the old porter who worked at the hotel. "Sir, could you give my friend here some mouth-to-mouth? He's having some breathing problems."

The old black porter's grizzled face broke into a wide grin, showing that he was missing several teeth. Realizing that Melaudra was joking, he played along as he allowed his long tongue to snake out before speaking. "Sure can. Let me help you, Sir."

Backing up, Emerson replied. "Funny thing. It's a miracle! I can breathe normal again. Guess I just caught my breath!"

Melaudra and the porter exchanged knowing glances.

"Well, then, shall we walk on over to the *Natchez?*"

"Sure."

They walked down St. Anne Street and turned right onto Decatur where they walked next to the fence encircling Jackson Square.

Crossing Decatur Street, they walked across the streetcar tracks and approached the *Natchez* at the Toulouse Street Wharf, behind JAX Brewery. The classic three-decked floating palace, owned by the New Orleans Steamboat Company, was resplendent with its brilliant white paint and its trimming in red with its red paddlewheel at the stern. In the fore structure, her two black stacks reached skyward like two football goalposts. Between the stacks was suspended a bale of cotton as the ship's official ensign. Perched on top of the Texas deck was the pilothouse, giving its captain a bird's-eye view of the river and its surroundings. Her custom-crafted, 32-note steam calliope was serenading the arrivees with lively tunes as steam plumes shot from her whistles.Emerson had always been fascinated by steamboats. It dated back to his youth and time spent in reading about Tom Sawyer and Huck Finn. This was not his first visit to the *Natchez*. On a couple of his previous trips, he had stepped back in time as he took cruises including the dinner cruise where he enjoyed the Cajun-Creole buffet. He had roamed the boat extensively and spent time in the engine room where he watched as the steam engines propelled the pitman arm, which in turn drove the giant oak paddlewheel, churning through the muddy Mississippi. As the *Natchez* glided past the French Quarter and five miles downriver, Emerson would relish the magic of the experience.

Producing her invitation, Melaudra handed it to one of the crew as they boarded the steamboat, which was draped with a number of banners regarding the St. Albans' Hospital Fund Raising event that evening.

"Get ready to mix it up with a lot of docs tonight," Melaudra said quietly to Emerson.

"Maybe one of them could prescribe something to get rid of my bouts of deafness and dumbness," Emerson joked about his reaction earlier at the sight of Melaudra in her outfit.

Giggling, Melaudra teased, "I think I have something that I could prescribe."

Surprised by what she said, Emerson asked, "What did you say?"

"Nothing, nothing," she said quietly and kept what she wanted to say to herself. She felt her attraction to this handsome reporter growing. But she kept reminding herself to be careful, she had been hurt by men too many times in the past. As tough as she was with her police work, she had vulnerability with some men, and Emerson was making her feel very vulnerable.

"Welcome aboard, folks," the nattily-attired crewman greeted. "Please proceed to the second deck."

"Mind if we take a quick look around the main deck?" Emerson asked the crewman.

"Not at all," he responded cordially.

"Let me give you a quick tour," Emerson said as he placed his hand in the small of Melaudra's back and gently guided her down the main deck. He talked as they walked. "They have a party private room on this deck for small parties. It's called the Magnolia Suite. Here are the boilers."

They peeked in the open doorway and saw two large boilers. Their names, Thelma and Louise, were painted on the side of the boilers.

"The boilers are put forward on the main deck to help counterbalance the weight of the steam engines and paddlewheel," he explained as they continued their tour past the galley and the engine room to the paddlewheel. Their passage to the fantail area next to the paddlewheel was blocked by a closed gate. "Guess we're not supposed to go over there," Emerson said as he observed the massive oak planks making up the blades of the paddlewheel.

"Isn't this beautiful?" Melaudra asked as they made their way to the stairs and began to climb to the second level, or boiler deck, and strolled toward the bow.

"I love these boats," Emerson replied and then began explaining. "If you look toward the bow, you'll see a tall flagpole. It's called a jack staff, and the pilots used them for sighting their course on the river."

They were leaning over the ornately-carved deck railing, which was painted in a brilliant white and trimmed in red. Emerson continued his explanation of the ship. "The deck above us is the Hurricane Deck, and then you have the Texas deck, and the pilothouse."

An authoritative voice behind them chimed, "Steamboats look like tiered wedding cakes to me. And better yet, they come without all the complications and responsibilities that marriage brings." The comment was followed by an evil chuckle.

Emerson and Melaudra whirled to confront the source of the comment.

"Truman Thibadaux. Dr. Thibadaux," he said to Emerson as he adjusted his bow tie carefully as he held a cocktail in one hand. He was wearing a tuxedo, and Emerson noticed that all the males were wearing tuxes. "We met the other day at the hospital."

"Emerson Moore," Emerson returned the stiff greeting, reminding Thibadaux of his name. Emerson felt uncomfortable since he was wearing a sport coat and khakis.

Ignoring Emerson, Thibadaux leered at Melaudra as his eye roamed over her skimpy attire. "What a pleasure to see you, Melaudra. Of course, I'd prefer to see more of you," he said.

The double meaning wasn't lost on Melaudra. She fully understood his intentions. When she spoke, she did so forcibly like she would to a suspect. "Get over it, Truman. I've told you before that I'm not interested in seeing you."

He was taken back by her serious tone. Thibadaux wasn't used to having females respond to him in that manner. He did his best to hide his surprise. "Of course, my dear. We shall continue to keep our relationship at a professional level." He turned and walked over to another group of partygoers, who were waving at him.

"Slimeball," Emerson commented as he watched Thibadaux slither away.

"I've dealt with his kind before. I won't pay him no never mind," she said as she flashed her dark eyes at Emerson. "One of my assignments for the department includes representing the department at some of the city's social functions. That's why we're here, tonight."

"Tough assignment."

"It can be. Some of the people are so full of themselves, but the majority of them are trying to do the right thing in helping the community raise money for charitable reasons."

"Did you have to pay for our tickets tonight?"

"Now, Emerson, you shouldn't ask a girl a question like that!"

He smiled. "Hey, I'm sorry about my attire. I feel a bit out of place with everyone else having tuxes on," Emerson said as Melaudra began steering him into the main cabin with its rose-colored walls and rose, cream, and burgundy-patterned carpeting.

From its ornate cream-colored tin ceiling hung several chandeliers that had been dimmed for the evening's event. Several guests were seated in the burgundy chairs, which surrounded a number of tables covered with white table-cloths. A Dixieland band was playing at the stern end in front of a large ship's wheel. It was mounted in front of a huge window, which overlooked the paddlewheel. There was an open bar and a sumptuous buffet awaited the partyers.

"Don't you worry about that," she replied. "You look just fine."

It didn't help. Emerson still felt a bit out of place. A shriek-ing whistle announced the departure of the *Natchez* from the dock, and the boat shook as its paddlewheel engaged and pro-pelled it forward for its cruise downriver.

"Let's grab a drink and then watch the river go by," Melaudra suggested as they walked to the ornate bar.

"What can I get you?" the bartender asked.

"A Bloody Mary," Melaudra ordered.

"Seven and Seven with a lemon twist," Emerson re-quested. The waiter quickly produced their drinks, and they stepped back outside to watch the river go by.

"Hmmm. They made this just right," Melaudra com-mented after taking a long sip of her drink. "How's your drink?"

"Perfect."

For the next 20 minutes, they talked about life in New Or-leans and watched as the sun began to fade in the west. "Ready for another?" Melaudra asked as she finished her drink. When she looked at Emerson's drink, she saw that he still had most of it. "I thought you said your drink was perfect."

"It is. I'm just careful."

"Careful?"

"I don't usually finish a drink."

"Why's that?"

Emerson then briefly explained the unexpected death of his wife and son during a tragic car wreck in Washington a few years earlier while he was out of town on assignment. Their loss had driven him to drink excessively, and he was leery about falling back into that trap. It had been his visit to comfort his aunt in the Lake Erie islands two years ago that had helped him to stop feeling sorry about himself and focus on others. It had been the catalyst to stop the heavy drinking.

Melaudra listened attentively until he finished his explanation. "I'm so sorry about the loss of your wife and son."

Changing the topic, Emerson suggested, "Let's go back in and get you a refill."

Smiling seductively, Melaudra asked, "You wouldn't be trying to get me drunk would you, Mr. Emerson Moore?"

With eyebrows raised in mock surprise, Emerson responded, "Who me?" Then, more seriously, he said, "I wouldn't do that."

"Oh damn," Melaudra commented half-heartedly.

"What did you say?"

"Nothing. Nothing at all."

They had reached the bar and ordered her refill. Afterward, they found a table, which had two chairs available and introduced themselves to the seated partyers who were enjoying the food from the sumptuous Creole buffet. Emerson and Melaudra joined the line at the buffet, secured their food, and returned to their table where they ate and chatted with their tablemates.

Following the completion of their meal, they took the stairs to the Texas deck, mingled with the crowd, and watched couples dancing in the subdued lighting. After a few minutes, the band began a slow song as the riverboat swung around and began its return trip up river. Emerson asked, "Like to dance?"

Before answering, Melaudra looked carefully at Emerson. She realized that this could be a step in a direction that she wasn't sure she wanted to go with any man at this time. But then again, here was a nice kind guy who was just in town for a few days. *What would it hurt*, she thought, *to go ahead and enjoy his company? But*, she realized, *she would have to keep her emotional guard up.* "That would be nice," she said as she finished her fourth Bloody Mary of the evening.

Holding her arm, Emerson guided her to the dance floor where he turned and swept her into his arms. Without thinking, he pulled the attractive detective in close to him, a little closer than he intended. He was then surprised when she didn't pull away. He smiled as he held her, and they danced to the music. He couldn't see her face. If he had, he would have noticed that her eyes were closed and a smile filled her pretty face.

When the song ended, the band saw how many dancers had crowded the small dance floor. They decided to play another slow song. Emerson looked at Melaudra and she nodded her head to his unasked question for a second dance. As the music played, she felt herself uncontrollably hold her body tighter against Emerson's body and put both of her arms around his neck. She smiled as she felt his arms tighten around her waist.

For her part, she could always put it off to the influence of the four Bloody Marys. She wasn't sure how Emerson would explain his actions—and she didn't quite care at the moment. She was going to enjoy it for what it was. A warm feeling began to spread through her body as she relaxed in the security of Emerson's strong arms.

It didn't last long. A shriek filled the air as a man who had been dancing nearby with his wife dropped to the floor and began gasping.

"Bradley! Bradley!" his wife shrieked. "Someone help him. He has a heart problem," she screamed.

The dancers stepped back to give him room, and the band stopped playing. Melaudra broke out of her trance-like state and rushed to the stricken man's side as did a number of the doctors present at the event.

"I'll handle this," Thibadaux said authoritatively as he pushed his way through the people around the fallen man and knelt at his side. "Is he allergic to anything?" Thibadaux snapped at the woman.

"No," she said.

"Somebody bring me a glass of water," Thibadaux ordered as he loosened the man's tie and shirt collar; then checked the man's pulse. "We need to get this man ashore right away," he yelled to one of the crewman who raced to inform the captain.

Thibadaux reached into the pocket of his tuxedo and produced the small bottle of pills, which he carried for emergencies like this. He popped the cap and spilled one of the pills into his hand. Taking the water glass that was quickly produced, he helped the man sit up and slipped the pill in his mouth. Holding the water glass to his lips, he instructed, "You've got to swallow this pill. Drink some of this water to help."

The weakened gentlemen did as he was instructed. He sipped the water and swallowed the pill as everyone on board felt the riverboat picking up speed to meet with a water taxi, which had been requested from Belle Chasse.

"What is it, Truman?" Melaudra asked as she leaned over Thibadaux.

"Cardiac arrhythmia. I just gave him a dose of digitalis to slow the ventricular rate during atrial fibrillation."

"How's that?" Melaudra asked, confused by the medical jargon.

"He's having a heart attack, and the pill I gave him should suffice until we can get him to a hospital." Turning to the crewmen, he saw a stretcher being carried. "Could we transport him to some place where it would be cool and quiet?"

"We'll carry him to the Magnolia Suite," one of the crewmen volunteered.

"We radioed for the water taxi from Belle Chasse. They'll be along side shortly and we'll transfer the gentlemen to the taxi. They'll have an ambulance on their dock, waiting to take him to emergency," the other crewmember volunteered.

They picked him up and carried him out of the room with Thibadaux accompanying them. Once they left, the band resumed playing. It was only a matter of minutes before the *Natchez* slowed to a stop, and the stricken patient and his wife were transferred to the water taxi. After one of Thibadaux's associates boarded the taxi and it departed for shore, the *Natchez* resumed cruising up river.

"Let's go outside," Melaudra suggested.

"Fine with me," Emerson agreed and followed her to a nearby door, which took them to an area overlooking the ship's stern and the paddlewheel propelling them up river. The approaching city lights could be seen on the right side of the ship, and the lights on Algiers's Point were on the port side.

"That was funny," Melaudra said as she stared at the sights.

"What's that?" Emerson asked.

"Most doctors don't have anything but their keys in their pockets. Truman had digitalis."

"Must have been a Boy Scout," Emerson teased. "Be prepared." He would recall later that the murders on Put-in-Bay had involved digitalis overdoses and that Thibadaux had visited the island, although he didn't know when.

Melaudra shook her head at the corny joke and leaned on the rail watching the paddlewheel. Standing close to her, Emerson slipped his arm around her waist and pulled her closer. Melaudra thought for a moment that she should resist, but then decided to allow herself to be pulled next to him. She'd later blame it on the Bloody Marys she had been drinking that evening.

Neither of them spoke. They stood together lost in their thoughts of the special bond, which was developing and bringing them closer together. There was a longing in their hearts for companionship.

Emerson was the first to take action. "Melaudra?" he asked softly.

"Yes?" she asked as she turned to face him and saw that his head was moving toward hers. She didn't turn away when his lips found hers and kissed her. He pulled back, looked at her as she smiled languidly at him, and kissed her again. Longer and with deeper feeling as their pent-up attraction for each other was released.

They turned their bodies to face each other and, with their arms, tightly pulled their bodies close to each other as they kissed several times as they passionately embraced.

Melaudra sensed that Emerson was the type of guy who didn't want to hurt anyone emotionally, and she was right. Emerson pulled away to look into her eyes and reached up with one hand to tenderly stroke her cheek with back of his hand, sending shivers down Melaudra's spine.

"You two should get a room!" the voice thundered.

Surprised, Melaudra and Emerson broke apart and turned to face the source of the comment. It was Thibadaux, and he had just finished a double Johnny Walker Scotch.

"Knock it off, Truman!" Melaudra warned as she smoothed out her dress and Emerson glared at him.

"It's my turn," Thibadaux said as he began to move in toward Melaudra.

"In your dreams. And then, it would be a nightmare!" Melaudra laughed as she easily spun away from the cardiologist.

When Thibadaux tried to grope her, Emerson stepped in. He grabbed Thibadaux by the shoulders and spun him around to face him. "The lady is not interested!" Emerson said firmly.

"Who do you think you are?" Enraged, Thibadaux took a step toward Emerson and began to swing a right hook. Emerson ducked under it and brought his two arms up quickly to

Thibadaux's chest and pushed him backwards. Thibadaux lost his balance and fell to the deck.

Taking Melaudra's arm, Emerson said, "Looks like we're back at the dock. Let's go."

"Good evening, Truman," Melaudra said as she stepped over him and walked to disembark from the cruise.

Emerson and Melaudra walked slowly through the warm evening on their way to Emerson's hotel. When they reached the front entrance, Melaudra turned to face him. "A part of me would like you to invite me to your room." Before Emerson could say anything, she continued, "But the better part of me is in control, and my answer would be no if you did ask. I just wanted you to know how I felt, I guess," she said as she looked softly into his eyes.

He smiled and sighed deeply. "I wouldn't want to do anything that would make you uncomfortable or that would be premature."

"You're such a gentleman," she cooed.

"Yeah, I've been told that. Sometimes, I think I'm too much of a gentleman."

"But I like the way you are," she smiled warmly and she moved in to kiss him softly on his mouth. He returned the kiss with his lips parted slightly. Reluctantly, she pulled away and began to walk to retrieve her car. "If I don't go now, I'll regret this in the morning! Thank you for a wonderful evening."

"The pleasure was all mine," Emerson called to the departing figure as he turned and walked into the hotel.

I'm not so sure about that comment, she thought and smiled wistfully to herself as her gait picked up.

St. Louis Cathedral
The Next Day

~

"You wanted to see me?" Alsandi asked as he walked into the garden behind the cathedral to meet with his unexpected visitor.

"Yes, I had a couple of questions I wanted to ask you. Do you have time now?"

"Yes, but I don't quite understand. Is there something about Father Maloney?"

"Yes and no. I hope you don't mind me asking, but could you tell me what was in the envelope that I gave you?" Seeing the look of dismay on the priest's face, Emerson quickly explained. "Call it a reporter's curiosity, but after seeing what I saw in his bedroom, I was curious if what I delivered to you had anything to do with it."

"What did you see there?" the priest asked nervously.

"There were a number of documents and reference books relating to various treaties between countries."

"Yes?" Alsandi asked hesitantly.

"What really grabbed my attention were a couple of documents which were stamped as property of the Vatican's Secret Archives. How do you think those documents ended up in the basement of a small church on an island in Lake Erie?" Emerson probed as he watched the priest's face closely for any reaction.

Alsandi's face turned gray. He could feel his heart rate quickening. "That is an interesting question you pose." His worst fears were realized. Maloney did steal other documents from the Vatican. He wondered which documents they were and what the erstwhile reporter had read. "Did you read the documents?"

"I couldn't. They were written in Italian."

Thinking for a moment, Alsandi suggested, "You should probably have them sent to me and I'll review them."

A grin spread slowly across Emerson's face. *Did the priest really think that he was that naïve?* Emerson wondered. "They've already been sent back to the Vatican." Emerson's instinct had told him that there was a possible storyline about the stolen documents. "I was curious. How did you know Maloney?"

Alsandi thought for a moment before answering. He didn't see any harm in responding and thought he might be better able to ascertain what the reporter knew. "We first met each other at the Vatican."

"Did you work together?"

"Not at first. In our free time, we spent time researching old documents in the library. That's where we first met. We had a common attraction to historical documents."

"So, you didn't work together?"

"Eventually we did. You may or may not know, but the Vatican has an area that strangely enough is called the Secret Archives. It houses old documents and letters between the Vatican and rulers or other documents of historical and religious importance." Alsandi saw Emerson listening intently. "Our mutual interest in historical documents had not gone unnoticed. Apparently one of the senior priests at the library noticed our research and the amount of time we had spent there. He recommended to Pope John Paul that we be assigned to work in the Secret Archives."

"You must have been excited."

"Oh yes. We were interviewed by the Pope and then transferred. To be able to go where only a few select people in the entire world were permitted to go was quite an honor for us."

Trying to put the priest at ease and lower his guard further, Emerson commented, "You both must have been highly trusted to have been given access to the archives."

Alsandi smiled. "Yes, we were known for our ability to maintain confidences."

Emerson began to push. "So, what kind of documents did you see there?"

Knowing that many of the documents were listed publicly, Alsandi began to recite the names of several. "There were documents listing some of the early supporters and enemies of the church. Other documents ranged from heretical and banned works to documents about the Inquisition, witchcraft, groups like the Knights Templar, and Protestantism. There were documents relating to papal complicity with the Nazis and the vices of priests over the centuries."

Emerson's eyebrows rose, showing his interest. "Sounds like a good place for me to research."

Smiling, Alsandi continued. "They'd never let someone like you in the archives. You've got to be a priest or a scholar researching a particular topic. Even then, and only if you can secure approval, you are only allowed access to a limited amount of archival material. There are a number of floors in the Secret Archives with study rooms lined with files or wooden cabinets filled with documents. Then, there's the Tower of Winds."

"Tower of Winds?"

"Yes, it's where studies were conducted on astronomy."

Emerson nodded.

"You'd be interested to know that there are files concerning the case of Galileo. He was condemned as a heretic during the Inquisition for saying that the earth revolved around the sun. There are files filled with letters, such as Henry the Eighth's request for a marriage annulment from his wife, Catherine of Aragon; a letter from the Great Khan of Mongolia to the Pope; and letters from Michelangelo to the Pope." Alsandi paused and looked at Emerson. "There's something else that many people don't know."

"What's that?" Emerson asked.

"Our Pope today, Benedict XVI."

"Yes?"

"As Cardinal Joseph Ratzinger, he headed the Secret Archives."

Emerson's eyes widened in surprise. "Is that why he is Pope today? Did he see something?"

Smiling slyly, Alsandi answered, "It wouldn't be appropriate for me to comment. I would say this, and you can't quote me, having access to anything in the archives would certainly place you in a possession of critical intelligence that you could wield at the right time. It doesn't matter whether it involves the church or other nations."

Emerson's mind raced with conspiracy theories. Putting them aside, he squinted at the priest in front of him. "With other nations?"

"Sure. The archives are filled with secret agreements between nations and treaties. Some of which could be devastating if they were made public."

"Did you see anything?" Emerson probed.

Alsandi didn't anticipate the question. He realized that he might have been too caught up in reliving a bit of his past life at the Vatican and revealed more than he intended. As a ruse, he glanced at his watch, "I didn't realize the time. I must run."

"You didn't answer my question. Did you see anything?" Emerson pushed.

"If I did, I certainly couldn't tell you, now could I?" Alsandi mused.

"You just answered my question. The right answer was no," Emerson responded firmly. Emerson glanced around the small courtyard and back to the priest. "How did you end up here?"

"It was time that I returned to the states to fill other duties," Alsandi replied.

"I understand that you and Maloney returned to the states at the same time. You both must have seen something that you shouldn't have seen," Emerson concluded as he realized that he might be bound by a gag order.

Shrugging his shoulders, Alsandi said as nonchalantly as possible, "You're going to draw your own conclusions no matter what I say. Now, I really must be going." He was stunned by Emerson's assumptions. Alsandi began to walk away.

"Oh, one more question, Father."

Alsandi stopped and turned to face Emerson. "Yes?"

"I've been doing some research about the rash of unsolved murders in the Quarter."

"Yes, there have been a few," the priest recalled nervously. "What is your question?"

"There was an incident the other night around the corner from here, across from Café du Monde."

"Yes?"

"The fellow died."

"Oh?"

"From a gunshot wound."

"Based on what I've read in the *Times-Picayune*, I don't believe that the other murders involved gunshot wounds."

"That's correct."

"What's your point?"

"Each of the other unsolved murders had one thing in common."

"The cross drawn in red on the victims' foreheads?"

"That and something else. The autopsies revealed unusually high concentrations of potassium chloride in the corpses."

"So? I'm missing your point." The priest was rocking nervously from one foot to the other.

"If potassium chloride is injected into the blood stream, it can kill a person within minutes and is not easily detected as the cause of death. It interrupts the heart's electrical signaling and induces cardiac arrest."

"I'm still missing your point."

"A small bottle of potassium chloride was found in the apartment where the last murder took place." Emerson confronted the priest with this piece of information which Elms had let slip during a phone conversation with Emerson that morning.

"That doesn't have anything to do with me. I really must go." The priest spun on his heels and began walking.

"Father, there's one more thing,"

The priest continued walking.

"The police found several strands of white hair in the apartment. They believe they belong to the killer," Emerson called out to the departing white-haired priest.

The priest's face, which Emerson couldn't see, was contorted with concern at the revelations from Emerson. He walked into St. Louis Cathedral and quickly went to one of the small offices. Closing the door behind himself, he went to the worn desk and sat down. Small beads of sweat were running down his face. They weren't due to the heat, but rather to his nervousness. He slowly reached for the cream-colored phone on the wooden desktop and began to punch in a New Orleans' number.

Place d'Armes Hotel
Later That Morning

~

The green pick-up truck pulled to a halt in front of the Place d'Armes. "Need a ride sailor?" the cheery voice called out.

Leaning against the wall and taking in the early morning on St. Anne Street, Emerson responded, "Aye aye, Captain," and reached for the truck's door. Pulling it open, he jumped into the passenger seat and thought how sharp Melaudra looked. She was wearing a blue and white polka dot sundress that ended at mid-thigh, showcasing her long legs. On her feet, she wore beige sandals.

"Looking good," Emerson said admiringly.

"Got to get dressed up for my daddy and the gang at home. Hope I don't distract you by wearing a dress," she teased all-knowingly.

"Oh no. Not at all," Emerson wasn't about to tell her how much he was enjoying the view. Besides, he figured, she knew that he would enjoy it.

She shifted the truck into first gear and began to move down St. Anne to take I-10 east out of town and toward Slidell.

"I'm looking forward to introducing you to my daddy. He's a real swamp man."

"Has he lived in the swamps his entire life?"

"Yep. He wouldn't have it any other way. He runs fish and trap lines. He's one of the hardest-working, fun-loving people I know. He can outwork, outfish, and outtrap virtually anyone in the swamp. He can probably outfox most of them too!" she grinned.

Emerson could sense the excitement she had in visiting her father. "Do you see him often?"

"Not as much as I'd like. Maybe twice a month."

"I understand you're Creole, but I don't quite understand Cajun. Can you help me?" Emerson asked as the truck picked up speed on I-10.

"Sure, Cajuns are the descendants of Acadians who came here from Nova Scotia in the mid-1700s. They speak a Cajun French that has developed into a unique dialect. Wait until you talk with my daddy. You'll love his accent and the words he uses."

"The words he uses?" Emerson questioned, not understanding.

Melaudra beamed. "He is so sweet. He still talks the old words. Just wait and you'll see. He has such a 'joie de vivre!' He's a real coon ass!"

"What did you call him?" Emerson couldn't believe she called her father a coon ass.

"Coon ass. Now don't you call him that. It's okay for Cajuns to call one another by that name, but it's not taken well when an outsider calls them by that. You probably didn't notice the bumper sticker on my truck."

"No, I just got in when you pulled up. What does it say?"

"Coon ass and Proud," she smiled. "Besides their great sense of humor, you'll see Cajuns love drinking and dancing."

"Sounds like the folks in New Orleans," Emerson mused. He then added, "Then again, it sounds like a lot of the folks up on Put-in-Bay."

"That's where you're from?"

"It's where I live now. It's an island retreat in the western basin of Lake Erie. Close enough to big cities like Cleveland and Detroit, but far enough away that you have a distinctive lifestyle like New Orleans."

"Yeah, but you've got them tough winters, I'll bet."

"Yes, we do," Emerson said as he thought back to his first winter on Put-in-Bay and how isolated it could get. He had tried talking his aunt into leaving for the winter but she would not have any of that. She had said that the isolation on the island provided a time for families and neighbors to get together and enjoy each other's company after a hectic tourist season.

The truck had crossed the long bridge over Lake Pontchartrain and exited onto Highway 263. When they reached Highway 90, they turned left and drove about five miles to Cajun Encounters Swamp Tours. They pulled off the road and into the parking lot.

"Cousins of mine run this," Melaudra explained as the truck slowed to a halt under the shade of a large cypress tree. "They'll give us a ride into the swamps to my daddy's place."

Within minutes they were walking down to the dock at the river's edge and being greeted by a tall, slender, dark-haired man who was wearing a red ball cap, gray T-shirt, and Levis. "Hey there, Melaudra. Going to see Mr. Bubbie today?" he asked as he grabbed one of the picnic baskets she was carrying.

"Yes," she smiled. "Can you run us out?" Luka nodded, and she introduced Emerson to the swamp guide as they boarded the boat and Luka started it.

Luka expertly spun the small boat away from the dock, and they headed upstream on the Pearl River and through the Honey Island swamps.

"Luka, why don't you tell Emerson a bit about the swamps?" Turning to Emerson, she added, "He's one of the best guides out here!" She gave Luka a warm smile.

"Now, how can any man resist a fine lady's request when she looks that good?" Luka lamented in jest. "You been out in the swamps before?" he asked Emerson.

"No, first time."

"You'll see that the Pearl River is just as muddy as the Missisloppy River," he teased as he called the Mississippi by the name the locals used. "We've got over 250 square miles or 77,000 acres in these here Honey Island swamps. Not a good place to go or to get lost if you don't know what you're doing."

Looking overhead, Luka pointed to a barn owl perched in a tree. "That one is a stealth hunter. You can't hear him coming until the last second. Over yonder," he pointed, "is a blue heron. I heard a guy tell a story about one that was caught by one of the locals. While he was wrestling to control it, it put its bill through his eyeball and pierced his brain. Killed him on the spot."

They eased under a bald cypress tree which was draped in Spanish moss. "They used to stuff mattresses with that moss. Look over there. See that!" Luka pointed excitedly. "That's a Nutria. It's a 30-pound rat with a beaver-like head. We eat them down here. You've heard about the Atkins diet?"

"Yes," Emerson responded not knowing where the rascally guide was going with the question.

"Down here, we have our own version. It's called the Ratkins Diet," he chuckled.

"We've got 28 different species of snake here. Some of the worst ones are the cottonmouth, copperheads, and the eastern coral snake. We've got all kinds of fish from striped bass to perch to five-foot-long gars. One guy caught a record 118-pound catfish. He had to use a hacksaw to cut the fish open!"

The boat had pulled into a tree-lined bayou, which widened considerably after the first 50 feet. Luka idled back the boat's engine and allowed the boat to float forward on its momentum. "Keep your eyes sharp. There are usually several gators around here. You really need to come back in

April or May when the bull gators are mating. It can get real nasty here."

Their eyes scanned the edges of the bayou to catch a glimpse of the gators. "There's two!" Luka called as two 14-foot gators approached the boat. He said to Emerson, "You can go to the bow and look over at the gators. Just be sure you don't slip and fall overboard. It's their lunchtime."

Emerson was anxious to see the gators in their natural habitat and as close as possible. He leaned over the edge to look more closely at them.

"Don't get too close. They can shoot up from the water and pull you in." The boat bumped against some low overhanging branches, which scrapped its rooftop. "Stupid branches. They're scratching up my roof, but I'd still rather have the roof. Sometimes snakes will drop off trees and into the boats. That's why I prefer boats with a roof over them."

Just then a snake dropped from the roof's edge onto Emerson's shoulder. Emerson shrieked with surprise and, fortunately for him, tumbled backwards into the boat rather than into the gator-infested water. As he frantically looked around to see where the snake landed, he heard laughter from the rear of the boat. It was coming from Luka and Melaudra.

Ignoring the laughter, Emerson continued to look for the snake. His hand griped an oar, which he had found in the boat's bottom. It was then he saw the snake. It was dangling from a wire at the front of the boat. The wire was attached to a rope, which encircled the roof lengthwise. When Emerson looked at the stern, he saw that Luka had one hand in the air and was gripping the rope.

"Works every time. I usually pull that rubber snake stunt on 12-year-old boys when they get too cocky on my boat tours. It usually quiets them down real quick. I've seen a couple of them wet their pants right in front of their school buddies." Luka grinned as he eased the throttle forward to break free of the branches.

"Emerson, you should have seen the look on your face! It was classic!" Melaudra chortled.

"You knew, didn't you? You knew that he was going to do that to me?" Emerson said as he pointed his finger at Melaudra.

"Why Mr. Emerson Moore, you getting a tad angry," Melaudra teased. "Actually, I did have an inkling when he allowed the boat to float towards the trees."

"And you enjoyed it, didn't you."

Melaudra didn't reply. She smiled provocatively at Emerson.

"There's a story about two city boys who came out here in the swamp. Snake fell off a tree into their boat, and they opened fire on the snake. There was only one problem," Luka grinned.

"What was that?" Emerson asked.

"They shot holes in the bottom of the boat, and the boat began to sink in an area full of gators."

"Gators get them?"

"Nah, A guy heard them screaming and got to them in time." While he was talking, Luka opened a chest, which contained raw meat. "Leftovers, mostly spoiled meat, but it don't matter to them gators," He said as he pulled out a bloody piece of meat and held it over the edge of the boat. "Watch this."

The words were no sooner out of his mouth than a gator shot three feet out of the water, and its lethal jaws snapped shut on the meaty treat. Luka's head spun around to Emerson. "Want to give it a try?"

"That one got pretty close to your hand," Emerson said without answering his question. "Anyone ever loses a finger feeding them?"

Luka displayed both hands and the fingers on them. "Not me. I'm too careful. A couple of guides over the years allowed their concentration to be broken when a pretty tourist asked them a question. They turned their heads to respond and didn't react quickly enough when the gator came out the water. One lost his arm from the elbow down and the other lost it just below the shoulder."

"That had to hurt," Emerson groaned as he imagined the pain.

"The good news was that neither of them fell into the bayou. Them gators would have been all over them."

"Yeah, I can imagine. I've seen what crocidiles do to zebras crossing rivers in Africa when I watch the History Channel. It's bloody!"

After five minutes of feeding the gators, Luka closed the lid of his ice chest. "All gone. We can head to your daddy's now, Melaudra." He returned to the stern and carefully eased the throttle forward, and the large craft moved down a short channel, which brought them back to the Pearl River.

"Hey, Mr. Emerson, do you know how a momma gets the baby gators to leave the nest when they're reluctant?"

"No, Luka. How does she?"

"She just eats a couple. The others get the message real quick and scram," he chortled.

Emerson shook his head and asked, "How much farther until we're there?"

"Oh, about a quarter-mile, wouldn't you agree, Luka?" Melaudra asked as the boat picked up speed on the river and the breeze brought some relief to the late morning heat.

"That's about right," Luka responded. "Whereabouts are you from?"

Emerson responded, "The islands of western Lake Erie. There's a small resort town on South Bass Island called Put-in-Bay."

Luka nodded his head. "Not too far from Cleveland, then?"

"Right. About an hour west."

"They've got a large Serbian and Croatian community in Cleveland," Luka observed.

Emerson was stunned. *How in the world would someone in the swamps of Louisiana know that,* Emerson thought. He had only learned of the large ethnic population in Cleveland when he had met with a Slovenian detective in Cleveland on a story he was researching. He had to ask. "How did you know that?"

"I'm Croatian. We all have a tendency to know where the other Croats settle."

"How did you end up here?" Emerson probed now that his curiosity had risen.

"My grandparents left Bosnia when the war started, and the whole family settled here. They had a relative here and that's what brought them to Louisiana. Then, my grandparents returned to Bosnia a few years ago. Ever been there during your travels?"

Emerson paused before responding. He remembered his early years when he went on assignment in the former Yugoslavia to cover the fighting between the Serbs and Croats in the town of Vukovar, located on the Danube River.

"Yes, I was there on assignment, but that's a story for another day," Emerson closed the discussion and turned his attention to the shanties that they began to pass. They were perched just inches above the water.

Seeing Emerson staring at the shanties, Luka opted to comment. "They're real Cajun homes. They live out here on the water's edge and fish and hunt to get by. Some of them will boat in to the highway and head up to Slidell for their work. Others will hardly ever leave the swamps. The river and bayous are their neighborhood streets."

Emerson found the structures unique. Many of the shanties had corrugated metal roofs and walls with aluminum windows. They all had a small boat or two tied up to their decks. The covered decks contained chairs, old sofas, picnic tables, and barbecue grills. Usually nets, traps, fishing rods, and skins hung from the walls or the porch rafters.

"Yesterday I saw an eight-foot gator sunning itself on that family's deck, right where those kids are jumping in the water and swimming," Luka commented as they went by one gaily painted home.

"Aren't they worried the gator'll come back?"

"Oh, they're keeping a sharp eye out for him and they got a dog standing there watching over them as they're swimming. He'll alert them to any danger, too."

"Hi, Luka!" a group of barefoot kids called from the porch of a shanty they were passing.

Luka slowed the boat and shouted back, "Hi, Kids!" and then to the tall bearded man wearing blue jeans and khaki work shirt who was grilling on the barbecue, "You cooking up a mess of fish?"

"I sure am. Come back in about 15 minutes and you can join us," the figure called back.

"I might just do that. I've got Bubbie Drencheau's daughter and her friend on board. Running them up to Bubbie's place."

"Hello, Melaudra. You tell your daddy that I said hello."

"I'll do that Mr. Simms," Melaudra called back. Turning to Emerson, she explained, "He's the sheriff for this parish."

Emerson was stunned. "He lives out here?"

"Best place to be, right with the people," Luka piped in.

They rode another eighth of a mile in silence as they took in the beauty of the river's lush vegetation, the clear skies, and the shanties. Some of the shanties were built on houseboats, which were tethered to nearby trees and rode quietly on the river's slow-moving current.

"We're here," Melaudra said as their boat neared a small shanty set just above water level.

Emerson eyed the dilapidated, unpainted shanty with a large deck and covered front porch. The deck ran down both sides of the shanty, and a pirogue was tied at one side. Cypress trees and lush vegetation seemed to threaten to overtake the shabby place. A weather-beaten sign hung from the porch. It read, "Honey Island Store," and faded tin signs advertising beer and bread were affixed on the wall. The front door was open as were two large windows, which overlooked the river. On the porch was a faded red cooler with Coke written in white paint. Christmas decorations hung from the porch even though Christmas was months away. To Emerson, the whole structure looked like it was on the verge of crashing to the ground at the next strong blast of wind.

Emerson helped Melaudra step off the boat onto the deck and then passed her the two picnic baskets, which she had carried to the boat from the truck. As Emerson stepped off the boat, Luka gunned the engine. "Be seeing you all." He then pushed the engine into gear and began to pull away from the deck.

"Thanks, Luka," Melaudra cried out.

"Thanks for the mini-tour, Luka," Emerson yelled.

"No problem. Just remember, Louisiana has the best politicians that money can buy," the affable tour guide called as he picked up speed and headed downriver.

A board squeaked near the open door, causing Emerson and Melaudra to whirl around and face the open doorway. They turned into the double-barrel shotgun, which was leveled at their chests. The shotgun was held by a 70-year-old black man wearing a threadbare blue cotton shirt and faded Levis, which were secured by red suspenders. On his head was a straw hat that had seen better days. An unlit cigarette butt was clenched firmly between his yellowed teeth. Behind horn-rimmed glasses, one side of which had tape holding it together, his dark-brown eyes stared menacingly at Emerson. He looked like he was on the verge of pulling the trigger.

"Hold on one second," Emerson started.

"Oh Mose, you do need to get your eyes checked," Melaudra said as she casually swept aside the gun's barrel and hugged the older gentleman.

"Can't be too careful. Who's your friend?" he asked as he held the lowered shotgun tightly, ready to swing it up at a moment's notice.

"Mose, meet my friend, Emerson Moore. It's his first time in the swamps. I bet he'll always remember meeting you the way you greeted him with that shotgun."

Mose relaxed his grip on the shotgun.

Emerson, now relieved, approached Mose with an outstretched hand. "Glad to meet you, Mose."

Mose looked at Emerson suspiciously and ignored his hand. "I don't know who you are and until I get comfortable with you, my name is Mr. Mose to you."

Taken aback momentarily, Emerson responded, "Okay then, Mr. Mose."

"Oh Mose, loosen up," she suggested. "Emerson, don't worry none about him. He's a sweetie, and that shotgun of his doesn't even fire."

Mose spoke quickly. "You needn't to have told him that." He leaned the shotgun against the front wall and next to the Coke cooler.

Emerson's mouth broke into a smile.

"My daddy helps him with running this little store." She walked into the store and added as her eyes surveyed the almost bare shelves, "Not that they make much money at it."

Emerson, closely followed by Mose, entered the small store. He leaned on an old cooler, which was full of beer and held four quarts of milk. Behind the sales counter were most of the shelves, and they held a variety of spices, cayenne pepper, canned beans, salt, a couple of brands of coffee, sugar, flour, paprika, horseradish, and green olives.

One set of shelves contained hunting and fishing gear. There were fishhooks, nets, ammunition, six rods, three lanterns, and lantern fuel.

"You're carrying Pampers!" Melaudra exclaimed as she saw them on the shelf.

"At your suggestion," Mose replied casually.

"Are they selling?" she asked.

"Yeah, when someone runs out and they don't want to run into town, just like about everything else in here."

Emerson continued to survey the room while Melaudra and Mose caught up. Two chairs sat next to an old table with a chessboard on it. It appeared that a game was in progress or else play had been interrupted. Next to the table was an old pot-bellied stove, which was used to reduce heating costs. Emerson couldn't see it, but a propane tank was out back and provided more costly heating fuel during especially chilly nights. A worn sofa, two aging lamps, and two overturned wooden crates, which served as small tables, completed the furnishings in the main room. On the wall behind the stove were mounted a boar's head and a snapping turtle's head with its beaked jaws wide open.

Through gaily beaded curtains, Emerson could see into the bedroom, which contained two single beds, each covered with a solitary blanket. Overturned wooden boxes served as nightstands. Each had a small lantern. A bare light bulb could be seen at the other end of a pull-chain that hung in the middle of the room. At the foot of each bed was a small wooden trunk that, Emerson surmised, held clothing.

"Emerson, come on out back," Melaudra called as she stood with her figure silhouetted in the doorway at the rear of the store.

Emerson joined her on the rear porch where he saw an old stove and a small refrigerator. It looked like something out of the 1940s. The back porch had a couple of rockers and a hammock hung between two of the roof supports. Scanning the porch's roof, Emerson saw two yellow bug lights hanging from the ceiling.

"Daddy," Melaudra called to a figure working at a makeshift table.

The figure turned around and smiled at his daughter.

Melaudra flew across the open space between her and her wiry father into his outstretched arms. He had a white beard and white hair pulled back into a ponytail. A black bandanna encircled his head and acted as a sweatband. His twinkling blue eyes stood out against a deeply tanned face filled with deep crevasses. This was a man who was used to hard life in the swamps and bayous. He wore a bloodstained, faded, white T-shirt which had printed in red, "Pearl River Souvenirs." At the side of his khaki workpants was a large knife in its sheath. His massive hands told a story of a man used to a life of hard work, including fishing, trapping, hunting, firewood cutting, and paddling his pirogue through the swamps.

"Why don't ma gurl come see me more often?" her daddy asked as he lifted her off her feet and spun her around in a circle.

"Daddy, you know it's hard for me to get away!' she squealed as he continued to spin around. "Daddy, put me down, you're going to hurt yourself!"

Her father held her tighter in response and spun her around harder. "You never too beeg for me to do dis!" A moment later he set her down on her feet and said, "Let me look at you. You look might fine, just lak you mudder did." He then looked over at Emerson. "Who dat man?"

"Daddy, this is Emerson Moore. He's a reporter for the *Washington Post.*"

Her father interrupted her. "Ah don't need no reporter da talk wit. You send him home."

Emerson took a step back.

"Daddy, he's not here to do a story. He's helping me with a case, and I wanted him to see the swamps." Turning to Emerson, she introduced her father, "Emerson, this is my Daddy, Bubbie."

"Hello, Mr. Drencheau." Emerson extended his hand, and Bubbie shook it cautiously.

"You don't do no story on me. You understand what Ah telling you?"

"Sure, no problem at all," Emerson replied with a grin. Emerson asked, "What do you have out there?"

Bubbie turned his head in the direction in which Emerson was looking. The small backyard, which was barely above water level and bounded on two sides by swamp, had a work area below a large cypress tree. It was a makeshift worktable consisting of a piece of chain length fence, supported by three two-by-fours on top of two sawhorses. On top of the chain link fence were six overturned snapping turtles. On the ground below the chain link fence were their heads, which had been chopped off with the axe that leaned against the tree.

"Cleaning ma turtles." His eyes twinkled momentarily and his face broke into a mischievous smile as he asked Emerson, "You want da help me?"

Wanting to start a friendship with Melaudra's father on the right foot, Emerson responded, "Sure. What do you need me to do?"

The two walked out to the makeshift worktable where a large pot of water was boiling on a grate over a hot fire. Bubbie picked up a pan and spoke as he dipped it into the boiling water. "Deese turtles, dey don't die right away. Even after you cut off eets head, it can still bite you."

Emerson eyed the massive heads carefully, mentally remembering the exact location of each one on the ground. He noticed that the ground was covered by blood from the six turtles bleeding out.

Turning to his worktable, Bubbie carefully poured the hot water around the edge of the turtle shell, where the turtle's muddy brown-green exterior skin was attached between the upper and lower shell.

"Dis balling water makes eet easier da cut," he explained as he withdrew his large knife from the sheath at his waist. Working quickly, he inserted the sharp blade into the hot water-drenched area and began to slice around the edge of the bottom shell and through the joints between the two shells. Within minutes he had lifted the bottom shell like a can lid.

He rolled back the skin and began to remove the yellow fat from the meat. "You don't want the turtle fat in de soup." He explained as he finished cutting out the fat and removing the entrails, which he threw into a nearby bucket. He then filleted the meat away from the top shell and placed it in a pot, which he had set on the table.

From the first turtle, he moved quickly to the next turtle as Emerson watched him make quick work on the cleaning process. When Bubbie got to the last turtle, he paused and looked at Emerson, extending the knife to him. "Dis one, she is yours to clean."

Emerson gingerly took the knife and turned to his waiting patient. *This was going to be interesting,* Emerson thought. "I'm going to need the water first," he said as he turned back to Bubbie who held the pan of boiling water in his hand.

"Dis is a very good start for you," he grinned. "You remembered de first ting to do."

Emerson poured the hot water between the two shells and set down the pan. He inserted the knife near the front right leg and began to cut.

In the house, Melaudra heard a scream and ran to the back porch.

"Aren't you two getting along?" the tough detective called. She saw her father rolling around on the ground. His arms were wrapped around his sides as he guffawed. Emerson stood next to the bloody knife that had been dropped to the ground. He held one hand to the side of his face, which had several bleeding scratch marks.

"What happened?" she called.

Emerson didn't respond, although his face was growing crimson in color. Bubbie rose to his knees and faced his daughter. Between laughter and tears, he answered her. "You friend, da reporter, he just learned dat de turtle's nervous system doesn't die right away. He put de knife in and hit de nerve. The turtle, his foot came up and clawed your friend on de face."

Sheepishly, Emerson spoke, "It's nothing. I'm embarrassed that I yelled. It was more of surprise than pain." Melaudra had reached his side and carefully dabbed her hand towel at the side of his face.

"Surprised you, huh? That's nothing. I was in the morgue one time when a fresh body was delivered. I was talking with the coroner, when the body suddenly sat up. I screamed and the coroner laughed. He said the same thing. It was just a reaction from the nervous system."

"I'd better finish my job," Emerson said, embarrassed by the attention this incident had garnered. He was a quick learner and finished cleaning the turtle within minutes.

"Good. You did a good job," Bubbie grinned with satisfaction at his pupil's prowess with the knife.

"It helps when you have a sharp knife," Emerson said as he handed the blade back to Bubbie who sheathed it. "What's next?"

"You take dis to the porch, and Mose will cook up some turtle soup for us. And here," Bubbie said as he passed the bucket of entrails to Emerson, "give him dis."

Emerson wondered what the entrails were going to be used for as he carried the two buckets to the house. As he walked, he eyed the swamp that was so dangerously close to the small backyard. On one side, he discerned a worn path, which led from the edge of the swamp to the side porch. *Must be a path for someone coming in from the swamps*, he thought. He had noticed a couple of pirogues on the swamp's edge.

"Here you go, Mose," Emerson said as he swung the two buckets up on the porch floor.

"I told you once before, my name is Mr. Mose to you. I don't know you from Adam," Mose said sternly.

"Sorry, I meant Mr. Mose," Emerson corrected himself hastily. "What are you cooking?" he asked as he leaned over a pot on the stove.

"Crawfish," he smiled. "I've got a special recipe for cooking them."

"Really, what's makes it special?" Emerson said as he turned his attention to the store and saw Melaudra busying herself with cleaning up some of the layers of dust inside.

"It's in the way I do it. First I start with a beer," he grinned. "After I finish the beer, I pop open another can and rinse the crawfish in the beer. Then I throw the crawfish in a basket and put it in a large 80-quart pot with water and bring it to a boil, like I'm doing now. Then, you throw in cayenne, pepper, herbs, salt, and lemon juice from a half a dozen lemons, then you throw the lemons in too! Now, you've got to watch it boil and, to help me watch it carefully, I drink another beer. It helps with your cooking senses," he chuckled.

"I'm not sure about that."

"Want a beer?"

"Sure. Just don't be offended if I don't finish it all."

"Not a drinker?"

"More like I had a drinking problem awhile back, so you just might say that I'm careful."

"I heard you two talking about beer, so I brought one to each of you," Melaudra said as she appeared in the doorway and handed them a beer. She popped open one for herself and raised the can to her dark brown lips where she allowed the cold liquid to run down her throat.

"Thank you," Mose said.

Mose popped open his beer and threw it down while Emerson slowly opened his beer as he watched Melaudra. *Pretty girl*, he thought as he watched her drink the cold beverage. She noticed Emerson watching her and stopped drinking to look into his eyes. She smiled softly and disappeared into the house.

"Pretty isn't she?" Mose said as he observed Emerson watching Melaudra.

"Yes, she is very pretty," Emerson said.

"So was her mother," Mose commented as he leaned on the back wall of the store.

"What happened to her mother?"

"Died of breast cancer just before Melaudra graduated from high school. Her name was Glory and she was my cousin. That's how I got hooked up with Bubbie. Glory's folks had left here when she was a kid and moved to Chicago. She graduated from college up there, but always wanted to come back to the swamps. She came back every summer and that's how she met Bubbie."

"What did a girl from Chicago see in Bubbie?" Emerson asked.

"A good strong man from the swamps. Oh, there's no doubt that he's a bit of a rascal, but he's a good Louisiana swamp man." He took a swig from his beer can and continued, "Melaudra followed in her mother's footsteps and went to Chicago to stay with her grandparents and go to college. Like her mother, she had to come back to the swamps too, although she joined the police force in New Orleans and did well for herself. She still comes back to the swamps to see her daddy."

"She never married?" Emerson asked as he looked inside the store again at Melaudra.

"Nope, she has had a few boyfriends that have come out here with her, but they didn't come back. Bubbie scared them. Looks like you're off to a good start with him. Don't know if she'll ever marry; she's one of those career women. She loves being a detective," Mose responded. "Want another beer?"

"No thanks." Emerson swished the beer around in the can and knew that he still had half a can left.

"Back to my recipe. I drop in halved onions, potatoes, and fresh garlic. Then I have another beer and drop in corn, sausage, and mushrooms. In about 15 minutes, it's ready to eat. Gives me time for another beer," Mose said as he stood away from the wall.

"What about the entrails?" Emerson asked as he eyed the bucketful on the edge of the porch.

Mose looked at the bucket and then at Emerson. His face broke into a smile. "Why don't you carry them around to the front of the store? Take the side deck over there," he was pointing to the right side of the store. "And don't make a lot of noise or thump anything on your way."

Emerson began to question him, but Mose cut him off. "No questions. Do as I say and carefully. I'll meet you out in front." And he turned and entered the store.

Emerson picked up the bucket of entrails and walked over to the side deck, which was just above the water's edge. He eyed the water carefully and looked toward the edge of the swamp and back out to the front of the building. He noticed that the path to the swamp ended at the edge of the deck, and that it appeared that the deck had been sanded. Seeing nothing to be immediately concerned about, he picked up the bucket and began to uneasily walk along the deck, which was overhung with swamp foliage. A couple of times the bucket bumped into the side of the store's wall.

When it banged against the wall loudly a second time, Mose appeared around the edge of the front porch. "I'd be a little more careful if I were you," he warned ominously.

Emerson's head quickly swung around, but he didn't note any danger to himself. He wondered to what Mose was referring. When he reached the front porch, he handed the bucket to Mose.

"You might want to step away from the side deck," Mose cautioned as he dumped the entrails on the deck. "Watch this," he said as he picked up a worn broom handle and thumped the deck several times. Within minutes, Emerson heard a noise along the deck on which he had just walked.

"You might want to step back a little farther from that side of the deck," Mose cautioned as the dangerous head of a hungry 14-foot-long alligator appeared as if by magic and quickly snapped at the entrails, pushing them into the water, and then followed them into the river where the alligator rolled over several times as it swallowed the sinking entrails.

Emerson stood frozen in his tracks as he watched the water churning and thought about his walk along that side of the deck.

"I call that bull alligator 'the Terminator.' He knows that when I thump the deck, I've got a treat for him. He rushes out of the swamp and along the deck like a freight train to get any food I have out for him."

"Why would you want to feed something like that and keep him around here?" Emerson asked aghast.

"He's our burglar alarm."

"Some alarm. Acts more like a food disposal if you ask me!" Emerson joked weakly.

"Having him around helps to keep any unwanted visitors away. It's not that we don't trust the locals, it's outsiders that he's good at scaring."

"I can see that!"

A noisy motor on the river caused them to look down river to see an approaching boat with three Cajuns aboard. There were two men and one woman. "That'd be Melaudra's cousin and her husband. The other guy is their neighbor," Mose explained.

Emerson turned his attention to the muddy river where the alligator had ceased its churning. "Do you need to warn them about that gator?"

Mose looked to where the alligator had been. "Nope. He's off to his den for a snooze."

Hearing the approaching boat, Melaudra joined Mose and Emerson on the front deck. Seeing her on the porch, her cousin, Bonnie, hollered as the boat drew near, "It's about time that you came out to see me."

Melaudra yelled back as the small boat's engine was cut and the boat glided the few feet to the deck where Moses was waiting to help tie it up. "I keep telling you to come into the Quarter to see me."

"Quarter's too wild for me, Honey. You got all kinds of strange creatures walking around there."

"And like you don't have strange creatures here in the swamp?"

"The only strange creature I've seen in this swamp is my husband and they don't come much stranger, but I guess I'll still put up with him. Right, T-Bone?" she said as she looked at her husband, who had garish tattoos on both arms and who was standing in the stern to hand a line to Mose.

The red-headed and bearded man was wearing a black tank top that fought to contain his large belly. He responded slowly to his chubby long-haired wife, "Pooh-yi mon Chere, where else would you find a good-looking man like me?"

"Pooh-yi?" Emerson muttered, not understanding the phrase.

Ignoring his question, Melaudra exclaimed, "Oh, where are my manners?" She quickly introduced Emerson to her two relatives and their lean, 50-year-old neighbor, Vernon. Vernon had long, black, scraggly hair and a black mustache.

"First time in the swamps?" Bonnie asked as she appreciatively eyed the handsome Emerson.

"Yes, and hopefully not the only visit," Emerson replied as he turned to give a warm smile to Melaudra. "You didn't interpret 'Pooh-yi' for me," Emerson reminded Melaudra.

"It's somewhat of a catch-all phrase. You have to listen to the tone in which it's said. It can mean anything from surprise and pleasure to being dismayed," Melaudra explained.

"Pooh-yi," Bonnie said quietly and seductively as she walked past Melaudra. "I wouldn't throw that one back into the river. Nice catch!" she added with a wink to Melaudra, who felt her face beginning to flush.

Attempting to recover her composure, Melaudra called, "Let's go on out back. I expect that the crawfish are about done."

Carrying the food that they brought and with Mose helping carry their musical instruments, they walked through the store to its rear porch, where they began to ready themselves for a crawfish feast.

While Bonnie and Melaudra spread newspaper on top of the picnic table on the back porch and Mose brought over the cooked crawfish, the visitors and Bubbie grabbed cold beers from an ice chest on the floor. Mose dumped the crawfish and lemon halves in a smoking heap on the tabletop.

"It is time to dig in!" Mose said as he took a deep breath to enjoy the unique aroma of fresh-cooked crawfish.

Bubbie was the first to act. With his left hand, he grabbed a crawfish off the pile and, while holding its head, gently twisted off it tail. Emerson watched as Bubbie raised the separated head to his mouth and sucked out the hot, spicy juices. Seeing Emerson watching him closely, Bubbie paused, "Dat's good. Ah like de crawfish brains in my mouth!"

Emerson swallowed hard at the thought of it.

"Daddy, don't," Melaudra warned. "It's not like that, Emerson, it's good."

Emerson smiled weakly. It looked like a lot of work to him, just like eating lobster was a lot of extra work. He was determined to be a good sport and try something new, but he wanted to understand how to eat them Cajun-style. He saw everyone else tackling their food and then turned back to watch Bubbie.

Bubbie had slid a finger under the first few segments at the top of the tail and peeled away the top to partially expose the tail. He then pinched the base of the shell and pulled out the tail meat, which looked like a tiny lobster tail. Grinning at Emerson, he popped it in his open mouth and gobbled it up. "You try, now!" he directed.

Emerson grabbed a crawfish from the pile and repeated the process he had observed Bubbie do while Melaudra intently watched him. He gently squeezed the tail end of the body close to where it joined the head and twisted off the tail end. He pulled back the shell and placed the tail meat to his mouth, giving it a hard suck. "Tasty," he commented as he turned his attention to the head which was oozing a brownish-yellow mystery mush.

"Nothing like savoring crawfish lungs to grow hair on your chest," Emerson teased as he placed the head to his mouth and sucked out the juicy meat.

"Good, isn't it?" Melaudra asked as she sucked a head.

"Better than I thought," Emerson replied as he reached for another crawfish from the shrinking pile on the picnic table.

"We've got red beans and rice over here," Bonnie called as she pointed to food on the table.

"And there's the jambalaya and cornbread I brought," Melaudra added as the group continued to feast and beer can lids popped.

Emerson stood and helped himself to the jambalaya, one of his favorite Louisiana foods. It was loaded with green peppers, onions, celery, hot peppers, and rice. When he returned to the table, he asked Melaudra, "I've never been clear on the difference between Cajun and Creole cooking. Could you explain it to me?"

"Sure, Creole cooking is not as spicy as Cajun. Cajun cooking typically is heartier and found out in the bayous. It uses what we call 'the trinity'—onions, celery, and finely-diced bell peppers. And you'll see a lot of rice with a dark thick gravy.

"You into cooking?" Mose asked.

"Oh, I was just a bit curious," Emerson responded.

"Bubbie and I can give you all kinds of recipes for swamp cooking, can't we Bubbie?" Mose looked at Bubbie for a response—only to get a smile and the sound of Bubbie sucking out the meat from another crawfish head.

"We got recipes like Deer in the Bucket and Deer Roast Surprise," Mose offered.

"Deer Roast Surprise?"

"Yeah. If you don't get sick from eating it, you'll be surprised," Bubbie chimed in as he used the back of his hand to wipe off the dripping juices from around his mouth.

"He's just funning you!" Mose said as he continued. "There's frog leg dumplings, alligator cacciatore, gator gumbo, gator tots, squirrel sauce picante, and turtle grits. We do it all out here," he beamed.

Ashe finished sucking another crawfish head, Emerson paused. "If it's as good as this, I'd like to give them all a try!" Turning to Melaudra, he asked, "With all of this good cooking, how do you stay so slim and trim?" He took a swallow from his beer can as he waited for her to swallow her crawfish. He noted that he was still on his first beer while the others had consumed mass quantities of the liquid refreshment.

"I'm careful. And I work out almost every day. Never know when I'll need that extra burst of speed to run after a perpetrator." She smiled warmly at Emerson.

An hour had passed since they had started consuming their meal. That's when Bubbie leaned back and emitted a loud burp. "Ma, dat was good!" he declared. He reached over to a washboard-like contraption and began strapping it to his chest. Seeing his actions, the others began to push away from the littered table and reach for a variety of instruments. Mose filled his hands with a fiddle while Vernon strapped on the accordion, which he had carried in from the boat. T-Bone picked up a guitar and everyone began to loosen up and tune their respective instruments.

Looking at the washboard Bubbie was fastening to his chest, Emerson asked, "It's a frottoir, right?"

"Very good," Melaudra was impressed.

"Whenever I visited the Quarter over the years, I've always taken time to listen to Cajun music. There's just something about that energetic melody and the singing that I find refreshing."

"It's party music, Emerson. It doesn't matter whether you're in one of the bars on Bourbon Street or the back porch in the swamps, it's good foot-stomping music for some good times," Melaudra said as T-Bone and Bonnie broke into a song, which was quickly picked up by the other players.

Melaudra and Emerson found themselves tapping their feet with the music. "Care to dance with a pretty girl?" Melaudra asked Emerson as she stood and held out her arms.

"You mean Bonnie?" Emerson teased as he looked over to Bonnie who was now two-stepping in place.

Feigning hurt feelings, Melaudra turned her back on Emerson, "Don't say that I didn't offer!" She was surprised when she felt arms surround her waist and she turned around to face Emerson.

"I was just teasing," he explained with a twinkle in his eyes.

"Teasing can get you in trouble," she warned as she began stepping to the music.

Emerson looked into her cute face and pretty eyes before responding. "I was kind of hoping it would," he replied mischievously.

She grabbed his hand and broke the spell of the moment. "Let's dance!" She moved quickly into a Cajun two-step, which Emerson picked up and followed.

The partying and music continued for another couple of hours, then everyone helped clean up and T-Bone, Bonnie, and Vernon left for home. Mose and Melaudra were finishing cleaning up, while Bubbie and Emerson drifted back to the turtle cleaning area.

"Ma gurl, she's a good one like her mudder," Bubbie said as he and Emerson watched her walking into the store.

"She's one fine woman," Emerson noted appreciatively.

"She don't hardly bring anyone out here."

"Really?"

"Dat de truth. Sometime, she worry dat her daddy gonna embarrass her."

"Do you?"

Bubbie's face broke into a wide grin. "Yes!" He heard Emerson chuckle and then said, "Maybe, sometime you come back and Ah take you out wit me to run my traps."

Before replying, Emerson tried to recall the phrase he had earlier in the day and then used it. "Pooh-yi! I'd like that."

Bubbie's smile grew as he spoke. "Dat's right! Pooh-yi! Now, you git up dere and help her." Bubbie turned his back and began to walk towards the swamp. He didn't want Emerson to see his growing smile.

Emerson headed for the store. He thought, as he walked, about how much he had enjoyed his visit. He loved the experience of breaking through barriers with people and getting a chance to learn their cultures and lifestyles. But this time, it was a little different. He was becoming more attracted to Melaudra.

A few hours later, as the night began closing in on the swamp, Melaudra leaned against the store's front porch post as Emerson stood nearby. "Did you have fun today?" she asked.

"Yes, I actually did. I've never experienced anything quite like this. The food was unbelievably great and everyone was so nice. That T-Bone certainly can sing—and they all played so well."

"They do, don't they? What did you enjoy most today?"

Emerson looked across the slow-moving river as the moon reflected its light, highlighting the muddy water with sparkles. Slowly, he responded, "Dancing with you."

Melaudra didn't say anything. She just smiled to herself. "Listen to the night. That's why I enjoy coming back here and getting away from the hustle of New Orleans." They stared across the river as Emerson stepped next to her.

"It is so soothing to hear the sounds of a night in the swamp. The frog's croaking out an evening melody. A gator or two roaring. The wind moving through the trees. Mosquitos buzzing," she added, aware that Emerson was standing next to her.

Leaning close to her ear, Emerson could smell the musky scent of her perfume. He lifted his hand to her face, turning her face so that she could look into his eyes. As he narrowed the distance between them, a voice interrupted them.

"Eets gitting late. Ah better git de two of you back to de landing."

Pulling back from each other, they turned and saw Bubbie standing at the front door.

"Sure, Daddy. Let me grab my things and Emerson can help you get the boat ready." She smiled at Emerson and hurried inside.

"Did Ah interrupt you?" Bubbie asked with a sly grin.

"No, not really. We were done talking," Emerson answered honestly. What he didn't say was what Bubbie had really interrupted him from doing. *But then again,* he wondered, *had Bubbie timed his interruption?*

Within minutes, they were seated in the small craft and motoring back down the river to the landing. The boat moved rapidly through the night as the moonlight played its silvery magic on the trees and vegetation surrounding the slow moving river.

Emerson and Melaudra rode quietly, disappointed that the magic of their moment together had been broken. Bubbie, on the other hand, was humming to himself nonchalantly and pleased with how he had interrupted them.

When they reached the landing, they said their goodbyes and Emerson and Melaudra rode back to the Quarter, talking seriously about the issues surrounding the serial murders. When they pulled in front of Emerson's hotel, Melaudra leaned over and kissed Emerson. Emerson, in turn, kissed her mouth, her hair, her neck, her cheeks, and her forehead.

"I could kiss you everywhere, from the top of your head to the bottom of your toes," Emerson said without thinking.

She smiled as she pulled away and looked at him. "I bet you could, but I'm not ready for that step. And it's easier to tell you that tonight than it was the other night when I had a few too many Bloody Marys," she said firmly.

"I was just going to suggest that we go over to Pere Antoine's restaurant for a few Bloody Marys," he teased.

"Not tonight, my friend. Now, I must really go." She leaned over and kissed him as her left hand reached for the door handle on his side and opened the door. "There you go," she sighed.

"Thanks for taking me out to meet your father," Emerson said as he stepped out of the truck.

"I enjoyed it," she said, as he closed the door and she drove away.

Place d'Armes Hotel
The Next Morning

Sitting on his balcony, Emerson was sipping coffee and reading the *Times-Picayune* when he was interrupted by the phone ringing in his room. He set down his cup and hurried inside to answer the phone. He hoped it was the return call he was expecting.

"Hello?"

"Emerson Moore?" the voice asked.

"Yes."

"It's Truman Thibadaux returning your call."

"Thank you very much."

"How may I help you?" the heavily accented Louisiana voice asked with a touch of arrogance. "Or were you calling to apologize for your behavior the other night? I'm sure that you accidentally stumbled into me and knocked me down," he stated presumptuously.

Gritting his teeth, Emerson apologized. "Well, that was one of the reasons that I called. I may have had a bit too much to drink and overreacted when you interrupted Melaudra and me." Emerson was willing to give in on this point, because he had a more direct question to ask, but he wanted to see Thibadaux's facial expression when it was posed to him.

Confidently, Thibadaux smiled to himself at Emerson's groveling apology. "Apology accepted. Now, what else was on your mind?"

"I wondered if you might have a few minutes for me to meet with you and ask you some medical questions. It's for a story I'm working on." Playing to Thibadaux's ego, Emerson suggested, "I could give your credit in the story as the source of my information."

Loving the spotlight, Thibadaux didn't hesitate. "I'm available later today. Why don't you come to my home?" He gave Emerson directions and they agreed on a time.

Garden District
New Orleans

Riding the St. Charles trolley through the prestigious Garden District was a visual treat to Emerson. He enjoyed travelling through the tree-lined streets and viewing the Italianate and Greek Revival architectural style homes, most of which had been built by early sugar and cotton planters. Some of the huge trees seemed to create a canopy over the streets and nestled up against the stately homes, which looked like candidates for the cover of *Southern Living*. Seeing the popular Cannon Restaurant, Emerson felt the trolley stop and rose from his wooden bench seat to exit near the rear. As people and cars whisked by him, he stopped to drink in the quiet majesty of the area even though the temperature was sweltering.

Glancing at the directions that he pulled from his shirt pocket, Emerson walked the short distance to the two-story white house, which was dominated by three neoclassical columns on its porch. He strolled along the walkway to the front entrance and mounted the steps to the porch and rang the doorbell.

"Mr. Moore, you found your way with no problems?" Thibadaux asked as he swung open one of the tall French doors to admit Emerson.

"No problem at all," Emerson responded as he entered the ornate home with its 14-foot high ceilings.

"Follow me, please," Thibadaux turned and led Emerson down the long hallway with its highly polished, glossy, wooden floor. There was an obviously expensive Oriental rug covering a portion of the long hallway's floor.

They walked past an ornate oak staircase, which curled its way upward. Thibadaux paused to open a pair of massive double doors, which led to his study. After they entered the study, Thibadaux went to an ornate serving table. "Care for a drink?"

"Yes. I'll take ice water."

Thibadaux stared at Emerson for a moment and then shrugged his shoulders as he reached for the ice bucket.

While Thibadaux was preparing the drinks, including gin and tonic for himself, Emerson looked around the massive study. There was a huge red-brick fireplace, which seemed to take up one whole wall to the left. Oak bookcases bearing shelves of leather-bound books competed with antique, gold-framed, oil paintings of life on Southern plantations. The study was furnished with a large, ornate, cherry desk and chair plus a gold loveseat and two dark-leather high-backed chairs.

"Here's your beverage. Hope I didn't make it too strong for you." Thibadaux said rudely as he raised his gin and tonic to his lips.

As he approached the serving table, Emerson noted a silver coat of arms mounted on the wall. It was obviously centuries old and bore the crest of the Knights Templar. A number of large swords were also displayed on the wall, but there was one item which captured Emerson's attention. It was a crossbow, which was also mounted on the wall.

Seeing Emerson drawn to the crossbow, Thibadaux remarked, "You may not have good taste when it comes to drinks, but you are certainly looking at the most rare of weapons in my collection."

"I've never seen one of these."

"This one dates back to 1200s." Thibadaux took another sip of his drink, then continued. "They originated in China and ended up in Europe. The Crusaders used them against the Arab archers with such unbelievable success that they quickly replaced longbow usage in battle."

"But, I thought everyone preferred the long bow," Emerson said, confused.

"The crossbow was more efficient. You could train someone to fire a crossbow accurately in a week whereas it took time to train longbow archers to develop their accuracy." Thibadaux took the oak crossbow off the wall and loaded it with one of the bolts, or arrows, from a container on the table below it. "These are really quite easy to operate," he said as he pulled it back to full draw and pulled the trigger, sending the bolt harmlessly into the fireplace opening. "Deadly, though."

He handed the weapon to Emerson who examined it more closely. "The stock resembles a rifle stock," Emerson observed.

"Notice the trigger?"

Emerson focused on the crossbow's triggering device.

"They became the basis for gun triggers, and our old friend, Mr. Leonardo da Vinci, designed what we call today a 'hair trigger.'"

"Amazing," Emerson said as he handed the weapon back to Thibadaux who placed it on the wall and then walked across the room to retrieve the bolt from the fireplace.

"Very deadly. So deadly that these bolts could pierce a knight's armor," he said as he stood with the retrieved bolt and returned it to its container across the room. "That's why Pope Urban II banned the use of crossbows. They may have been banned, but they became the weapon of choice for snipers in that time period."

The comment about the Pope triggered a thought in the back of Emerson's mind. "Speaking about the Pope, I understand that there are quite a few Catholics in New Orleans," he set the bait for a possible line of questioning.

"Yes, there are. Although I'm not one."

Not the answer that Emerson was hoping for. If Thibadaux had been a Catholic, then Emerson had planned on asking him about St. Louis Cathedral and the priest he had met there. Emerson then switched to the real reason he was there. "I talked with the chief of police for our little island village early this morning."

"Yes?"

"He told me that you were identified as being one of a group of doctors who visited the island a couple of weeks ago."

"Yes, I was there. I believe I told you when we first met that I had visited that little island of yours." Thibadaux's mind was racing as he tried to ascertain where this line of questioning was headed.

"Did you know that we had a couple of murders that weekend on the island?"

In addition to his mind racing, Thibadaux felt his heart begin to race. "No," he lied.

"Based on what the coroner and the police have been able to determine, the two deaths may have been committed by someone with a medical background."

Turning his back to Emerson, Thibadaux walked to the sideboard and began to fix himself another drink. "And what does this have to do with me? Why are you here in my home asking me questions regarding murders on your island? You're not the police!"

"Oh, I'd say it is just a matter of curiosity, Doctor."

"And what raised your curiosity with me?" Thibadaux had turned to face Emerson and was looking over the rim of the glass from which he was sipping his drink.

"Two things. First, two people die when you visit our island. Second was your treatment of the fellow on the *Natchez.*"

That was the confirmation he was looking for. *Trudy had been killed by the digitalis,* Thibadaux thought. "To your first point, I'd answer coincidence. I don't understand your second point."

"What did you treat the gentleman with on the *Natchez?*"

"Digitalis," Thibadaux answered before he could catch himself.

"Exactly what was used as an overdose in the island murder. I noticed that you had pills readily available on board the *Natchez* the other night."

Beneath his icy exterior, Thibadaux was beginning to fume. He tried to dismiss Emerson's analysis. "Purely coincidental."

Emerson began to walk toward the hall and the front door. "There's one more thing."

"What's that?"

"The other island murder was caused by a stroke."

"So, people have strokes all the time."

"This one was caused by someone cutting off the blood supply to the brain. It was caused by someone who knew what he was doing and how to hide it. The only problem was that the coroner found marks from someone's fingers on the arteries to the brain."

Swearing under his breath, Thibadaux had followed Emerson to the front door. "Conjecture, Mr. Moore. Nothing more than conjecture. I would be very careful how you draw your conclusions and any besmirchment of my good name will find you with your own legal problems," he threatened.

"I'll have my proof when I go to press. Thank you for your time, Doctor." Emerson walked out the door, which Thibadaux slammed shut.

He watched Emerson descend the steps and begin to walk away from the large home. A floorboard creaked, warning Thibadaux of someone approaching him. He whirled and confronted the intruder.

"How did you get in here?"

"I have a key, remember?"

"Yes, I do. I should take it away!" he snapped. "How long have you been here?"

"Long enough. And don't worry, I came in the back so that no one would see me and ruin your precious reputation."

Thibadaux breathed a sigh of relief.

"That was him, though."

"The reporter?"

"Yes."

"He's the one you told me about on the phone?"

"The very same."

"Nosy, isn't he?" Thibadaux asked.

"It would seem so."

"What was he interested in knowing?"

"He seems to have multiple interests. He wanted to know about my friend, Father Maloney."

"The one who was kicked out of the Vatican with you?" Thibadaux leered at Alsandi.

"Yes," Alsandi responded slowly at the harsh tone used by Thibadaux.

"What did he want to know about him?"

"He had some questions about why we were asked to leave," he replied, choosing his words carefully.

"And what did you tell him?"

"Nothing, just like I tell you nothing about what happened."

"Makes you wonder what you two did?" Thibadaux leered suggestively.

Alsandi's face reddened at the innuendo. "It's not what we did. It's what we discovered. And that's all I can tell you," he stormed.

"Okay, no sense in getting yourself worked up. You said he had questions about a couple of things. What else did he ask you about?"

"The murders."

"The murders?"

"Yes. It seems that he is interested in doing a story about the murders here in the Quarter."

Thibadaux leaned forward with interest. "Did he say anything in particular?"

"Not really, he just asked questions. He did mention one thing."

"And that was?"

"Apparently the killer has white hair," Alsandi said nervously. "They found samples in the apartment."

"Hmmm." Thibadaux muttered as he looked at the priest standing in front of him. "Anything else?"

"No."

"Okay then." Thibadaux looked at his watch. "I've got to get ready. I've got plans tonight. Is there anything you need?"

"Not really. I just wanted to sit and talk with you like we used to."

"Not tonight. I'll call you and have you over sometime in the next few days."

"I miss those days. Mother wanted us to grow closer together. She didn't want any walls between us."

Thibadaux looked at his stepbrother for a moment and then replied, "I don't think we ever let that come between us. It was your lifestyle choice that made the wall."

"We need to break down that wall."

"Yeah yeah," Thibadaux muttered sarcastically.

The priest turned and walked to the rear of the house where he allowed himself out and slipped away. Thibadaux walked to the rear door and watch through the etched glass as Alsandi left. The stress of the last hour was gnawing at his stomach. He knew that it wasn't from his spicy dinner. It was more of a growing concern about his stepbrother, the only person who knew many of the dark secrets from their childhood. It was a childhood during which they were physically abused by two separate strong-willed fathers who had domineering personalities. He and his stepbrother were powerless to stop the abuse that their mother had tolerated.

He slowly turned away from the door and walked to his sidebar where he poured himself an extra large brandy.

Honey Island Swamp
The Next Day

"Pooh-yi. Just get in de boat!" Bubbie exclaimed with consternation as Emerson looked at the pirogue that was little more than a hollowed-out log that they would use to navigate through alligator-infested swamps.

With his eyes sweeping the water for gators in front of the dilapidated store perched on the Pearl River, Emerson stood precariously on the edge of the dock and looked at Bubbie Drencheau, who was perched carefully in the pirogue's stern. "I thought we were going in a real boat."

"Dis is de real boat! Git yourself in heah!" Bubbie said to his reluctant passenger.

"What's all the racket about?" Melaudra asked as she walked out of the store, followed closely by a grinning Mose.

Bubbie was the first to speak. "You fren won't git in de boat. Iffen he gonna go wit me to check ma traps, he got to git in de boat!"

Emerson smiled weakly at Melaudra. "I'm not sure that it's a wise decision to paddle around the swamps in something that small. I've seen alligators bigger than that boat. Why they'd just nudge it over and have themselves a free lunch!" Emerson said worriedly.

"Not to worry, Son," Mose quipped. "They spit out white meat. It's not as tasty as us black folks."

Emerson shot him a look, which did little to wipe the snickering smile from Mose's face

Melaudra resolved the issue. "Emerson, my daddy started taking me into the swamps in pirogues when I was a little girl. Nothing ever happened to us." Bubbie was beaming as his daughter spoke. "He's one of the most careful people around in these swamps. He can smell the gators before he sees them."

"That's right. Ain't no man around here who know them swamps better than Bubbie," Mose added.

"You guys sure about that, Melaudra?" Emerson asked.

She nodded her head.

"Mose . . . err, Mr. Mose?" he corrected himself and saw the scowl disappear from Mose's face as he nodded in affirmation.

Steadying himself, he cautiously stepped into the bow of the pirogue as he muttered, "What I do to please a woman!"

"What was that?" Melaudra asked.

"Nothing. Nothing at all," he responded as he picked up a paddle and dug into the slow-moving water as Mose pushed them off from the dock. In the stern, Bubbie expertly wielded his paddle twice as fast as his passenger.

They moved up stream several hundred yards before Bubbie turned them into a bayou where tree limbs hung low to the water. They paddled quietly as Emerson thought about the unexpected phone call from Melaudra and the invitation to join her on another trip to visit her father and Mose. He could get a chance to learn more about the swamps by accompanying her father to check his traps. Emerson had quickly thrown on jeans, a T-shirt and pair of sneakers. She had picked him up within the hour and they had driven to Slidell where they met up with Luka, who gave them a ride to her father's place.

"We go in dere." Emerson turned around and saw Bubbie pointing toward a spot on the bank, which appeared to have been worn by boats going ashore. As the pirogue bumped into the dry land, Emerson carefully stood and jumped from the pirogue and pulled the bow ashore.

Items started flying out of the hull of the pirogue and falling on the ground by Emerson's feet. "Put de pack on. Here carry dis. You'll see what to do." Emerson slipped one of the backpacks on his back as he watched Bubbie do the same. He picked up and held the pole, which was rounded at one end. He then followed Bubbie, who had turned and began walking down a well-worn path along the edge of the swamp.

"Where are we headed?" Emerson shouted as he walked briskly to catch up with the swift moving swamp man.

"Shhh! Talk softly, you'll scare off de game," Bubbie warned.

They had barely hiked 50 yards when Bubbie slowed and carefully approached the edge of the bank. Sticking the sharp end of the pole into the water, he pulled out a steel trap, which had been sprung. "Dis one, he de smart one. He got de bait and git away. Ah git him another dey." He worked quickly in resetting the trap, baiting it, and sliding it back into the water's edge.

Scratching his beard as he stood, he looked at Emerson. "Pooh-yi, we have better luck at de next one." He broke into a brisk walk with Emerson moving quickly to keep up with him.

In another 50 yards, Bubbie slowed and cautiously approached another trap. This time, as he neared it, he deftly jumped to the side as a trapped angry raccoon charged at him from the water's edge. He didn't get too close to Bubbie, as the trap's chain served as a tether and restrained him.

"Dis is a good one," Bubbie smiled as he held the long pole and swung the larger, unsharpened end at the raccoon's head. The pole connected with a loud crack and the raccoon was knocked unconscious. Moving quickly, Bubbie freed the raccoon from the trap and picked him up, holding the large raccoon's back to his chest. He then placed the pole, which he was holding with both hands, under the raccoon's neck and pulled it back sharply. It broke the raccoon's neck, killing it. Turning his back to Emerson, he instructed, "Throw him in ma backpack."

Emerson moved quickly to pick up the dead raccoon and threw him in the backpack.

"Dis is easy, right?" Bubbie asked as he turned and grinned at Emerson before resting and baiting the trap.

"No problem," Emerson responded slowly.

At the next trap, they found it had been sprung. They reset and baited it. The following trap had an angry raccoon wherein Bubbie repeated his unique killing process. When they found the largest raccoon of the day in the next trap, Bubbie turned to Emerson and said, "Dis one, he yours."

"Mine?" Emerson asked as he looked at the large angry raccoon pulling at its trap.

"Yeah, dis one is yours. Go ahead, Ah hep you iffen you need it."

Emerson held the pole in one hand and swung at the raging animal. It dodged the blow and Bubbie chuckled. "Dat one, he de mean one."

Emerson focused on the scrambling animal and swung again. This time he connected with a glancing blow off the animal's head.

"Hit de thing. Don't give em de love taps. Knock em out!" Bubbie encouraged.

Trying to anticipate which way the animal was going to dodge, Emerson guessed and swung hard. He connected with the big animal's head and the raccoon dropped to the ground. Emerson moved quickly to free the unconscious animal from the trap, as he had seen Bubbie do, and then picked him up. Positioning him against his chest, he carefully placed the pole underneath the animals head and pulled back to kill it.

"Dat's de way," Bubbie called as he bent over to pick up the dead raccoon and spun Emerson around so that he could deposit it into Emerson's backpack. Bubbie reset the trap and they began walking to the next trap.

They were halfway there when Emerson felt the first movement. He shook it off as his imagination and continued following Bubbie. A moment later, he felt a stronger movement in the backpack. It was quickly followed by a snarl and the backpack seemed to come alive as the now-conscious and very angry raccoon began to scramble to the top of its temporary cage to seek an escape. With a quick yell to Bubbie, Emerson shucked the backpack off his shoulder just as a set of claws took a dangerous swipe at his neck, narrowly missing it.

As he was dropping the pack, Emerson heard deep laughter coming from Bubbie who had dropped on the ground and was rolling around in absolute mirth at Emerson's predicament. Emerson turned his attention back to the backpack in time to see his prisoner freeing itself and, after a wild-eyed glance at its former captor, waddle hurriedly into the lush undergrowth.

"You didn't break its neck!" Bubbie squealed as he tried to stop his laughter. "Dis is one of de funniest tings Ah've seen in deese here swamps."

Emerson didn't say anything. He was embarrassed that he hadn't killed his captive.

After a few minutes, Bubbie began to compose himself and stood to his feet. Leading the way, he began walking to the next trap, still chuckling as he walked. At the next trap, Emerson took control and, this time, made sure he broke the raccoon's neck before it was placed in his back pack. They found two more raccoons in traps and then began the trek back to the beached pirogue.

Returning to the store, they paddled in silence.

"How did you boys do, today?" Melaudra called from her seat on the front porch as they neared.

"Pooh-yi. Dis man of yours had a live coon in his pack," Bubbie yelled as they bumped against the dock and Mose appeared to lend a hand. Between laughs, Bubbie recounted Emerson's confrontation with the irritated raccoon.

"Oh, Emerson," Melaudra cooed as she tried to ease Emerson's embarrassment.

When Bubbie asked him to help skin the raccoon, Emerson decided to pass and went inside to join Melaudra.

Once they finished dinner, Bubbie ran Melaudra and Emerson down river to the dock where the truck was parked and the two drove back to the Quarter. Melaudra and Emerson spent five minutes in the truck's front seat kissing each other goodbye before Melaudra allowed her better judgment to rule and drove to her apartment. Alone again, Emerson walked into the hotel lobby and to his room.

Saturday, August 27th
St. Albans Hospital

~

"This is the complete list?" Melaudra asked the administrator.

"Yes," the 50-year old man responded as he peered over the tops of his eyeglasses at the determined detective in front of him.

"Let me see it, Mel," Elms asked his partner, who handed it to him.

"It's just not sitting right in my gut. There's more here," Melaudra said as the two of them walked into a nearby conference room which had been provided for their use. She plopped into one of the chairs as Elms sat next to her.

"There's something not right here and we're overlooking it," she said with a puzzled look on her face. "Bear with me." She slid one of the reports in front of Elms. "You take a look through them, while I check these."

Knowing better than to argue with his partner, Elms started to review the report of early morning visitors to the hospital on the day that Fordham had died as well as the day before and the day after he died.

After an hour, Melaudra inquired. "Find anything?"

"I saw your buddy, Thibadaux, who was signed in on all three days."

"But he practices here. You'd expect him to be here. Anything else?"

"Yeah, about the same time each of these three days, a priest was signed in."

"A priest?"

"Probably making his morning rounds like the docs do."

Looking up from a stack of reports in front of her, Melaudra asked, "Would the priest's name be Alsandi?"

With a look of surprise, Elms looked at Melaudra. "Yes, how did you know that?"

"Three weeks ago, there was another of the mysterious deaths in the Quarter. The victim was rushed here around five in the morning. He died two hours later."

"What's the connection to Alsandi?"

"He signed in at six that morning."

"Coincidence?"

"Don't know."

"How about your boyfriend? Was he signed in?"

Before double-checking through her list, Melaudra shot Elms a look of dismay for his tasteless comment. Elms shrugged his shoulders and grinned.

"No, not signed in."

"Interesting," Elms concluded. "Maybe we should meet with this priest."

"Why don't you arrange it? I'll gather these reports and return them"

"Sure."

Ten minutes later, Melaudra and Elms walked out of the hospital lobby and crossed the street to return to their offices. They had been able to quickly secure a phone number for the priest and had called to set up an appointment with him in two hours.

St. Louis Cathedral
French Quarter

Sitting in one of the small offices available for the priests, Alsandi was shaken by the phone call. *Why would the detectives want to meet with me,* he wondered. He was still shaken by the death of Maloney and the reporter's visit. Now he was having a visit from the police.

He stood and walked over to the door, which he closed. Returning to the chair, he leaned over the desk and dialed a number.

The phone rang three times and was answered.

"Truman?"

"Yes, what it is it?" Thibadaux stormed.

"I just got a call from two detectives. They want to meet with me in two hours."

"Damn it!"

"Watch your language," the priest chided the cardiologist.

Ignoring him, Thibadaux probed as his mind raced, "Why do they want to meet you?"

"The detective wants to ask me some questions regarding the serial killings."

"Where are you meeting them?"

"In the cathedral's entrance."

A thought crossed Thibadaux's mind. *Maybe it was time to end the serial murders in the Quarter for once and for all.* "Meet them outside the entrance. Right there, across from Jackson Square. Can you do that?"

"Yes, but why?"

"Don't ask questions, just do as I say. I'll handle everything for you," Thibadaux said as he ended the call and dialed another number.

"Yes," the voice answered softly.

"I have a job for you." Thibadaux quickly outlined his plan.

Across from Jackson Square
St. Anne Street

~

Returning from a brief respite of chicory coffee at Café du Monde, Emerson found himself walking down St. Anne Street toward his hotel. As he walked, he allowed his eyes to wander from the vendors set up in the street along Jackson Square to the windows of the nearby shops.

He wasn't paying attention when he almost tripped over a young boy, seated on the sidewalk.

"Hi, Mr. Moore," the boy called as Emerson quickly side-stepped him. The voice sounded eerily familiar, and Emerson looked down into the smiling face of Austin Tobin.

"Austin! My how you've grown since I saw you last," Emerson exclaimed as he bent down and gave the six-year-old a bear hug. "Where's your mother?" he asked as he stood. He began looking around for the beautiful redhead, who had tortured his heart a couple of years earlier when they met on Put-in-Bay. They had a mutual attraction to each other until he learned that she was very married—although not happily. Since then, he had thought of her often and chased her in his dreams. Catching her was like catching an elusive shadow.

Before Austin could reply, Emerson spotted the tall red-head inside the Ma Sherie Amour Gift Shop, a Victorian style teashop. An idea surged through Emerson's mind. "Austin, here's what we're going to do. We're going to surprise her." Pointing to a small ice cream stand close to Decatur Street, Emerson said, "I'm going to run up there and buy a couple of ice cream cones for you and me. When she walks out, you and I'll be sitting here, eating them. Won't she be surprised?"

"But Mr. Moore, I'm not . . ."

Emerson cut him off. "Don't worry. It won't ruin your meal. You stay here and I'll be right back. What flavor do you want?" he asked as he walked briskly away.

"Strawberry," the boy yelled with a look of consternation.

Moving quickly, Emerson placed the order and was in process of paying for the two ice cream cones. He glanced down the street and saw a very beautiful Martine standing with Austin. She was wearing a white, short-sleeve, cotton blouse and a short skirt, which highlighted her long legs. Austin was talking and was pointing at Emerson. Emerson's face broke into a large smile and he waved.

What happened next was a nightmare and seemed to take place in slow motion. Martine returned his smile with a glare and tugged at Austin's arm. When Austin didn't move, she raised her hand in the air and dropped it quickly, slapping the six-year-old across the face. The boy broke into tears and allowed himself to be dragged along to the corner of St. Anne Street and Chartres Street.

"Martine!" Emerson yelled as he pushed the two ice cream cones back into the vendor's hands and began to run after her and Austin. Martine had hurriedly stepped into one of the cabs lined up on Chartres Street and sped away; leaving behind a very confused Emerson He leaned against the wall of Madeline's Coffee Shop to catch his breath.

"Trouble?" Melaudra's voice appeared out of nowhere.

Surprised, Emerson looked around and saw Melaudra and Elms approaching him as they walked across Chartres Street along St. Anne Street. There was a coolness in the tone of Melaudra's voice, which had not been there before. What Emerson didn't know was that she and Elms had observed Emerson's warm response and the passionate look in his eyes when he saw the object of his affection. Melaudra was hurt by the excitement and the spark that Emerson displayed. Having been hurt so many times before, she had expected to be hurt by this reporter also. Now, her guard was up, and she felt the need to protect her heart.

Sensing that something had changed with Melaudra, Emerson replied, "Oh, I thought I saw an old friend."

"Must have been a very special old friend the way you got excited," Melaudra observed coolly. Elms didn't say anything, he just watched as his partner's heart was hurt once again by a man.

Trying to change the topic, Emerson asked, "So, what brings you two deep into tourist territory today?"

Seeing that Melaudra was not responding, Elms replied. "We've got a meeting with one of the priests today."

"Going to confession?" Emerson teased.

Breaking her silence, Melaudra replied tersely, "I'm not so sure we're the ones who should be going."

Across the street and through the doors of St. Louis Cathedral, Alsandi stepped into the late morning sun. As he looked around for his visitors and enjoyed the bustle of Jackson Square, a shot rang out from a balcony on the Upper Pontalba overlooking Jackson Square and St. Peter Street. The bullet ricocheted off the wall near Alsandi's head, as the air filled with screams from the tourists and vendors who ran from the scene.

The priest dropped to the ground as Melaudra and Elms, with guns drawn and followed closely by Emerson, raced to the priest's side.

"Are you okay?" Melaudra asked as she knelt next to the priest.

"Yes. Yes, I am."

Elms made the mistake of walking in front of the priest when a second shot filled the late morning air. The bullet caught Elms in the shoulder, spinning him to the ground.

"Harry, you alright?" Melaudra asked worriedly as she moved to her partner and looked anxiously at him and the direction from which the shot had originated.

"Oh, I'll be okay." Elms said as blood flowed from his shoulder wound. "Some luck, I'm having. I've been hit twice in the shoulder now in the last couple of weeks!"

"Officer down in front of St. Louis Cathedral. Requesting back up and EMTs." Melaudra called into the police radio, which seemed to appear magically in her hands. "Let's pull you inside the door." She then noticed that Emerson had already shoved the priest into the cathedral's doorway. Seeing Elms' wound, the priest disappeared inside the cathedral, but quickly returned with wet towels, which he applied to stem the bleeding.

Melaudra eased herself around the corner of the doorway and looked in the direction where the shots were fired. She didn't see anything, but was greeted by two out of breath detectives, Morris and his partner, Scully Jones. They had their handguns drawn.

"Who's hit?" Morris asked as he stopped to capture his breath. Jones took a position by the doorway and scanned the streets for any shooters.

"Elms caught one in the shoulder. It was meant for the priest," Melaudra explained as she stood to her feet.

"The priest? Now, why would anyone want to shoot a priest?" Jones asked in amazement.

"Got me," Melaudra responded as two police cars and an ambulance pulled in front of the cathedral. The EMTs replaced Alsandi at Elms' side and quickly addressed his wound. They produced a gurney, assisted him in rolling on to it, and loaded him in the vehicle for the short run to St. Alban's Hospital.

After Melaudra told the arriving police officers what had transpired, two of the police officers and Morris and Jones began to walk toward the building from which they believed the shots originated.

Watching them walk away, Melaudra noted, "It's too late."

"To find the shooter?" Emerson asked.

"Yes. He's long gone." Melaudra said as she turned to the priest. "Would you happen to be Father Alsandi?"

"Yes."

Stunned, Emerson asked, "You were coming here to meet him?"

"Yes, why the surprised look?"

"This is the priest whom I flew down to see." Emerson explained his relationship and meetings with the priest.

"Hmm," Melaudra murmured. "Father, it's obvious that the shooter had you targeted. Any reason why anyone would want to shoot you?"

Visibly shaken, the priest shook his head from side to side. "No, not that I can think of."

Thinking quickly, Melaudra probed, "Did anyone know that you were going to meet with me?"

"No." The priest paused after responding as a look of realization crossed his face.

"Remember something?"

"No," he answered quickly. There was uneasiness in his response, which was not lost on Melaudra.

"Father, are you telling me the truth?"

The priest didn't respond. Instead he busied himself with picking up the towels, which he had brought to use on Elms.

"Father, I've been around the block enough times to know when someone is holding back." She looked him square in the eyes. "Tell me what's going on."

The priest tried to avoid eye contact, but his efforts were fruitless.

"Father, did anyone know you were going to meet with me?"

The priest thought back to the phone call he had made. *Surely, that call wouldn't have triggered a violent response,* he thought. He decided to reveal a touch of the truth. "Yes, I called someone."

Melaudra's brow furrowed as she probed. "Was it anyone who would be concerned with you meeting me?"

The priest awkwardly cleared his throat before answering. "Yes."

"Did you tell whoever it was that my meeting with you concerned the unsolved murders in the Quarter?"

"Yes, but I was just trying to be honest," the priest explained.

Melaudra shot a look of exasperation at Emerson. Turning back to the priest, she instructed him, "Tell me what's going on."

"I can't."

"Do you know who the murderer is?"

"Yes, I believe I do," the priest responded awkwardly.

"Listen, Father, if you want me to help you, you need to help yourself. Tell me who murderer is."

"I can't do that."

"You're going to stand here and not tell me?" Melaudra stormed. Passersby looked at her with dismay as she raised her voice at the priest.

"Yes." It was obvious that the priest was growing more uncomfortable with the questions.

"And what about other future victims? You're going to be as guilty as the murderer for protecting this psychopath!" Melaudra continued drilling in, trying to get the priest to realize the gravity of the situation.

"Are you the murderer?" It was Emerson's turn to throw a question at Alsandi.

Alsandi was taken aback by the unexpected question. "Why would you ask that?"

"Emerson, I'm asking the questions here." She was surprised how Emerson had interrupted her line of questioning. She was sure that he didn't know about the trip, which she and Elms had made that day to St. Albans to review visitor records. "Go ahead and respond to his question." She realized that the priest had not answered Emerson's question as to whether or not he was the murderer.

"Don't I have the right to counsel?" Alsandi questioned apprehensively in return.

"Why? You're not being charged for anything. We just came here today to ask you some questions." She paused before continuing. "You seem to have gone on the defensive."

The inner devils that Alsandi wrestled with were now tormenting him again. "I'm just uncomfortable talking about this right now."

"With someone shooting at you, I guess I'd understand that. Would you like us to take you into protective custody?"

"At the station?" Alsandi questioned.

Melaudra nodded her head.

"No, they can still get at me. I'm not comfortable there."

"Who's this that you're talking about?"

The priest dropped his head and looked at the ground. "Just give me some time. I need to sort this out, but you've got to protect me."

"Melaudra?"

She whirled to look at Emerson.

"I know the perfect place where no one would ever bother him."

"Where, Emerson?"

"Your father's place. Who'd go out in that swamp to find him?"

Titling her head, she thought about his idea. *Who'd think about looking for him there,* she wondered. Her head snapped around at the priest. "We have just the place for you." She took one of the priest's arms in her hand and began to walk him to where her car was parked. "Coming?"

She had caught Emerson off guard. "Sure. Thanks for letting me," he said as he caught up with her and began walking down St. Anne Street to where she and Elms had parked. As they turned onto St. Anne, Emerson thought briefly about trying to track down Martine and find out why she exhibited such abnormal behavior with Austin. He hoped that she wasn't on drugs. He shook off his thoughts to concentrate on the situation at hand.

Neither Emerson nor Melaudra saw a man following them at a safe distance. He had a cell phone glued to his ear as he instructed an accomplice driving another car as to where he was headed.

Honey Island Swamp
Bubbie's Store and Home

~

The night was full of sounds from the swamp: the random hooting of owls mixed with frogs croaking their lullabies, the splashes of fish, and the sound of a gentle breeze blowing through the trees, rustling its leaves. The dark sky was empty of clouds and dotted by the twinkling starlight. It was peaceful, like the calm before the storm. But all hell was about to break loose as a hurricane named Katrina was bearing down on the Louisiana coast. However, Katrina wasn't the only danger on the horizon.

With engines now shut off, the stolen boat glided slowly across the slow-moving river toward the little store whose windows were lit with a soft warm glow. The store's occupants were apparently unconcerned about any uninvited guests that evening.

"See anybody?" Morris called to the bow where his partner, Jones, peered into the darkness.

"Naah, doesn't look like they expect anyone," Jones sneered as he looked from the approaching dock to the two menacing passengers in the boat. They were two burly ex-New Orleans policemen who had been fired from the force and now worked seedy jobs. Their names were Lester and Damien. Morris had invited the two armed thugs to accompany them on this perilous mission.

"Good."

Morris expertly guided the craft against the dock, and the four of them quietly stepped off the boat. They didn't need to worry about making noise based on the loud Cajun music and conversation emitting from inside the structure. Morris motioned for the two henchmen to walk along the side deck to cover the rear of the house, while he and Jones would enter through the front.

With guns drawn, Morris burst into the store first, quickly followed by Jones. At the same time, Lester and Damien charged through the back door. What they found before them caused a chuckle to emerge from Morris' throat as he looked at the group in front of them. "Well well. What have we here? The pretty detective, Melaudra Drencheau, some nosy newspaper reporter, a priest, and Melaudra's papa."

"Thank you, but I'm not her papa," Mose replied brusquely. "However, it would be an honor to have someone like her as a daughter."

"Thanks, Mose," Melaudra beamed at Mose.

"Thanks, Mose," Morris mimicked sarcastically. "Speaking of papa, where is he?"

Melaudra responded hurriedly, "He's out on Pontchartrain. How did you find us?" She asked as she looked at the four pistols leveled at them. Her mind was groping, searching for the answer hidden beyond her reach.

"Your chubby buddy, Elms."

"Elms?"

"Yeah, we caught up with him at the hospital after our tail on you lost you. I told him that we learned that a contract had been put out on you and we had to warn you. He couldn't talk fast enough about where you might be headed. This sounded like the most logical, so here we are. The only place where Elms is lightweight is in his brains." Morris smirked as he looked at Melaudra. "Of course, it didn't hurt that he was on drugs when he told us. That made it easier to get the information."

Melaudra started forward, but stopped suddenly when Morris leveled his gun at her. "What do you think you're doing, Morris?"

"Something that no one else has been able to do with you."

"What's that?"

"Tame you!"

"You think you're man enough?" Melaudra's eyes narrowed as fury filled her. The muscles in her face were working as she fought back further comment.

Smiling, Morris motioned with his pistol for her to turn around. "You'll see, soon enough." A sly smile crossed his face as he approached her. He grabbed her arms roughly behind her and placed his mouth next to her ear. "I'm the man you've been waiting for all of your life. Problem is you didn't ever give me a chance."

Morris' preoccupation with what he was saying prevented him from seeing Melaudra slowly raise her foot. With a burst of energy, she brought it down hard on his instep. Morris released her and spun around in pain. "Bitch, I'm going to kill you right now." He steadied himself as the aching pain continued. Morris leveled his gun at Melaudra, now facing him and staring at him with a cold glare. With an evil grin he pulled the trigger. As the gun fired, Melaudra stood still and didn't flinch as the bullet whizzed by, narrowly missing her.

Morris turned and swore at Jones, who had at the last minute pushed the gun's barrel to the side. "What in the hell did you do that for?" Morris scowled at his partner. "You want me to make you my ex-partner?"

Jones shrugged. "We've got orders and they don't include killing her, at least right away."

Emerson stepped forward. "Okay, Fellows, what's this all about?" he asked as he surveyed the four gunmen.

"We're not interested in you, Mr. Nosy Reporter. But it's too bad that you're here because you're just going to end up disappearing in the swamp. You and her friend there," he said as he smirked at Mose.

Mose threw Morris a look filled with anger.

"You still didn't answer my question. What's this about?" Emerson pushed.

"Father, you want to tell them?"

The priest stared at Morris. "Tell them? Tell them what?"

"You really don't know, do you?" Morris cackled.

The priest looked blankly at Morris.

"Never mind. You'll soon find out."

"I think we've had about enough of this. You owe us an explanation. Is this a matter of taking the priest into protective custody?" Emerson asked as he became irritated. "What's this about?" Emerson saw Mose edging next to the kitchen counter where a large iron skillet rested next to a butcher's knife. Emerson caught Melaudra's eye and saw that she too had seen Mose moving toward the kitchen counter.

Emerson walked to the other side of the room in order to draw the thugs' attention away from the kitchen area.

"Where do you think you're going?" Jones asked belligerently.

Emerson stopped and turned. "Away from the rotten stench you guys brought into the room."

Before anything more could be said, Mose picked up and swung the skillet into the back of Damien's head. At the same time he grabbed the knife and lunged at Lester, penetrating his shirt but missing his flesh. With a look of evil on his face, Lester's large hands grabbed Mose's hand and snapped it back, as the sound of a breaking bone filled the air.

Emerson jumped on Jones, knocking him to the ground as they wrestled for control of his gun. At the same time, Melaudra charged into Morris and with her fingers outstretched raked his face with her long nails, causing Morris to screech with surprise and pain as he recoiled away from her.

Emerson rolled on top of Jones and dug the fingers from his left hand deep into Jones right eye socket, threatening to rip out his eye. Jones screamed as he fought back and lost control of his weapon. Emerson, with Jones' gun in his right hand, rolled off of Jones and to his knees where he began to take aim at Morris.

Morris saw Jones' predicament and swung Melaudra around in front of him as a shield, even though she continued to struggle like a wildcat. Seeing how strong she was, Damien stepped up to help subdue Melaudra by grabbing one of her arms.

"The odds are against you," Morris said ominously before Emerson could speak. "There are three of us with guns, and one of you. On top of that, I suspect that you're no expert with a weapon."

Glaring, Emerson responded, "Don't be too sure of that." *If only they knew how familiar he had become with weapons during the war in Yugoslavia,* Emerson thought proudly.

"Still, by the time you fired, the three of us would have fired. The odds are against you," Morris said logically.

"This time, they're against me. Next time, they won't be," he said as he reluctantly handed the gun back to Jones.

"Don't be too sure of that, you cocky son of a bitch," Morris said as he released Melaudra to Damien's grip and suddenly swung his steel-toed shoe at Emerson. The kick caught Emerson off guard and, even though he started to turn his head, it caught in the side of his jaw. The crunching contact of steel on bone made everyone else in the room shiver.

"Jones, cuff her and the priest." When Jones approached Melaudra, she began to crouch in preparation to spring at him. The movement was observed by Morris. "Melaudra, don't even try it." He stepped next to Emerson and placed the barrel of his gun against the back of Emerson's head. "Try anything, and the first bullet will find itself buried in his brain matter."

Melaudra looked at Emerson, who winked at her. She thought for a second and then relaxed, allowing Jones to place the handcuffs on her. He produced a second pair and cuffed the priest. "All set."

"Take these two out to the boat," Morris commanded as he then turned to Lester and Damien, who were positioned by Emerson and Mose. "Tie their arms behind them." The two found pieces of rope and quickly secured Mose and Emerson.

"We're going to New Orleans. You take these two out front on the porch and sit them down like you're just having a nice visit. When her father returns, kill them all and then take his boat and catch up with us."

"Got it," Lester responded as they herded Mose and Emerson to the front porch where they forced the two down onto an old worn glider. Lester leaned against one of the porch posts while Damien eased his large frame into a rocking chair, which he scooted close to Mose so that he could watch their two captives closely.

Morris joined Jones, the priest, and Melaudra in the small boat, which Jones had running. They moved into the current and headed the boat to where they had parked their car. As the noise from the boat's motor faded down river, it was replaced by the cacophony of noise from the swamp animal life.

Thirty minutes passed in relative silence on the porch, broken from time to time as Lester or Damien slapped at an errant mosquito trying to land on their flesh.

"Let's do them now," Damien said, breaking the uneasy silence as he rocked in the chair.

"Can't"

"Why not?"

"We was told to wait until the bitch's father showed up," Lester replied menacingly.

Damien looked around from his seat to the river and cocked his ear. "I don't hear nothing. What if he don't come back until tomorrow?"

"Then, we wait," he said as he rubbed his back up and down against the porch post.

Fifteen minutes later, they heard the sounds of an approaching boat on the river.

"Must be him!" Damien said excitedly as he rocked vigorously in the rocker in front of Mose. It was about that time that Mose began to thump his foot hard on the wooden floor.

"What are you doing, old man?" Damien shot the question at Mose.

"Damn foot fell asleep. I'm trying to restore my circulation. Mind if I stand up?"

"Yes, I do. You just sit there. You can stamp your feet as much as you want," Damien said as he continued rocking.

Mose just smiled to himself and continued to stamp his feet. Within a minute, they heard a noise along the side deck of the house.

"What in the hell is that?" Damien asked as he leaned back in his rocker to peer around the corner. As he leaned back, Mose gave the rocker a push backwards, causing Damien to somersault onto the edge of the deck. As he looked up at the cause of the noise, he saw the wide-open jaws of Mose's gator charging at him.

Damien screamed as he tried to roll to the side. It was too late, as the gator's jaws clamped down on his neck. Three splashes were heard hitting the water. One was from the gator as his momentum carried him into the river. The other two splashes were Damien's body and his head that had been severed from his body by the gator's first bite.

Lester had been frozen by the shock of what had transpired. Waking from his shock, he aimed his gun into the water and began to fire several rounds. Unseen to him, Emerson had lowered his arms, which had been tied behind his back, and dropped them to the behind his heels. He then stepped through his arms and brought his arms to the front of his body. Seeing Lester peering into the water, Emerson rushed him, carrying them into the river.

Lester fought to climb to the surface, but Emerson, who had taken a deep breath as they fell into the water, was able to throw his tied arms over Lester's shoulders and drag him down towards the muddy river bottom where he held the struggling thug.

As Lester weakened, Emerson allowed the two of them to float to the surface where they broke the water to find themselves staring into the barrel of a shotgun. The barrel swung away from Emerson to aim at Lester.

"Pooh-yi. What you boys doing in deese river when you got a gator feeding over dey?" asked Bubbie.

Lester, who was gasping for air, and Emerson turned to see the gator turning and twisting as it snacked on its unexpected treat before taking it to its lair to rot.

Within seconds, Emerson and Lester were out of the water and seated safely on the deck. Bubbie held his shotgun on Lester after untying Emerson, who in turn untied Mose. He then used the rope to secure Lester's hands behind his back.

"What you doing all the way out heah?" Bubbie asked Emerson. "Ma little girl heah wit you?"

Emerson aided by Mose, who was nursing his broken left wrist, quickly explained what had transpired. As they explained they saw Bubbie's face change with concern for his daughter. His eyes blazed with anger as he scowled at Lester.

"Where dey take ma girl and da priest?" he fiercely asked Lester.

"That's for me to know and you to find out," Lester gloated as his belligerence returned.

"You don't know what you jes sed, boy!" Bubbie said in response to the challenge. "Ah got de ways to make people tell me what Ah want to know." Looking at Emerson, he said, "Hep me git him in ma boat."

"What are you going to do?" Emerson asked.

"Dat's ma business."

"I can't let you hurt him," Emerson said. "We need to take him to the police."

"Ah am de police out here. Ain't dat right, Mose?" Bubbie looked at his friend.

A smile crept across Mose's face. "Yes, he is. He's a deputy sheriff out here."

"You release dis man into ma custody. Ah'm taking him in to axe him some questions."

Emerson stood to his feet and started to help place Lester into Bubbie's boat. "I'll come along, too."

Bubbie pushed him back as Emerson tried to follow Lester into the boat. "No can do. You have to be da police to go into the questioning room. You stay heah wit Mose. Ah'll be right back."

"Don't count on it. I'm not telling anyone anything," Lester called haughtily from his seat in the bow. "When we get to the station, I want to call my attorney."

Bubbie looked at Lester with a smug expression on his face. "We see about dat. People jes have a way of telling me everyting Ah wanna know." Bubbie turned his head to look at Emerson as Lester swung around in the bow and faced forward. "Maybe, one of deese days, Ah teach you how to interview people better." He grinned mysteriously as he stepped into the boat's stern and started its motor.

As the boat picked up speed and headed down the river, Mose appeared at Emerson's side and handed him a cold beer. "Thought you might want one of these."

"Thanks," Emerson said as he sat back on the glider with Mose and looked toward the river where the gator had been snacking. The water was relatively still now.

"You did good tonight," Mose said as he swallowed his beer and held the cold can against his wrist to relieve the pain.

"So did you, Mr. Mose. Nice move with calling the gator and flipping the rocker over!" Looking at Mose's damaged wrist, Emerson offered, "We need to wrap that up in something to give it some support."

"I'll bring a wrap out here," Mose said as he stood and started to walk inside. He paused and turned to look at Emerson. "Oh, one thing, Emerson."

"Yes?"

"You can drop the Mister, now. It's just Mose."

Emerson turned his head and saw Mose smiling at him. "Why, thank you, Mose!"

Mose returned and they wrapped his wrist. It seemed like only a few minutes had passed before the air was filled with an inhuman scream from down river.

"Mose, what was that?" Emerson asked as he stood and walked to the porch post where he stared down river.

Mose didn't respond. He just took another swipe of his beer and looked in the opposite direction.

A second scream followed.

"You heard that, didn't you?"

"Yes, I heard it."

A look of realization crossed Emerson's face. He looked at Mose. "It's Bubbie interviewing Lester, isn't it?"

Mose didn't respond at first. He finished another swallow of his beer and then looked at Emerson. "People who live in the swamp don't like outsiders messing with them. We've got our own laws out here. They're quick and speedy."

Emerson's face crinkled up as he anguished over the thought that someone, apparently, had taken the law into their own hands.

"I can tell what you're going through, Emerson. You're good people. Just don't forget, she's Bubbie's daughter. She's all that he has."

The comment didn't give Emerson much solace. A few minutes later, Bubbie returned in his boat and tied up to the dock. As he stepped from the boat two more agonized shrieks interrupted the evening sounds. Emerson put his hand on Bubbie's shoulder and spun him around. "I want to know what you did."

"Ah got de truth out of him," Bubbie spat out angrily as he started to go inside.

"Wait," Emerson called. "What did you do?"

"Dat's none of your business. We gotta get ma gurl."

"I want to know what happened. I thought you were taking him to the police station? He was going to call his attorney."

"Ah didn't say nothing about taking him to de police station. Ah jes sed Ah was going to take him in for questions."

"Where did you take him?"

Bubbie looked into Emerson's eyes and realized that Emerson wasn't going to back off until he got the whole story.

"Ah took him down in a bayou about 200 yards from here. It's got two big gators in it. Ah hung him from a tree limb with his feet about a foot out of de water."

Emerson's eyes widened.

"Ah ask de boy nice de first time where ma gurl is. He said something very nasty about ma gurl. So, Ah cut his two feet and let de blood drip into the water. Den, Ah told him de dripping blood would attract de gators. Ah told him iffen he'd talk, Ah'd cut him down and put him back in ma boat."

Emerson could picture the scene vividly in his mind. "Did he tell you anything?"

"Not at first. Ah told him dat de gators would jump out of de water and first tear off one leg, den dey tear off the other and he'd bleed to death or when dey tear off his second leg, sometime de whole body come down. Den dey eat him."

"Did he tell you then?"

"Oh yeah. He told me where dey took ma gurl. He'd quote the whole Bible if Ah asked. Now we git another shotgun and den we go get her."

Emerson looked back at the boat and saw that Lester wasn't in it. "Where's Lester?"

"Oh, dat was him you heard screaming. Jes when Ah was going to cut him down, he sed another nasty ting about ma gurl. So Ah left him hanging. Teach him a ting or two," Bubbie grinned crazily.

Emerson groaned and looked at Mose.

"It's called the law of the swamp," Mose said firmly.

A moment later, Bubbie reappeared. In his arms were two more shotguns, two pistols, and a box of shotgun shells. "You coming wit me?" he asked Emerson as he walked toward his boat.

Without hesitation, Emerson scrambled after him. "Where do we start?"

"The city," Bubbie answered as he started his boat and pulled it quickly into the river. Emerson found himself thrown back in his seat as the craft leapt forward with a burst of speed.

"You know where you're going?"

"Yep," Bubbie replied with a determined look on his face. His jaw was set like that of a man on a singular mission. "Dat boy, Lester. He tole me everythin Ah need to know."

The boat accelerated down the river as it carried its occupants into the heart of the storm. They had no idea that the National Hurricane Center had alerted New Orleans city officials at 7:00 p.m. that Katrina was a Category 5 Level hurricane and on a path for a direct hit on the city. Reacting to the alert, city officials issued a voluntary evacuation order.

Driving over Lake Pontchartrain in Melaudra's truck, Emerson, who had found her keys hidden under the seat, and Bubbie noticed the steady flow of traffic streaming out of New Orleans.

"Seems strange that so many cars are heading out of town this late at night?" Emerson commented as he glanced at his watch and saw that it was nearing 11 p.m.

"Dat very unusual," Bubbie said in response.

"Let's check the news. Maybe that hurricane is headed this way after all," Emerson suggested as he recalled earlier news reports about Katrina and her progress in the Gulf.

The radio news announcer filled the air with reports regarding the approaching hurricane and the voluntary evacuation order as well as traffic reports. It seemed like most of the traffic was headed west toward Baton Rouge although a substantial amount was headed east toward Biloxi where it would then turn north and run inland.

"This is going to make things very interesting," Emerson said as he looked at Bubbie out of the corner of his eye.

"We gotta git ma gurl." Bubbie was very focused on the task at hand as he stared straight ahead.

Esplanade Avenue
In the Quarter

~

The fast moving vehicle made an abrupt right hand turn. "Change of plans?" Jones asked from the backseat, directly behind Melaudra. The priest was seated next to Jones in the backseat. Both the priest and Melaudra were blindfolded.

Morris, the driver, had just finished a cell phone call. "Yep. We're going to take them to a safe house rather than here in the Quarter. It's because of the hurricane." He reached down and turned the radio's volume up so that he could hear the latest news about the approaching storm.

Melaudra had cocked her head at the comment. "Morris, what's this all about?"

"Sorry, my dear. I can't say anything."

"I know it's about the priest, but why are you doing this to me?"

"Call it being in the wrong place at the wrong time, Sweetheart."

Bristling at the comment, she replied, "I'm not your sweetheart. Never was, never will be."

"By the end of the night, you may have wished you had been. Because if you were, I may have been able to protect you. Now, who knows what's going to happen to you?"

Esplanade Avenue
Two Hours Later

~

The truck that had slowly driven by the darkened building drove to the end of the street. There, it turned around and drove back in front of the building. Seeing no activity, the driver slowly eased the truck into a parking space two doors down. The driver and his passenger, carrying shotguns, emerged from the truck and approached the building.

"I don't think anyone is around." Emerson whispered softly as he peered through the dirty window into the unlighted office. "Are you sure this is the right address?"

"Yes. And Lester wasn't lying. Dat boy wuz telling de truth." Bubbie had moved next to the door and was checking the lock. "We look anyway." He stepped back and threw a shoulder against the door. The door creaked as it fought to withstand the force thrown against it. When Bubbie pushed hard a second time, the door burst open, followed by Bubbie tumbling to the floor. He stood to his feet and swept the room with his shotgun as Emerson walked in.

Emerson's hand searched the wall until he found the light switch and flicked the lights on. Blinking their eyes quickly, they went through the building, but didn't find anyone.

"All clear," Emerson noted as they returned to the front room.

"Dis doesn't make any sense."

"How's that?"

"Dere was no doubt in my mind dat Lester was telling de truth."

"Maybe they changed their plans." Emerson paused. "The hurricane coming in may have been responsible for that." Looking around, Emerson had an idea. "Let's go to the hospital. We'll ask Elms for help."

The two men quickly left the building and drove the short distance to St. Albans Hospital. After parking the truck and entering the building, they stopped at the information desk to inquire for directions to Elms' room. Getting the room number, they took a nearby elevator to his floor and after a short walk, strolled into his room.

Elms was asleep, but Bubbie didn't let that slow him down one second. "Wake up," he bellowed. The abruptness not only caused Elms to open his eyes wide, but caused him to sit up suddenly. He winced as the sudden movement shot pain in his shoulder and down his arm. He turned his head to look at Bubbie and relaxed when he recognized him from photos on Melaudra's desk. "Bubbie, right?" he asked.

Before Bubbie could respond, a nurse appeared at the doorway. "Everything okay in here," she said as her eyes darted from Bubbie to Emerson to Elms.

"Just a couple of my rowdy friends," Elms assured her. Hearing his comment, she spun on her heels and walked briskly to the nurses' station.

"Why isn't it nice that you two came in at this late hour to visit me?" When he saw the serious looks in their faces, he asked, "Oh oh. This looks like trouble. Where's Melaudra?"

Emerson quickly filled him in.

"So Morris and Jones are in on this, huh?"

"That's what it appears is happening."

"Never trusted those two," he said as he swung his legs to the side of his bed. "Hand me my clothes and shoes. They're over in that closet," he ordered.

"What are you doing?" Emerson asked.

"Getting out of this place. There's a hurricane coming, and we don't have any time to lose in finding Melaudra." Wincing as he eased his arm and shoulder out of the gown, he dropped the gown to the floor as he stood. Emerson was relieved to see that he still had his boxer shorts on as Elms slowly put on his shirt. "We'll start with finding out who owns the building."

"Where you gonna find help dis late at night?" Bubbie asked with a look of consternation on his face.

"I'd think you've got people you need to talk to who are already evacuating," Emerson added.

"I've got my ways," Elms grinned as he pulled on his slacks and slipped his feet into his well-worn loafers. "Let's go."

After a heated discussion with the nurse, who had blocked Elms' path when he tried to leave, Elms produced his badge to dramatically calm the nurse. The three left the building and ran across the street to the police station where they found the elevator broken as was typical. Elms looked at his companions, shrugged his shoulders, winced as a result, and pointed toward the stairs.

When they arrived on the third floor, they found a mostly deserted office. Elms sat down as Morris' desk and directed Emerson to Jones' desk. "Look through here to see if we can find anything which will give us a clue at to what they are up to," Elms ordered.

As he began to rifle through the papers and files on the desktop, Emerson asked, "Do you really think they left any incriminating notes around here?"

"You never can tell. Just check it out." His stomach began to growl, reminding him that he hadn't eaten since lunch. Elms looked at Bubbie. "Mr. Drencheau?"

"Yes?" Bubbie asked as he stood shifting his weight from one foot to the other.

"How about doing me a really big favor?"

"Yes?"

"There's a little all-night restaurant around the corner from here. If they're open, could you grab us some chicory coffees and beignets?"

"I can do dat."

Elms gave him $20 and directions and watched as Bubbie descended the stairs.

"Got to have your sweets, huh?" Emerson teased as he began to open the desk drawers and look through them.

"Not this time. I wanted to get him out of here so that we could talk."

Emerson sat straight up and looked squarely at Elms. "About?" he asked with a serious tone.

"Morris and Jones. This isn't for print, but Melaudra and I are on special assignment for Internal Affairs."

Emerson's mouth dropped. "You are?"

Elms paused as he beamed with pride, "We were placed on this special assignment, focused on corruption in the department. Our investigation is centered on Morris and Jones."

"There's a drug dealer in town that we have been trying to catch. His name is Toma. Every time we get close, he seems to be able to slip through our hands. That's what began our suspicions. There was a growing concern that Morris and Jones are linked to this dealer. They seem to always be involved whenever a bust is going down. This last time, we caught one of Toma's dealers. Her name was Snow White. But as usual, Toma got away."

"So, just keep Morris and Jones off the busts. Reassign them."

"Not quite that easy. We want to nab them, too."

"So what's this have to do with Melaudra? You don't think they've figured out that you two were working for Internal Affairs, do you?"

"No."

"What about the priest?"

"We're trying to link the priest to the murders here in the Quarter."

"So why were they interested in taking him?"

"Ever since you told me about that tonight, I've been trying to figure it out. I just don't know." Elms began looking through files with chicken-scratched markings and notes on the margins. Emerson looked through Jones' desk.

"You figure out where ma girl is?"

Bubbie's voice surprised both of them.

"Not yet. We're still figuring," Elms replied as he took one of the cups of coffee from Bubbie and grabbed a beignet from the bag, at the same time covering his fingers with the powdered sugar.

"Ah'm telling you two. Don't take long. Ah'm not a patient man." Bubbie picked up one of the coffees and began to sip on it as he nervously began pacing around the department.

Sunday, August 28th
The Police Station

~

As the morning dawned, Elms and Emerson were still working their way through files. Elms had gone online and was trying to determine who owned the building as a starting point.

Bubbie had hidden himself near the top of the stairs in hopes that Morris and Jones would report in for work on Sunday. He had his own plan for making them talk and reveal what had happened to his daughter. He was becoming more impatient by the minute due to the lack of progress made by Elms and Emerson.

"Let's go and find ma gurl! Why can't you two hep me?" a very frustrated Bubbie fumed.

"We're trying," Elms answered. "This may take awhile. People aren't in their offices on Sunday, and we've got people leaving the city."

"It looks like it just got worse," Emerson said. He had turned on a nearby TV and switched to live news coverage. City officials had just finished ordering a mandatory evacuation of the city. It was 9:30 a.m. The news report went on to say that mandatory evacuations were also issued for many of the surrounding parishes. It also suggested that people could seek shelter at the Superdome and the Convention Center.

"Now, we're in for it," Elms mused.

"You gonna be in for it iffen we don't find ma gurl pretty damn quick," Bubbie stormed.

Footsteps on the stairs announced the arrival of a number of detectives, who were reporting for duty, even though it was their off-day. Bubbie hid himself again, waiting for Elms to point out Morris and Jones. He was disappointed when he realized that they were not part of the group.

The arriving detectives gathered around Elms to hear about his sniper wound from the previous day. Elms quickly filled them in and then excused himself and, accompanied by his two guests, began to descend the stairs. "Getting a little too crowded up there."

"What we gonna do?" Bubbie asked eagerly.

"I've got the name and address of the building's owner and also the home addresses of Morris and Jones. I thought we'd go make some house calls."

"I'll drive," Emerson volunteered as he remembered that the weapons were in Melaudra's truck. "Besides, you'd have a hard time driving with that shoulder of yours."

"Fine with me," Elms agreed.

Within minutes they were seated in the truck As they pulled out on the street, they entered a massive gridlock as people evacuating the city clogged the roads with their vehicles. They ended up spending most of the day slowly working their way from one traffic jam to another, as they made their rounds to each of the three residences. Their efforts were to no avail, as they found no one at home at any of the three.

"Now, what do we do?" Bubbie agitated.

"We better find a place to hunker down. We'll go back to the Quarter. It's above sea level if we get any flooding," Elms suggested.

"You ting they'll be flooding?" Bubbie asked.

"If the news reports we've been hearing are correct, there will be."

"Den, Ah don't want to be in de city." Bubbie leaned towards Emerson who was focused on navigating the vehicle through traffic. "You take me home. Ah'll ride dis out at ma place."

Emerson was surprised that Bubbie would abandon the search for his daughter. "Are you sure?"

"Yep. Ah got de plan." He sat back in the seat with a sly grin spreading across his face.

"Okay then." Turning to Elms, Emerson asked, "Drop you off at the police station?"

"Might as well," Elms replied. "This traffic is something else. As it is, it'll probably take you two a week to drive over to Slidell and the swamps." He glanced skyward at the approaching dark clouds, which heralded the arrival of Katrina.

They drove past the Superdome where they saw people waiting in line to enter the structure. They observed police searching each person for weapons or drugs before they were allowed to enter. Other citizens were making their way to the Convention Center, which overlooked the Mississippi River.

Dropping Elms at the station, Bubbie give Emerson directions through a number of backroads, until they arrived at the edge of Lake Pontchartrain to a dock that was owned by one of Bubbie's friends. They were then transported by boat across the lake to Slidell and made their way back to Bubbie's place where Mose had food cooking. They ate hurriedly and grabbed a few hours of sleep before helping Mose secure the small store as best as possible.

Monday, August 29th
Katrina Hits New Orleans

~

When Katrina hit on Monday, she had weakened to a Category 4 hurricane with 145-mph winds and came ashore at Buras, Louisiana. Although the direct hit on New Orleans was avoided, there was significant damage caused by the winds. Most of the windows on the north side of the Hyatt Regency New Orleans were blown out, and many other high-rise buildings had extensive window damage. Brick facades on several buildings had crumbled into the streets.

As of midday, the eye of Hurricane Katrina had swept northeast. It subjected the city to hurricane conditions for hours, but spared New Orleans the brunt of the storm. The city escaped most of the catastrophic wind damage and heavy rain that had been anticipated.

But New Orleans had a bigger problem as levees began to fail, and the city experienced widespread flooding. The east side of New Orleans was under five to six feet of water. Entire neighborhoods on the south shore of Lake Pontchartrain were flooded including the Ninth Ward, housing built on relatively low land and where three pumps failed. The 17th Street Canal off of Lake Pontchartrain had been breeched, causing flooding in the Bucktown and West End areas.

In St. Bernard Parish, a levee had broken on the Industrial Canal, a five-and-a-half-mile waterway that connected the Mississippi River to Lake Pontchartrain.

As the flood waters rose and submerged homes, many stranded residents became trapped in their attics. Unable to escape through their homes, they chopped holes into their roofs with hatchets and sledge hammers, stored there since a close encounter with Hurricane Betsy years earlier. They then scrambled through the holes to await rescue from the Coast Guard choppers flying overhead. Some people were not so lucky as reports began to pour in regarding floating bodies.

Throughout the day and the next few days, rescue coordination efforts were hampered by the inability to communicate. Many telephones, including most cell phones, were not working due to line breaks, base station destruction, or power failures. In some cases, amateur radio provided tactical and emergency communications, as well as health-and-welfare enquiries

Without power, local television broadcasting was disrupted, causing news crews to work closely with sister stations in nearby cities. The New Orleans *Times-Picayune* had a cadre of reporters and editors hunkered down in a bunker-like section of the offices where they rode out the storm and then wrote stories. Coordinating their efforts with *The Cleveland Plain Dealer*, news reports were updated to an Internet Web site until a hard copy could be printed a few days later in Baton Rouge.

That night, New Orleans was dark—no power and drinking water. There were reports that 80 percent of the city was flooded, with water reaching as high as 20 feet in some places. Both airports were underwater; gas leaks and fires were reported throughout the city; and the "Twin Spans" over the east end of Lake Pontchartrain were damaged and impassable.

Tuesday, August 30th
Canal Street

~

From the back of the four-wheeler, Toma surveyed flooded Canal Street and saw opportunity in front of him. "Boys," he said, "let's go over to Best Buy. I want to get me one of those plasma TVs."

The two gang members with him grinned in anticipation.

"The Big Easy just became Easy Pickings! Let's go shopping!" Toma smiled.

The truck moved forward carefully in the hip-deep water and pulled up in front of an electronics store. One of Toma's men jumped out of the truck and hitched a chain to the steel gate protecting the store from looters. He affixed the other end to the truck and signaled the driver to yank the gate open. When other looters saw the open store, they began to approach, but backed away quickly when Toma and his men waved their weapons menacingly at them.

In the main downtown business district on Canal Street, looters sloshed through hip-deep water and ripped open the steel gates on the front of several clothing and jewelry stores. Others were loading up large plastic containers and laundry baskets with stolen goods and walking away. The few isolated policemen were helpless to take action and, especially in cases where looters were after daily essentials such as food and medical supplies, reluctant to take action.

Rescuers begin picking up stranded people with boats and helicopters. Coast Guard choppers filled the skies as they swooped in to rescue shell-shocked and bedraggled flood victims, especially those in the Ninth Ward. Across the Industrial Canal, St. Bernard Parish had more than 40,000 flooded homes. Corpses were found throughout the flooded areas as fights and fires broke out, and storm survivors, who were tired and hungry, felt they had been forsaken. A sense of gloom seemed to settle over the city that had been so full of life just a few days earlier.

On the Highway
Outside of Slidell

~

When he saw the gator in the middle of the road, 75-year-old Watson Williams swerved his lumbering Mercury to the left and lost control. The car flew into the water-filled median area, which separated the two roadways, and became stuck in the mud. Williams' 71-year-old wife began screaming when she saw that the water was rising. The electric door locks and the open windows shorted out due to the rapidly rising water.

"Now, don't you worry," he began. "We'll just ease ourselves out of the windows, Coo Coo." He called her by the loving nickname he had given her when they had first started dating 50 some years ago.

Ignoring his advice, she countered, "You better think twice about that, Watson. Look at that sign."

Watson's eyes followed her finger and the direction in which it was pointing. There across from where they sat, was a damaged sign. The sign read, "Alligator Farm." Next to the sign a large cypress tree had fallen and crushed the fence which had kept the alligators captive. The portion of the fence along the roadway now lay submerged under the rising waters, and the captive alligators were able to escape from their confinement.

The hungry gators hadn't been fed in a couple of days, and they were looking for prey. To them, meals-on-wheels had just arrived. A number of the gators slithered across the roadway and began circling the car, much to the horror of its two occupants.

"Roll up the windows," Coo Coo commanded.

"I can't, Sweetie. They shorted out."

"I can't believe this is happening to us," she said softly as she began to cry, accepting her fate.

Watson, on the other hand, was looking into the back seat for anything he could use. But, the seat was empty. He only had his bare hands, and those old hands were certainly no match for the gators, one of which tried to reach up and stick its jaws inside the open window. It didn't succeed, but within a few minutes, when the water rose higher, it wouldn't have a problem.

Watson shuddered at the thought of being cornered in the car with a gator inside. Suddenly, he saw an approaching four-wheel-drive pick-up truck. He took off his red cap and took a chance of sticking his arm out the window and waving his cap to attract attention. It worked.

The truck came to a sudden stop and Emerson, who had dropped Bubbie off at a friend's in order to borrow a bigger boat, stepped out of the cab.

"You folks, okay?" Emerson yelled with concern as he saw three gators circling and a couple more on the opposite roadway.

"We're not hurt, if that's what you mean," Watson yelled back. "But, we can't hold out much longer. One of them gators tried to get in the window a minute ago!"

"Let's see what I can do." Emerson scanned the ground leading down to the where the car was stuck and tried to determine if the muddy water in the median had any sink holes, but he couldn't tell. He also knew that he couldn't wait any longer.

He hopped back into the truck and carefully began to back the truck down the slight embankment and toward the trapped car. The truck slide sideways, and Emerson waited until it stopped sliding. Adjusting the steering wheel, he feathered the gas pedal and began backing slowly backwards until the bed was within three feet of the stranded vehicle and on the driver's side.

Opening the truck door, he swung around and up into the bed of the truck. With a shovel he found in the bed, he held it as he made his way to the rear. He opened the tailgate and shouted to Williams.

"You get yourself ready to crawl out that window when I get there. We're going to have to move pretty fast."

"Take my wife first," he pleaded as he looked at her.

"I'll take you first. You're closer, and I don't have time for you two to switch places in the front seat."

Nervously, Williams answered as he pulled himself up into a crouching position near the window. "I'm ready."

With that Emerson jumped out of the bed and splashed into the water next to the car. When the nearest gator started to close in on him, he raised the shovel and brought it down sharply on its snout, causing it to reel back in surprise. It was at that moment that Emerson pulled Williams from the car and took the two steps to the truck bed where he heaved Williams in. Emerson jumped in the bed also and took a quick breather as he surveyed where the gators were. He noticed that the two gators, who had been on the opposite roadway, had now entered the water and were approaching the passenger's side of the car.

"Coo Coo. You've got to be ready when he comes for you," Williams shouted to his wife who had scooted across the seat to the driver's side.

She held back a bit as one of the gators was moving in. As it stuck its opened jaws through the driver's window, Emerson, who had jumped out of the truck, dropped the shovel squarely on its head, causing it to recoil angrily and withdraw. "Watch it or I'll turn you into a wallet," Emerson threatened. Dropping the shovel, Emerson reached into the car to pull out the woman. As he did, Emerson saw another gator start to enter through the open passenger window.

He quickly jerked the woman out of the driver's window as the gator's powerful jaws closed on empty air. Moving quickly as a ten-foot-long gator began to close on him, Emerson threw Mrs. Williams into the rear of the truck. The gator ignored the woman and zeroed in on Emerson, who now was parallel with the truck door. As the gator's jaws opened in preparation for taking a chunk of Emerson, Emerson reached into the open truck door and grabbed the loaded shotgun. Quickly he turned and stuck the barrel down the gator's jaws, pulling the trigger as he did. "Take a bite of this," he chortled.

A scream from the truck bed interrupted his sense of accomplishment and Emerson saw that one of the gators, with the assistance of the rising water, was starting to crawl into the truck's open tailgate.

Emerson jumped into the cab where he had left the engine running and threw the truck in gear. The wheels spun momentarily before finding traction and the truck leapt forward, depositing the hungry gator in its wake.

Emerson stopped the truck about a half-mile down the road where he checked on his two rescuees. Other than being shocked by their close encounter, they were fine. He jumped back into the cab and took them to a small gas station where the attendant offered to help them. Emerson looked at his watch and realized that he was late for his rendezvous with Bubbie and Mose. He jumped back into the truck and sped off to their meeting point. They were heading back into the Quarter to meet with Elms, who had a lead as to where Melaudra might have been sequestered.

As he drove, he thought back to the time he spent with Bubbie and Mose at their place in the swamp during the hurricane. The winds had ripped off a portion of the roof of the small store and the Pearl River had flooded over onto the porch, but fortunately did not flood into the house. Trees were down all around the house and some of the neighboring Cajun homes had been severely damaged or destroyed. It was an experience that he didn't want to relive. They had paddled out of the swamp that morning and borrowed the four-wheeler, which Emerson was driving around Slidell, while he quickly assessed the damage, and avoided downed power lines, fallen trees, and debris scattered on the roadways.

St. Albans Hospital
Ramparts Street

The first floor of the 500-bed hospital was flooding and the exhausted staff worked unendingly in the horrible conditions as they moved the emergency room operations to the second floor. They tried to care for their patients and many of the last minute refugees who took shelter there. Back-up generators were providing limited power to keep alive the more serious cases. Some patients were transported to the helipad for rooftop extractions to functioning hospitals.

The dead were stacked in a second-floor operating room. Patients requiring ventilators were kept alive with hand-powered resuscitation bags, with staff members taking turns operating the hand pumps. Many of the hospital workers sacrificed their own personal concerns and had volunteered to stay at the hospital during the crisis.

Several doctors were meeting to discuss potential outbreaks of food poisoning, hepatitis A, cholera, typhoid fever, yellow fever, malaria, and West Nile Virus. There was growing concern about E. coli contamination of food and drinking water, compounded by the sweltering heat and stifling humidity.

Throughout the city, the hustle and bustle of normal everyday life filled with tourists and jazz music was replaced by the sounds of chain saws, heavy equipment, and generators. The streets were lined with ruined refrigerators, freezers, washers, and dryers. Abandoned cars and trucks littered the once-proud roadways, sidewalks, yards, and—in some cases—front porches.

In place of tile, tin, and shingles, blue tarps were being stretched across many of the roofs of homes damaged by the hurricane. The new roofing technique was branded "FEMA roofing."

A new aroma replaced the sweet seduction of Creole and Cajun cooking. It was a melting pot of rotting food, sewage, and petrochemical toxic sludge.

Many holdouts in the French Quarter, which did not flood, had stored water in bathtubs and dipped water from neighboring swimming pools to use for bathing or flushing toilets. Neighbors without power were generously giving away steaks and fish, which wouldn't last long in the humid heat, or throwing cook-outs on their balconies or inner courtyards. The people of the Quarter were innovative survivors and exchanged news at several Bourbon Street bars, which stayed open during the hurricane.

Garden District
Thibadaux's Home
~

In one of New Orleans' wealthiest areas, back-up generators provided power at several homes, showing that their owners were guarding them from being looted. Damage in the upscale Uptown and Garden District was limited to fallen trees, downed electric lines, minor water damage, and limited flooding.

Many of the residents had heeded the warnings and had been among the first evacuees. Some returned quickly or had additional food, water, and weapons delivered to them.

This was the case at Thibadaux's multimillion-dollar home, where he and his guests had moved from their refuge in his basement to his first-floor library. He had arranged with a Baton Rouge vendor to deliver ice and food via helicopter to his home. In a corner of his library sat a large lavender ice chest. It was filled with iced champagne.

Picking up one of the exquisite champagne glasses, Thibadaux refilled his glass and turned to look at his guests. "My oh my," he began as he sipped on his third glass of liquid gold. "What a dilemma we have here tonight!"

No one replied.

"We have a priest who is murdering people in the Quarter . . ."

"I didn't kill anyone!" the priest interrupted as he struggled to free himself and started to rise from his chair. He found himself pulled roughly back into the chair as Jones grabbed his shoulders.

"That's not what the good detective believes, is it?" he asked as he played with the champagne glass.

Melaudra returned his question with an icy stare.

Thibadaux continued. "It would seem that, based on police reports which our good friend Detective Morris has provided me, that the suspected murderer has white hair. People also noticed on several occasions that the murderer was well built. As I look around the room, I only see one person with white hair, and everyone knows you have a penchant for maintaining your muscular body." He shifted from one foot to the other as he spoke.

Morris smiled evilly as Thibadaux paused and looked at the white-haired priest. "It also seems that a certain priest was observed, or should I say 'is on record,' as having visited St. Albans Hospital near the times that two of the victims died."

"Truman, you know that I didn't kill anyone," the priest said.

Thibadaux, who had turned his back to the group, spun around and shot back, "How dare you say that you didn't kill anyone? You killed our mother!"

"No, I didn't. I wasn't here when she died."

"That's why she died. You weren't here! If it hadn't been for you getting this call on your life to go into the priesthood, then leaving to go to Rome, she would still be alive today. You abandoned her, and you abandoned me." Thibadaux cast his eyes downward before he spoke again. "She died of a broken heart."

Melaudra, Morris, and Jones looked at each other in shock at the revelation that the two were siblings.

"Oh, don't be so dismayed," Thibadaux said in response to the shocked facial expressions.

"Truman," the priest started, "you have a dark cloud around your soul."

Scowling, Thibadaux responded to Alsandi, "Let he who is without sin cast the first stone."

The priest bowed his head, shaking it from side to side.

"Father," Melaudra began, "I know that Truman is lying."

The priest turned his head and leveled his eyes at the defiant female detective. "How's that?"

"We're trained to spot when someone is lying."

A sly smile crossed Thibadaux's face as he leaned casually against a chair back.

"Did you notice how fast he talked as he mentioned the murders in the Quarter? Did you notice how the pupils of his eyes narrowed as he talked about the murders? Did you notice him playing with the champagne glass or shifting from one foot to another when he spoke about the murders?" Melaudra asked.

The priest shook his head negatively.

"Well, I did."

"Bullshit!" Truman screamed. He had enough of her assessment.

"Now, he's trying to drown me out," she added.

"That's quite enough out of you, Drencheau," Thibadaux bellowed.

"Not quite yet," she responded. She turned toward the priest. "What he didn't tell you was that the white hair samples we discovered were synthetic. This serial killer was wearing a wig." A look of satisfaction beamed from Melaudra's face at the revelation.

Thibadaux stared at her with fury in his eyes, then glared at Morris and Jones. "You knew this?"

"Nope. I didn't see the lab reports," Morris hurriedly answered.

"I wouldn't be surprised to find a white wig in your brother's possession," Melaudra added.

"Nice try, Detective. But I'm not reacting."

"You don't need to react. I know you're the serial killer, and you were trying to divert attention to your brother. Maybe it was to pay him back for leaving your mother," she suggested. Noticing his hand on the champagne glass, Melaudra observed, "You're doing it again."

"What?"

"Lying. You were unconsciously playing with that champagne glass again."

Picking up the glass, Thibadaux threw it across the room where it smashed to pieces upon hitting the richly wallpapered wall. "There, that should resolve your fixation on the champagne glass," he cackled although inwardly he had been surprised how Melaudra had pinpointed him as the killer. It just seemed like something had snapped within him in the last few months, driving him to kill. To protect himself and to pay back his stepbother for abandoning their mother, he created a killer who resembled his stepbrother.

"Not my fixation. It was yours."

The sound of a vehicle pulling up to the house caused the room to quiet. "Jones, go check it out!" Thibadaux ordered.

Carrying his gun at waist level, Jones hurriedly left the parlor and walked to the front of the house where he peered through the lace-covered glass door. Two figures had emerged from the parked truck and were making their way to the front door. Recognizing them, Jones opened the door to allow them to enter.

In the dark shadows of the evening, three armed men watched from across the street as the newcomers arrived and entered the house.

Speaking in hushed tones, Elms said, "That was Toma, who just walked in there. And Jones let him in."

"So your assumption was true. With Jones there, Melaudra and the priest are probably there, too!" Emerson concluded.

Elms had found Thibadaux's home address on a card inside of Morris' desk, which made him suspect that Melaudra may be at Thibadaux's house. Elms had indicated that it was worth checking out and Bubbie had volunteered to question Thibadaux.

Bubbie said impatiently. "Let's go get ma gurl!"

"Counting Morris, there's at least five of them and three of us," Emerson cautioned.

"Four of us, iffen you count Mose back in the boat. We outnumber them," Bubbie grinned as he hefted his shotgun.

Looking at the swamp man, Emerson grinned back. "This is one that I want a front seat for." He could only imagine how Bubbie would act once he got his hands on Morris and Jones. "Here's an idea," Emerson said. He quickly outlined a plan, which surprised Elms with its simplicity and probability of success. When Emerson tried to coordinate their watches, he saw that Bubbie didn't wear a watch. "Here, take mine," he offered and handed his watch to Bubbie who took it and scurried off to prepare for his part.

In the meantime, Emerson and Elms crept across the street. As they began walking along the front porch, Emerson froze causing Elms to bump into him.

"What's wrong?" Elms hissed.

"Something just slithered across the ground in front of me and headed toward the porch." Emerson responded.

"With all the high water, it could have been one of the snakes seeking dry ground. There was a report of snakes escaping from the zoo. It's not too far from here."

"Poisonous?"

"I consider all snakes as poisonous," Elms replied with a shudder. "Let's move it. We're wasting time."

The two continued their way to the rear of the house where they tried the rear door and found it locked. Emerson pulled out a credit card and slipped it between the doorjamb and was able to spring the lock. Slowly he opened the door, fearing that an unexpected creak would divulge their presence.

Inside the house, Thibadaux was greeting his visitors. "What a surprise!" he said as the two walked into his library.

The taller of the two saw Melaudra guarded by Morris and Jones. "It is I who should be surprised. She's been trying to catch me for some time and now it appears that she is the one who is caught."

Melaudra's eyes narrowed. "Don't count on it, Toma!"

The drug dealer's eyes focused on the priest. "And a priest. How convenient! Perhaps he can hear your confession before I kill you."

"I'm not Catholic." She smiled coolly as she wondered what linked the drug dealer to Thibadaux.

"You might want to consider converting," he said with sarcastic laughter.

"What are you doing here?" Thibadaux quizzed.

"I've got a proposition for you."

"Yes?"

"What are the chances that I could get in to some of the hospitals here and tap into their drug supplies?"

A look of concern crossed Thibadaux's face. "Didn't I supply you with enough drugs from St. Albans?"

"Piecemeal, you did. But now is the time for me to stock up! I could have more drugs than Walgreens!" A thin smile crossed Toma's lips. "You know what they say about supply and demand. And now is the opportune time for me to build up my supply because, once things start to return to normal, the demand is going to skyrocket—and I'll be sitting pretty!"

Thibadaux thought momentarily about the probability of lax security at the area hospitals. "Shouldn't be a problem at St. Albans. I can sketch a map for you so you know where to go. There's hardly any security there now."

Toma looked at his driver and allowed his face to break into a large smile as Thibadaux walked across the room to a cherry secretary and pulled open the desktop.

In the rear of the house, Elms bumped into a chair, which scraped the floor, sending a noise echoing down the hall.

Furrowing his brow, Thibadaux asked, "Did anyone hear a noise out back?"

Toma's driver, who had been leaning in the parlor doorway, responded, "Yeah. I'll check it out." Drawing a gun from his waist, he carefully walked down the well-decorated hallway toward the rear of the house.

Hearing the approaching footsteps, Emerson and Elms looked for hiding places. Emerson stepped into a small walk in pantry, pulling the door shut behind him. At the same time, Elms scooted his overstuffed body underneath the kitchen table, which was covered by an oversized tablecloth.

Within seconds, the driver cautiously poked his head around the corner and looked into the dark kitchen. Not seeing anything, he walked through the kitchen and opened the back door to peek into the back yard. Seeing nothing, he walked back down the hallway to the parlor. "Nothing back there," he reported.

"Check out front and use this. I should have given this to you earlier when you went to check." Thibadaux handed the driver a flashlight that he quickly turned on and walked with to the front of the house. He opened the front door and stepped onto the front porch where he looked around. No one was in site. He walked down the steps and sensed something slithering by his foot. He whirled and saw whatever it was disappear under the edge of the front porch.

Curious, the driver switched off the flashlight and knelt by the edge of the porch. Carefully, he bent closer to the ground and raised the flashlight next to his face. Holding the edge of the porch trim with one hand, he ripped it upward and, at the same time, turned on the flashlight. It was a fatal mistake.

Philippine pit vipers are deadly venomous snakes with one peculiar trait. Contrary to other snakes, they are one of the few who strike at light. It's like waving a red cape in front of a charging bull. When the light came on, the pit viper, which was trying to find a new home since its escape from the New Orleans Zoo, struck suddenly at the flashlight. Its semi-triangular head struck a second time at the driver's face and then slithered under the porch.

The driver's screams filled the quiet night air and echoed down the hallway to the parlor, as the bluish-green snake with dark blotches on its back retreated farther under the porch.

"See what's wrong!" Thibadaux ordered Toma and Jones who, with guns drawn, ran to the front of the house. Thibadaux pulled open one of the secretary's drawers and turned around with a .38 revolver in his right hand. He aimed it at Melaudra.

"What's this about?" she asked.

"Just a precaution."

Morris took his cue from Thibadaux and withdrew his revolver from his holster and held it loosely in his right hand as he stood behind Melaudra and the priest.

Outside, Toma knelt next to his driver while Jones scanned the dark street. "Calm down. What happened?"

Lying on the ground, the driver was beginning to go into shock. "It was a snake. It was under the porch and it bit me."

"Where?" Toma asked as he picked up the flashlight and shined it on the driver's hand.

"No. Up here. On my face."

Directing the light to the driver's face, Toma saw the two skin punctures from the viper's fangs.

"You got to get me some help."

"No, it can't be anything bad. Probably just a watersnake. I've seen snakebites before. This one isn't poisonous," Toma stormed. Toma's arrogance was confusing poisonous snake bites, which leave fang holes, with the horseshoe-shaped mark left by nonpoisonous snakes.

From the porch, Jones called. "What you got there? A little snake, rattle, and roll?"

Even in the darkness, Jones could see the glare that Toma threw him. He quickly changed his tone. "You know that the zoo lost some poisonous snakes?"

Before Toma could respond, a sudden deafening clamor drew their attention to the nearby flooded intersection. Flying around the corner and across the flooded intersection toward them was a rapidly approaching airboat.

"What in the hell is that doing here?" Toma asked out loud to no one in particular.

As the craft neared, he saw a figure laying prone in the bow. The figure was holding a weapon, and it appeared to be pointed directly at Toma. Toma had been around long enough to know not to wait to ask questions. He made a decision and acted on it. This time, it would turn out to be the wrong decision.

He raised his handgun and fired a round at the airboat. That was the first mistake. His round was returned with two shots that found their target. The first shot caught Toma in his upper body. The second round fired by the marksman in the bow smashed into Toma's right eye socket, carried into the brain, and exploded out of the rear of his head. Toma dropped to the ground.

From the porch, where Jones had been frozen by the surprise appearance of the airboat, Jones opened fire. Two shots were returned from the airboat and Jones's legs crumpled under him, He tumbled down the stairs to land on the ground next to Toma. He was dead before he hit the ground.

The airboat, which had crashed over the low ornate iron fence in front of the property, came to a halt and Bubbie Drencheau leapt from the bow. He dropped the rifle, which he had been holding, and reached back for his shotgun. The airboat's driver started to follow Bubbie, but Bubbie stopped him. "Mose, you stay out heah and keep watch. Ah'm gonna find ma gurl." Bubbie began to climb the front steps. He had a very deadly and determined look about him. Mose picked up the discarded rifle and took a defensive position next to the airboat.

Hearing the noise from the approaching airboat, Emerson and Elms made the decision to rush the parlor. They had heard the screams and knew that at least two people had run to the front porch. They figured that there were at least two armed people in the parlor.

When they appeared in the doorway, Elms shouted, "Drop your weapons!"

Morris, with a patronizing smile on his face, swung his weapon to point at Elms. "Elmo, your contract has been cancelled." He began to pull the trigger when the first and second rounds from Elms' weapon exploded in his chest. His gun dropped from his hand and hit the floor, quickly followed by Morris' body.

Simultaneously, Thibadaux spun around to face Melaudra. "Fare thee well, Beautiful Maiden!" He pulled the trigger as Melaudra cursed him. Thibadaux's concentration on Melaudra prevented him from noticing that the priest had been slowly preparing to interrupt Thibadaux's plans. Just a second before Thibadaux fired, the priest launched his body through the short distance to cover Melaudra. The bullet intended for her caught the priest in the chest, and he slumped on top of Melaudra, protecting her with his body.

Thibadaux grinned sardonically. "My brother was always so stupid. Try this one, Drencheau!" Thibadaux had again pointed the gun at Melaudra's head when a shout distracted him. Squeezing into the parlor's doorway next to the pudgy Elms was Emerson. "Lower your weapon," he ordered Thibadaux as he pointed his shotgun.

Elms started to push his way into the room, bringing his weapon to bear on Thibadaux. "I'll take care of this, Emerson."

"Not this time. He's mine," Emerson said firmly as he gripped the shotgun.

Thibadaux swung his weapon around to aim at Emerson. "You've certainly created a stir since you came to town. Goodbye, Mr. Emerson Moore." Without waiting for a reply, he pulled the trigger. The bullet missed Emerson as it splintered the molding next to where Emerson was standing.

Emerson returned fire with both barrels of the shotgun. The blast echoed through the house and tore into Thibadaux's midsection. Thibadaux dropped his gun and clenched the cabinet next to him as he tried to maintain his footing. It was a useless attempt as he lost his grip and fell to the floor.

A moan emitted from where Melaudra sat with the priest shielding her body. She awkwardly tried to roll the priest off of her.

"Help her. I'll check Morris," Elms instructed Emerson as he handed him a set of keys to unlock the handcuffs before checking to be sure that the other two were dead.

"What took you so long, Elmo?" Melaudra called as Emerson undid her handcuffs and she rubbed her wrists briskly.

"Just a little bad weather by the name of Katrina!" he responded as he checked Morris, who was dead.

Melaudra staggered to the wall, while Emerson moved to uncuff the priest. Blood was gushing from a wound in his chest and gurgling from his mouth. His color was fading as Emerson looked at the priest, then noticed movement from Thibadaux.

Thibadaux had pulled himself to his elbows and was now pointing his gun at Emerson. "I don't die quite that easy, but you will."

A swooshing sound filled the air and Thibadaux's eyes widened in surprise. Protruding from his ear was an arrow from his crossbow. He turned his head and a look of disbelief filled his face. Standing next to the wall was Melaudra. She was holding the discharged crossbow. Melaudra smiled dangerously at him as his eyes glazed over and he fell to the floor, dead.

"Nice shot!" Emerson called after taking a deep breath.

Melaudra cocked her head, then replaced the crossbow on the wall. "I think I made my point."

Melaudra and Elms approached Emerson and the dying priest.

"Let me help you, Emerson," Melaudra said as she positioned a throw pillow from the elegant sofa under the priest's head.

"It's too late," the priest gasped between breaths as he peered through squinted eyes at Melaudra and Emerson. He was fumbling for his rosary, which was in his pocket.

"Here, let me help you," Emerson said as he tried to assist in pulling it from his pocket. Something seemed to snag in his pocket, so Emerson gave the rosary a tug and it came out. Entangled with the rosary was his apartment key. Emerson passed the rosary and key to the priest to hold in his weakening hands.

"The key," the priest mumbled as his strength faded.

"Yes?" Emerson asked.

"Take the key and go to my apartment." The priest gasped slowly. "It's the secret . . ." Before he could finish, he took one last gasp and died.

"The secret?" Emerson asked as he looked at Melaudra and Elms.

"Guess it's yours to discover, Mr. Reporter," Melaudra teased. "He gave you the key, and I'm a witness, although a very curious witness, I might add."

"Dere's ma gurl," Bubbie shouted from the doorway where he stood with his reloaded shotgun. "Everytin okay in heah?"

"Yes, Daddy. But everything is really okay now that you're here," she said as she walked cross the room into her father's arms for a huge bear hug.

Elms and Emerson were standing and watching the two reunite.

"Hey, Mel, why don't I ever get a hug like that from you?" Elms asked.

Melaudra spun around from her father's grip and began to wiggle her fingers as she approached Elms, saying, "I'm going to give you something better. I'm going to tickle you, Elmo!"

Elms took three steps backwards. "I realize that women find me irresistible. But I really must ask you to try to control yourself, Mel!"

Melaudra stopped. "Oh, if you insist, I guess I can."

"What happened to the guys out in front?" Emerson asked.

"Dead." Bubbie responded. "You should da seen da look on dere faces when Ah come around on de airboat!"

"By the way, I've got a surprise for the two of you," Melaudra said as she looked at Elms and Emerson.

"What's that?" Emerson asked.

"Thibadaux and Alsandi were stepbrothers. They had the same mother."

"What?" Emerson asked in disbelief.

"Yes, I know it's hard to believe, but it's true."

Elms thought for a moment and said, "I think I know now why Thibadaux was the way he was."

"How's that?" Melaudra asked.

"Thibadaux must have been the brother who was stuck in the birth canal too long." He began chuckling at his own joke, which was a good thing since no one else found it to be funny. "Hey, look here." Everyone turned to see what Elms found and saw him pull a white wig from the bottom drawer of the secretary. "I bet this wig matches the hair samples from the murders. Now, I'll just take a couple of his." Elms bent over Thibadaux's body and plucked a few strands of hair from his head. "Let's see if these match any samples inside the wig." He produced a small plastic bag from his pocket, and dropped the newly acquired samples inside.

"I'm sure we found our serial killer," Melaudra stated as she looked at Thibadaux's body. "How's the city?" Melaudra asked and they quickly brought her up to date on the damage caused by the hurricane and the disastrous flooding.

They secured the area as best as they could and boarded the airboat for the ride back to the police station. When they arrived at the station, Elms jumped from the airboat and began to walk into the station.

Emerson stepped from the airboat and waited for Melaudra to finish hugging and saying goodbye to her father and Mose.

"You be careful now, gurl," Bubbie called to his daughter after she stepped from the airboat. Mose gunned the airboat's engine and put it in a tight turn before heading east and back to the swamps.

Melaudra looked at Emerson. "Thank you."

"I didn't do anything. It was really your father and Elms. I was just along for the ride." Melaudra looked softly into Emerson's eyes and was about to kiss him, when she abruptly pulled back. "I've got to go. There's probably all kinds of things going on with this flooding. I need to help." Melaudra ran up the stairs and shouted to Emerson just before she entered the building. "I enjoyed meeting you." She turned quickly and went into the building. She didn't want Emerson to see the tears in her eyes.

As she entered the building, Elms walked out. "Hey, Emerson, Old Buddy." He had seen the tears in Melaudra's eyes when she flew by him. "You blew it, my friend."

"I blew it? How's that?"

"Our pretty friend, Melaudra, was falling for you."

"Yeah, I thought things were going quite well. Then for some reason, she started giving me the cold shoulder."

Elms cocked his head to one side. "Think back to what may have triggered that."

Racking the recesses of his mind, Emerson recalled her reaction after seeing him chase after Martine. "Was it the redhead on St. Anne Street?"

"You seemed pretty interested in that redhead."

"We're just friends. We go way back," he tried to explain.

"Based on your reactions—and you may not have realized what we saw—it appeared to Melaudra and me that the two of you may have had a relationship and that you still cared deeply about that redhead. Do you?"

Thinking back to their time together on the Lake Erie islands, Emerson said, "Not really."

"Wrong answer. The only right answer would have been 'no.'" Elms commented. "For your information, that redhead has a pretty bad reputation in the Quarter. When Melaudra saw your interest, you killed any opportunity for a relationship with her. And that's just too bad, because Melaudra is one of the finest women I know."

Extending his hand to Emerson, Elms said as they shook hands, "It was nice meeting you and thanks for your help tonight. I've got to go."

Shaken, Emerson said, "Good-bye, Elmo."

"To each his own," Elms said cryptically and with a raised eyebrow as he turned and walked into the building, leaving Emerson looking puzzled.

Outside James H Cohen & Sons *Royal Street*

~

It was around 11:00 in the evening, and Emerson was making his way through the French Quarter from the police station to his hotel. He was taking a circuitous route so that he could observe the damage caused by the hurricane's strong winds and rain. As he passed Antoine's Restaurant, he saw that one brick wall had partially collapsed. Turning onto Royal Street, he was approaching Cohen's, which was across the street from the massive stone building housing the Louisiana Supreme Court. It was there that a gang of six young thugs confronted Emerson.

"What do we have here?" one shouted as he danced around Emerson.

The others began to encircle him as Emerson asked, "Something I can do for you guys?"

"Oh, most certainly, there is!" the first thug taunted.

Emerson didn't like the way the odds were shaping up against him.

"You can start by giving us your wallet," a second thug said menacingly.

Never having been robbed, Emerson was not going to allow it to happen here. "If you want it, you boys will just have to take it," he said, mustering as much bravado as he could.

From the shadows of Cohen's doorway, a stern voice bellowed, "And you better plan on trying to take mine, too."

Everyone turned to face the source of the voice. Stepping out of the shadows and brandishing a cane was Jimmie Cohen, the spry, 80-year-old owner of Cohen's who looked like he was more ready to play the role of Douglas Fairbanks Jr., than retire to a rocking chair.

"Nah, we don't bother old people. You don't have anything more than your monthly welfare check," the first thug said as he moved in a little too close to Cohen. Cohen raised his cane quickly and brought it sharply across the side of the thug's head, causing him to reel from the blow.

"Mind your manners, Son," Cohen cracked.

The second gang member darted at Cohen, who pointed his cane straight at him. The boy grabbed hold of the cane and pulled. The cane came free in his hands like a sword's sheath and he lost his balance. With his eyes popping, he stared at 14 inches of cold steel, pointed at his gut. The blade had been concealed in Cohen's sword cane, just one of the many weapons featured in his store.

"You boys are not acting like southern gentlemen, now are you?" Cohen moved forward slowly and carefully jabbed the sword at the gang members who were preparing to charge at the brave storeowner. Emerson was calculating quickly how Cohen and he were going to overcome these assailants, when two gunshots rang out. The bullets ricocheted off the sidewalk near the gang. The thugs looked around the dark street and couldn't see how many shooters they were facing and decided to run.

Cohen began laughing. "Those boys can't run much faster than that," he laughed as they disappeared in the darkness.

"Thanks, Mr. Cohen. But you shouldn't have risked yourself."

"Wasn't any risk about it. I was just taking my normal evening stroll and, just before you came by, I took a peek into my store. When you needed help, I stepped out."

"But it still was risky."

"Not with Rafael and Tony on the roof," he grinned and pointed to the top of the Louisiana Supreme Court building, across the street.

"Rafael and Tony?"

"Sure, they're a couple of SWAT team snipers assigned to protect this side of the Supreme Court building from anyone trying to break in. I was hoping that they wouldn't take too long before they got themselves involved."

"How'd they see us? It's so dark."

"Night vision goggles. They told me about them during one of their visits to the store."

Smiling at the wily storeowner, whom Emerson had admired for years, he said, "You always have an ace up your sleeve."

With a twinkle in his eye, Cohen replied, "You always have to have the ace, but you don't always have to play it!"

"Thanks, Rafael and Tony!" Emerson shouted into the darkness

"You're welcome," Rafael yelled from the rooftop.

"I'm going to head on home. Why don't you stop over tomorrow morning and I'll show you the damage to the store."

"Is it bad?"

"No, just some water damage, and one of the walls on the third floor is damaged. But you come back tomorrow and we'll show you."

"Need an escort back to your home?" Emerson asked recalling that Mr. Cohen lived in one of the Quarter's condos.

"No, I'll be quite fine," he said as he placed the sheath over his sword cane and began walking toward his home.

Emerson turned and made his way the short distance to his darkened hotel which had a few generators running to provide limited electrical service. It was going to be an uncomfortable night with the late summer heat and humidity— and no air conditioning. For people trapped in the Ninth Ward or housed in the Superdome or Convention Center, it was even more uncomfortable.

The Next Day
Place d'Armes

~

Feeling sticky from the heat and a mostly sleepless night, Emerson dressed in the light from his balcony and walked to the first-floor breakfast area. There, he snacked on the small breakfast that the hotel's staff had scrounged together. They had stocked up on bottled water and food as the hurricane approached, but were being careful as they distributed the food sparingly.

After his light breakfast, Emerson decided to survey the Quarter's hurricane damage and went for a walk in its deserted streets. As he walked, he encountered debris blown from the second- and third-floor balconies or off building roofs. He chuckled when he stumbled across a defaced sign for ghost tours. A red circle had been drawn around the sign with a red line cutting diagonally through it. The sign had been altered to read "Ghost Town."

As he walked down Royal Street, Emerson saw the garden behind St. Louis Cathedral where he had met with the priest. Two large trees had fallen on each side of the statue of Jesus, leaving the statue undamaged other than a piece missing from the thumb.

Crossing St. Louis Street, Emerson peered upward at the rooftop of the Supreme Court building as he tried to spy the shooters from the previous night. Not seeing them, he walked into Cohen's store and stopped to stare after taking three steps. Where a few days before, the walls had displayed rifles, swords, and other weapons, display hooks were now revealed. The display cabinets filled with rare weapons and coins were also empty.

"Looks different, doesn't it?" Steve Cohen asked as he emerged from a rear office.

"I can't believe my eyes," Emerson said as he thought about the work that went into taking down the huge inventory of antique and rare weapons.

"Yeah, we took everything down and shipped it to our off-site storage vault for security purposes," Steve explained. "Heard you and my dad had a little run in with some guys last night."

"Yes, we did. He told you?"

"As only my father can tell a story," he grinned. "Did he really slash the letter 'C' on the guy's shirt?"

Laughing, Emerson replied, "I think he was having a little fun with you when he told you that story!"

"I thought he was funning me. I'm glad it worked out the way it did."

"Me too. It could have become ugly." Looking around at the bare walls, Emerson asked, "Is he here today?"

"Upstairs. We had some water damage in the front room of the apartment. Come on up and I'll show you." As they walked to the stairs, he called to his brother Jerry, "We're going up to see Dad."

"Okay. You're seeing a different side of the Quarter these days," Jerry said to Emerson as he walked by.

"Something I certainly didn't expect."

They climbed the stairs to the third-floor apartment, which was now being used as a warehouse. Walking down the narrow hallway to the front of the apartment, they found Jimmie and his grandson, Barry. They were pulling drywall and shreds of rose-colored wallpaper from the damaged wall. The large narrow windows, which opened unto the balcony overlooking Royal Street, provided light for the room.

"Recover from last night?" Emerson asked as he walked into the room.

"Nothing to recover from," Jimmie replied and turned back to helping his grandson. "This used to be my grandfather's apartment. And, as you can see, we've got a bit of a mess here," he said as he tore away a piece of drywall.

A red-brick chimney ran up the wall from a fireplace, which had been bricked in years ago. A few of the bricks had become loose and fell to the ground when Jimmie bumped them. He bent over to replace them when something hidden in the fireplace caught his eye. "What's this?" He dropped slowly to one knee and looked into the fireplace. "Help me with this, Barry."

Barry dropped to his side and the two spent a few minutes in working loose more bricks to expose a portion of the firebox. Jimmie then reached in and extracted an object wrapped in oilskin. "Well well. What do we have here?" he mused as he stood and walked to a dusty table in the middle of the room. "It looks like my grandfather may have hidden a gift for us."

As the four of them gathered around the table, Jimmie began to slowly unwrap the oilskin to reveal an eight-inch-long gold cross set with a deep-green emerald. "Take a look at this, Fellows," Jimmie said as he slowly examined the cross and then passed it to the other three.

When it was handed to Emerson, he carefully inspected the cross. "Hey, it looks like this is a lid. Does this come off?" He returned the cross to Jimmie, who closely reexamined it.

"You may have something here," Jimmie said as he spotted a small, indented area near the top of the cross. He tried to pry it open, but couldn't.

"Try this," Emerson said as he produced a pocketknife and opened the blade.

"Thank you," Jimmie said as he took the knife, and began to pry at the recessed area. After a few minutes with Barry holding the cross, while Jimmie pried, the top of the cross popped off and fell to the table. Jimmie peered inside the hollow cross and saw a document. "Now, this is getting interesting." He pulled out a rolled document that was hidden inside.

The room was hushed as he delicately unrolled the document and began to read it aloud:

13 May 1805

The Vatican
Rome, Italy

The Honorable President of the United States, Thomas Jefferson

I am corresponding with you about an item of grave concern and consequence to the United States with regards to the procurement of the Louisiana territory from France.

There was a preliminary and secret treaty between the French Republic and His Catholic Majesty, the King of Spain, agreed and signed, on 1 October 1800 and known as the Secret Treaty of Ildefonso. The treaty concerned the aggrandizement of His Royal Highness, the Infant Duke of Parma and the Retrocession of Louisiana to France. To their mutual satisfaction, the French Republic agreed that the aggrandizement to be given to His Royal Highness, the Duke of Parma, would consist of the domain of Tuscany. In return, Spain agreed to retrocede to the French Republic, the province of Louisiana.

In 1803, the French Republic, in violation of the Secret Treaty of Ildefonso, consummated a sale of the Louisiana territory with the United States of America and transferred ownership. Under the terms of the Secret Treaty of Ildefonso, the French Republic was precluded from transferring the Louisiana territory to another nation.

Since legally, there could not be an ownership transfer of the Louisiana territory to the United States of America, the territory continues to be owned by Spain, and you should take every effort to conduct talks with Spain to secure legal ownership of the aforementioned territory.

Godspeed,
Pope Pius VII

"This is serious," Jimmie said as he broke the silence. "We need to figure out what we should do."

Barry and Steve nodded their heads in unison.

"I think you have the answer," Emerson suggested.

The other three turned their heads and stared with perplexed looks at Emerson.

"Since the cross and its contents belong to the Catholic Church, I'd suggest returning it to them."

"But we've got a responsibility to report this memo and the impact it will have," Steve offered.

"That's right, I agree with my son," Jimmie stated firmly.

"What I mean by returning it to them is through the media. I'd like to do a story exposing the illegality of the Louisiana Purchase so that it can be addressed through proper channels. As part of the story, I'd arrange for the return of the cross to the Vatican—since it's their property—and donate the letter to our National Archives in Washington."

A silence filled the room as each of the occupants weighed Emerson's suggestion and the historical significance of their discovery.

"Gentlemen, I suppose we should do as he proposes," Jimmie said.

"Of course, I'd detail that we found the cross in your store filled with antiquities. It couldn't be any more serendipitous than that!" Emerson smiled.

Convinced that they were doing the right thing, Jimmie concluded, "It's the right thing to do."

"Why don't you keep the cross here until I'm ready to return it? I'll take the document with me so that I can start my story," Emerson suggested.

"Come on down to the office and I'll give you an envelope to protect the document," Jimmie said as he turned to walk out of the room.

The meeting broke up and Emerson headed for the priest's apartment. He had found the address in Cohen's phone directory. As he walked through the humid morning, he could see clouds of black smoke billowing on the skyline from warehouse fires down river.

Reaching the apartment, he pulled aside a damaged shutter, partially blocking his access to the stairwell to the second floor. Climbing the stairs, he entered the dark hallway and had to peer closely at the apartment numbers to be sure he was entering the correct apartment. Finding the priest's apartment, he inserted the key and swung open the door.

The small studio apartment consisted of a living room with cooking facilities. There was a large worn overstuffed chair with a reading lamp and a desk. On the wall opposite the chair was a picture providing a bird's-eye view of the Vatican. Emerson glanced around the small apartment and then walked down the narrow hallway, which opened to an even smaller bedroom, containing a bed, small nightstand, dresser, and exercise equipment. Above the bed was a crucifix and the opposite wall had a painting of the baby Jesus and the Virgin Mary.

Returning to the living room, Emerson looked through the desk for the envelope, which he had delivered to the priest just a few days earlier. He couldn't find it. He then pulled the desk away from the wall and found two, large wooden pockets, which had been nailed to the rear of the desk. One pocket held the envelope that Emerson had delivered. The other pocket held two more envelopes, one of which carried the Vatican logo and return address.

Emerson carried the envelopes to the chair and sat down with his back to the window so that he would have reading light. He read the letter from the Vatican, which was dated a number of years earlier and officially castigated Alsandi for reviewing and discussing highly sensitive documents in the Secret Archives relative to a specific unnamed incident. Emerson suspected it regarded the Louisiana Purchase. The letter to Alsandi strictly forbade him to discuss any of the contents of the Secret Archives at the risk of excommunication from the Catholic Church and eternal damnation.

Emerson set aside the first letter and read the letter from Father Maloney to Father Alsandi which he had delivered. It concerned their discovery of evidence in the Secret Archives that the Vatican had threatened on several occasions to reveal the illegality of the Louisiana Purchase unless the United States would align itself in support of key Vatican political positions. Maloney's letter had begged Alsandi to take a stand against the Vatican's coercive practices with the United States by revealing what they had discovered.

Emerson slouched in the chair. After the events of the last few days and the magnitude of the hidden document and the letters, Emerson felt emotionally and physically drained. He stood and folded the two letters, placing them in his pocket. Walking out of the apartment, he locked its door and descended the stairs and emerged at street level.

He decided to take a walk through the devastated Quarter. The absence of people walking the streets was noteworthy. With his mind racing with ideas for this remarkable news story, Emerson decided to head for Bourbon Street to survey people traffic and devastation to the Quarter. As he walked down Toulouse, he noticed that several of the antique street lamps were leaning at an angle, and several had broken glass panes. Even the metal street signs had been bent by the strong winds.

He rounded the corner and looked down the nearly barren party street. Rather than jazz and Cajun music blasting from the bars lining the once raucous street, there was an eerie silence. He looked into the Tropical Isle at the corner of Toulouse and Bourbon, which was the home of the famous Hand Grenade drink. They had a generator going in the bar, which was crowded with hardy Quarter residents. Hanging above the bar was a hastily made cardboard sign. It read: *France—Want to buy us back?* Emerson smiled at the irony of the sign in light of what he had seen that day.

A few doors down, Emerson came to a sudden stop. There, on the wall was a photo of Martine in short revealing clubwear on a poster. She was a dancer at the club and used the stage name Ginger. Stunned Emerson stepped back and bumped into a man, who Emerson didn't realize was walking behind him.

"Oh, excuse me," he offered still in shock. He couldn't understand why she would be dancing on stage in that type of club.

"Hey, no problem." The sandy-haired, slightly built man allowed his eyes to follow Emerson's. When he saw him staring at the poster, he asked, "Did you know Ginger?"

Emerson groaned at the nickname and the use of the past tense. "Yes. Why did you ask did I know?"

"They found his body this morning. He drowned."

Emerson's mind was spinning. "You said his body? Martine, err Ginger was a guy?"

"Yeah, one of the best female impersonators in the Quarter. He danced here ever since he arrived about two years ago. He lived here in the Quarter, right down the hall from me."

Waves of shock and revulsion filled Emerson's mind. He looked more closely at Martine's poster to ascertain it was her. There was no doubt in his mind. He noticed that she had let her hair grow longer, she looked the same as she had the last he'd seen her in Port Clinton. "I'm sorry, I'm just surprised. That's all."

"He fooled a lot of people. I think the breast implants had something to do with it."

Emerson's memory flashed back to one particular sunny day in which he and Martine had gone swimming, and how good he had thought she had looked in her bikini. He shuddered again, as he thought about the kisses they had shared.

"Did you know him?" the stranger asked.

"In a way, I did." Emerson was still reeling.

"You look like you could use a drink. Come on down to the Tropical Isle with me. It's Hand Grenade time."

A dazed Emerson responded, "I think you're right. I could use a drink. In fact, I might need several and that's something I haven't done in years—to drink several, that is."

"I'm Wayne Weathersbee. I live here in the Quarter."

"Emerson Moore." As they walked, Emerson recalled Elms' cryptic message about each to his own. He then realized that Melaudra thought he had a thing for Martine or Ginger. No wonder she suddenly became very cool to him.

They walked the short distance to the bar and ordered their drinks. Wayne took a Hand Grenade and Emerson ordered a double Seven and Seven with a slice of lemon.

"You're not from around here, are you?"

"No, I was just in town visiting."

"Wrong time to visit!" Wayne said as he sipped his drink. "Got a place here?"

"Yeah, I'm staying at Place d'Armes."

"Good thing you're not over at the Superdome. When they say a shelter is a 'last resort,' you don't want to be there. Would you want to spend several days in the Superdome with no electric, water, or sewage with 20,000 people?"

Emerson smiled as he raised his glass to his lips and allowed the warm liquid to provide him relief.

Wayne continued. "If you decide to ride out the storm and are told to have a three- to five-day supply of water and food and there will be no power, you need to be prepared for the worst and have extra. You should always have cases of bottled water stashed away for emergency use. Have you seen all of the reporters in town? It's like an invasion."

Emerson smiled at his chatty acquaintance and decided not to reveal his profession.

"There's a lot of sensationalism going on. The TV cameras don't begin to show the suffering and losses the residents are experiencing." The talkative Wayne turned to Emerson and asked, "Do you know who Jim Cantore is?"

Emerson nodded as he took a long drink from his glass.

"I'd say any time Jim Cantore from the Weather Channel comes to your town to cover a hurricane then it's time to evacuate," Wayne grinned as he sipped his Hand Grenade. "I was in the Lower Ninth Ward today. The destruction is total. I have no idea what the future holds for that part of town or the other areas that suffered severe damage. I'm not sure anyone could have prepared for a disaster of this magnitude," he mused.

"National TV is doing a poor job of covering the heroes who worked long hours under unimaginable conditions during and after the hurricane. For the most part, our police, firefighters, medical workers, and emergency operations people stayed in town. They worked long hours despite being separated from their families and being concerned about their own homes. Some of the NOPD officers I know had to discharge their weapons to defend themselves and other rescue workers."

Emerson was listening intently.

"And another thing. FEMA can't just call up Paw-Paw's Camper World and order 250,000 trailers. There probably aren't that many in the whole country. They will have to be built and that takes time. FEMA can't stockpile them just in case they'll need them some day. They had some looters. It should be okay to shoot looters who are stealing non-food items. However, if someone is stealing food to survive I think we have to show compassion. I just don't know what one does with a big-screen TV when there is no power!"

"I'd agree with you on that," Emerson smiled.

"We all need to take care of each other and pull through this. We can rebuild the city. It will have a smaller population, but hopefully, will still be a great place to live and visit. But it will take all of us who live here to help and all of those that used to visit to come back and visit again, often. I think New Orleanians will work together and show the world that New Orleans will once again be a place that people from across the globe want to visit."

The bar was getting more crowded as people came in to hear the news and grab a drink before the evening curfew set in.

"Wayne, I enjoyed talking with you. Perhaps, I'll see you again." Emerson said as he rose from his bar stool. His head was now spinning faster, thanks to the drink he had finished.

"You can usually find me here at the Tropical Isle," he replied. "Hey, Earl, I'll take another Hand Grenade."

Emerson shook his hand and left cash on the bar for his drink before heading towards the street and walking slowly back to his hotel. His mind went back to what he had learned about Martine and the Vatican intrigue.

The Next Morning
Place d'Armes
~

From his balcony, he could see smoke arising above the skyline as water continued to pour into the city from the damaged levees. Parts of the city were becoming like a large lake of toxic oil, gas, chemicals, and sewage that morphed from brown to a greenish-black.

In some areas, houses and trailers were rolled end-to-end and split at the seams. Caskets floated away from their crypts. The Mississippi River had been driven backward by the hurricane's force. Barges and commercial fishing ships had been tossed about like children's toys.

Emerson sat at his laptop and began writing his story about the discovery of the cross and its hidden document, as well as the letters in Alsandi's apartment. Over the next few weeks, Emerson would balance his time between writing this earth-shattering story and reporting on the recovery and re-building of New Orleans. He vowed to do his best in reporting the facts and avoiding hype.

Aunt Anne's House
Put-in-Bay
~

Sitting on the front porch and enjoying the warmth of the mid -October afternoon as he watched the boats moving in and out of the harbor, Emerson was deep in thought as to the repercussions his story on the Vatican had caused. The United States government had moved quickly to work with France and Spain to resolve the illegality of the Louisiana Purchase and was making headway in its negotiations. The revelations about the Vatican's coercive practices contributed to additional hue and outcry about the contents of the Secret Archives and the Vatican's long history of political manipulations.

Emerson's contemplations were interrupted by the phone's ring. He stood and walked into the antique- filled living room.

"Hello."

"Emerson, I've found you," the feminine voice said excitedly.

Stunned, Emerson sat down in a nearby chair. "Martine?" he asked.

"Hi, Emerson. It's been so long since we talked."

Dazed, Emerson said, "I thought you were killed by Katrina."

There was a moment of silence before she responded. "That wasn't me. Martin was my twin brother."

Emerson let out a deep sigh of relief at the news. His emotions were stretched again as he was elated by the news that Martine was not only alive, but a female. At the same time, he shared in her loss and wanted to be sympathetic to her. "I am so sorry," he said.

"Thank you, Emerson. I was in the Quarter to pick up his belongings. A guy who had an apartment next to Martin's was helping me pack up Martin's belongings, and we got to talking about all sorts of things. I think he was trying to take my mind off the task at hand. But the Lake Erie islands came up in our discussion, and he mentioned that he had met a reporter from the islands a few weeks earlier. I asked him if it was you and he said it was. He also said that you seemed shocked that Martin was dead so I figured that you thought it was me."

"You figured right." Emerson searched his memory and then asked, "The guy's name was Wayne, right?"

"Yes. A real nice guy. And then Austin had told me that he saw you in the Quarter when he went shopping with Martin, but I didn't believe him. It was the day that Martin slapped his face. I can tell you that Martin and I had a pretty serious discussion about him slapping my son."

"That was very confusing. I couldn't imagine that you would ever slap a child in the face."

"No way. I saw your story about the Louisiana Purchase. Nice job."

"Thanks. It sure has created a stir."

"That's an understatement," she chuckled. "And how's your aunt?" Martine had loved the dear lady from the first time she met her.

"Fine. She's at a meeting with the OWLS. That's the Old Women's Literary Society."

Martine chuckled.

"Are you still living in New Orleans?"

"No, we evacuated before Katrina hit. We're living in Pensacola now."

Emerson asked the question he dreaded to ask. "How's your husband doing?"

Martine heard the change in tone in Emerson's voice. Her heart wanted her to respond that he wasn't around any longer, but she knew better. "Tim's doing fine. His company has operations here, and it looks like we'll be staying here permanently." She took a deep breath. "You didn't ask, but he's doing so much better. He's trying to follow the straight and narrow."

There was an uncomfortable silence as they thought back to their first meeting.

"Martine?"

"Yes?" she asked softly.

"I still think about you."

"I thought so. I think about you, too, and about something that can never be," she said sadly as she thought about her time with him at Put-in-Bay a couple of years earlier.

"You never know what will transpire in the future."

Tears began to well up in Martine's eyes. "I'd better go. I just wanted to call to let you know that I was okay." She wanted to tell him that she wanted to hear his voice again, but decided it would be wiser not to disclose it.

They ended their call and Emerson slowly rose to his feet. He walked back to the front porch and settled into one of the white rockers. Without thinking, he picked up a brochure about the Cayman Islands and began to read through it.

In a few months, he would be accompanying legendary island singer, Mike "Mad Dog" Adams to Key West for "Put-in-Bay Day," and then on to the Caymans where Mad Dog had a series of singing engagements.

PostScript to Readers
The Adams-Onis Treaty

The storyline regarding the illegality of the sale of the Louisiana Purchase to the United States by France in 1803 was true. The sale violated the Treaty of San Ildefonso between Spain and France, which stipulated the French could not transfer Louisiana to a third party.

The matter was resolved in the Adams-Onis Treaty of 1819 in which the United States paid $5 million for the rights to Florida and relinquished its claims to parts of Texas and other Spanish areas. The treaty also formalized the boundary of the Louisiana Purchase.

Coming Summer 2007
The Next Emerson Moore Adventure

The Other Side of Hell